A SEASON AT
SANDITON

A Completion of Jane Austen's Manuscript

Dedicated with eternal love to Netty, Jonnie, Mags, Kevin, Sheamie and Paudie – the best co-adventurer-sibling-friends a girl could ask for.

ROSE SERVITOVA

A SEASON AT SANDITON

A Completion of Jane Austen's Manuscript

WOOSTER PUBLISHING

First published in 2022 by
Wooster Publishing
Limerick
Ireland

Paperback	ISBN: 978 1 78846 270 9
eBook – mobi format	ISBN: 978 1 78846 279 2
Amazon paperback	ISBN: 978 1 78846 280 8

Produced by Kazoo Independent Publishing Services
222 Beech Park, Lucan, Co. Dublin
www.kazoopublishing.com

Kazoo Independent Publishing Services is not the publisher of this work. All rights and responsibilities pertaining to this work remain with Wooster Publishing.

Kazoo offers independent authors a full range of publishing services. For further details visit kazoopublishing.com

Cover design by Andrew Brown
Printed in the EU

ACKNOWLEDGEMENTS

F irstly, to all my Jane Austen friends – I can never thank you enough for walking along this road with me – true kindred spirits. To Mark Brownlow for always playing Mr Bennet to my Mr Collins and to Lynn Henry who told me to get a move on. Lynn's humour and faith in me steadied my shaking quill on more than one occasion. I really appreciate Karen Ievers of Mount Ievers Court and Emily Smith of the Jane Austen Society of North America for launching *A Season at Sanditon* in true nineteenth century style. A quick mention for those who reviewed early drafts of this book for me – Katherine Cowley and Melissa Makarewicz – thank you for your professionalism and knowledge of what makes an average book, better and to all at Kazoo Independent Publishing Services for their consistency and excellence. Thank you to Limerick City and County Council Arts Office and the Arts Council of Ireland for supporting this fledgling writer to upskill over the years. Thanks to Mam, Dad and Uncle Mike and my darlings, Filip, Laura and Charlie. They are my most loved and if I am not writing, it is probably because I'm thinking of you, doing something with you or driving you somewhere. Finally, a massive thank you to my friends and extended family – a very funny, patient and good sort of people and to Fluffy the cat.

Lord, what fools these mortals be!
– A Midsummer Night's Dream,
WILLIAM SHAKESPEARE

CHAPTER ONE

A gentleman and a lady travelling from Tunbridge towards that part of the Sussex coast which lies between Hastings and Eastbourne, being induced by business to quit the high road and attempt a very rough lane, were overturned in toiling up its long ascent, half rock, half sand. The accident happened just beyond the only gentleman's house near the lane. It was here that their driver, William, on first being required to take that direction, had believed to be necessarily their destination and had with most unwilling looks been forced to pass by. He had grumbled and shaken his shoulders and pitied and cut his horses so sharply that he might have been open to the suspicion of overturning them on purpose. He might have been blamed if the road had not become worse as soon as the premises of the said house were left behind and he had not warned, with a most thunderous countenance, that, beyond it, no wheels but cart wheels could safely proceed. The severity of the fall was broken by their slow pace and the narrowness of the lane. Subsequent to the gentleman scrambling out and helping his companion, they neither of them at first felt more than shaken and bruised.

But the gentleman had, in the course of the extrication, sprained his foot. Once sensible of it, he was obliged in a few moments to cut short both his reproaches to William and his congratulations to his wife and himself and sit down on the bank, unable to stand.

"There is something wrong here," said he, putting his hand to his ankle. "But never mind, my dear" – looking up at her with a smile – "it could not have happened, you know, in a better place – Good out of evil. The very thing perhaps to be wished for. We shall soon get relief. *There*, I fancy, lies my cure," pointing to the neat-looking end of a cottage, which was seen romantically situated among wood on a high eminence at some little distance. "Does not *that* promise to be the very place?"

His wife, neither able to do or suggest anything, fervently hoped it was. She stood, terrified and anxious, until receiving her first real comfort from the sight of several persons now coming to their assistance. The accident had been discerned from a hayfield adjoining the house they had passed. And the persons who approached were a well-looking, hale, gentlemanlike man, of middle age, the proprietor of the place, who happened to be among his haymakers at the time, and three or four of the ablest of them. They were summoned to attend their master, while the rest of the field – men, women and children – came of their own accord to observe the curious scene before them, that they may have something to talk of later.

Mr Heywood, such was the name of the said proprietor, advanced with a very civil salutation, concern for the accident, much surprise at anybody's attempting that road in a carriage, and ready offers of assistance. His courtesies were received with good breeding and gratitude, and while one or two of the men lent their help to the driver in getting the carriage upright again, the traveller laid out a request.

"You are extremely obliging, sir, and I take you at your word. The injury to my leg is, I dare say, very trifling. But it is always best in these cases, you know, to have a surgeon's opinion without loss of time. And as the road does not seem in a favourable state for my getting up to his house myself, I will thank you to send off one of these good people for the surgeon."

"The surgeon, sir!" exclaimed Mr Heywood. "I am afraid you will find no surgeon at hand here, but I dare say we shall do very well without him."

"Nay, sir, if *he* is not in the way, his partner will do just as well, or rather better. I would rather see his partner. Indeed I would prefer the attendance of his partner. One of these good people can be with him in three minutes, I am sure. I need not ask whether I see the house," (looking towards the cottage) "for excepting your own, we have passed none in this place which can be the abode of a gentleman."

Mr Heywood looked very much astonished, and replied: "What, sir! Are you expecting to find a surgeon in that cottage? We have neither surgeon nor partner in the parish, I assure you."

"Excuse me, sir," replied the other. "I am sorry to have the appearance of contradicting you, but from the extent of the parish or some other cause you may not be aware of the fact. Can I be mistaken in the place? Am I not in Willingden? Is not this Willingden?"

"Yes, sir, this is certainly Willingden."

"Then, sir, I can bring proof of your having a surgeon in the parish, whether you may know it or not. Here, sir," (taking out his pocket book) "if you will do me the favour of casting your eye over these advertisements which I cut out myself yesterday from the *Morning Post* and the *Kentish Gazette*, I think you will be convinced that I am not speaking at random. You will find in it an advertisement of the dissolution of a partnership in the medical line in your own parish – extensive business, undeniable character references – wishing to form a separate establishment. You will find it at full length, sir," offering the two little oblong extracts.

"Sir, if you were to show me all the newspapers that are printed in one week throughout the kingdom, you would not persuade me of there being a surgeon in Willingden," said Mr Heywood with a good-humoured smile. "Having lived here ever since I was born, man and boy fifty-seven years, I think I must have known of such a person. At least I may venture to say that he has not much business. To be sure, if gentlemen were to be often attempting this lane in post-chaises, it might not be a bad speculation for a surgeon to get a house at the top of the hill. But as to that cottage, I can assure you, sir, that it is in fact, in spite of its spruce air at this distance, as indifferent a double tenement as any in the parish, and that my shepherd lives at one end and three old women at the other."

He took the pieces of paper as he spoke, and, having looked them over, added, "I believe I can explain it, sir. Your mistake *is* in the place. There are two Willingdens in this country. And your advertisement refers to the other, which is Great Willingden or Willingden Abbots, and lies seven miles off on the other side of Battle – quite down in the weald. And *we,* sir," he added, speaking rather proudly, "are not in the weald."

"Not *down* in the weald, I am sure," replied the traveller pleasantly. "It took us half an hour to climb your hill. Well, I dare say it is as you say and I have made an abominably stupid blunder – all done in a moment. The advertisements did not catch my eye till the last half hour of our being in town – when everything was in the hurry and confusion which always attend a short stay there. One is never able to complete anything in the way of business, you know, till the carriage is at the door. And, accordingly satisfying myself with a brief inquiry, and finding we were actually to pass within a mile or two of a *Willingden,* I sought no farther … my dear," (to his wife) "I am very sorry to have brought you into this scrape. But do not be alarmed about my leg. It gives me no pain while I am quiet. And as soon as these good people have succeeded in setting the carriage to rights and William turns the horses round, the best thing we can do will be to measure back our steps into the turnpike road and proceed to Hailsham, and so home, without attempting anything farther. Two hours take us home from Hailsham. And once at home, we have our remedy at hand, you know. A little of our own bracing sea air will soon set me on my feet again. Depend upon it, my dear, it is exactly a case for the sea. Saline air and immersion will be the very thing. My sensations tell me so already."

In a most friendly manner Mr Heywood here interposed,

entreating them not to think of proceeding till the ankle had been examined and some refreshment taken, and very cordially pressing them to make use of his house for both purposes.

"We are always well stocked," said he, "with all the common remedies for sprains and bruises. And I will answer for the pleasure it will give my wife and daughters to be of service to you in every way in their power."

A twinge or two, in trying to move his foot, disposed the traveller to think rather more than he had done at first of the benefit of immediate assistance. Consulting his wife in the few words of "Well, my dear, I believe it will be better for us," he turned again to Mr Heywood, and said: "Before we accept your hospitality, sir, and in order to do away with any unfavourable impression which the sort of wild-goose chase you find me in may have given rise to, allow me to tell you who we are. My name is Parker, Mr Parker of Sanditon; this lady, my wife, Mrs Parker. We are on our road home from London. My name perhaps, though I am by no means the first of my family holding landed property in the parish of Sanditon, may be unknown at this distance from the coast. But Sanditon itself – everybody has heard of Sanditon. The favourite for a young and rising bathing place, certainly the favourite spot of all that are to be found along the coast of Sussex – the most favoured by nature, and promising to be the most chosen by man."

William, who was still attempting to right the carriage, turned towards his master at this moment as if to speak, but on hearing the topic, lifted his eyes heavenward and returned to his task.

"Yes, I have heard of Sanditon," replied Mr Heywood. "Every five years, one hears of some new place or other starting up by the sea and growing the fashion. How they can half of them be filled is the wonder! *Where* people can be found with money and time to go to them! Bad things for a country – sure to raise the price of provisions and make the poor good for nothing – as I dare say you find, sir."

"Not at all, sir, not at all," cried Mr Parker eagerly. "Quite the contrary, I assure you. A common idea, but a mistaken one. It may apply to your large, overgrown places like Brighton or Worthing or Eastbourne but *not* to a small village like Sanditon, precluded by its size from experiencing any of the evils of civilisation. While the growth of the place, the buildings, the nursery grounds, the demand for everything and the sure resort of the very best company whose regular, steady, private families of thorough gentility and character who are a blessing everywhere, excited the industry of the poor and diffuse comfort and improvement among them of every sort. No sir, I assure you, Sanditon is not a place—"

"I do not mean to take exception to any place in particular," answered Mr Heywood. "I only think our coast is too full of them altogether. But had we not better try to get you—"

"Our coast too full!" repeated Mr Parker. "On that point perhaps we may not totally disagree. At least there are *enough*. Our coast is abundant enough. It demands no more. Everybody's taste and everybody's finances may be suited. And those good people who are trying to add to the number are, in my opinion, excessively absurd and must soon find themselves the dupes of their own misleading calculations. Such a place as Sanditon, sir, I may say was wanted, was called for. Nature had marked it out, had spoken in most intelligible characters. The finest, purest sea breeze on the coast. It is acknowledged to be so – excellent bathing – fine hard sand – deep water ten yards from the shore – no mud – no weeds – no slimy rocks. Never was there a place more obviously designed by nature for the resort of the invalid. It is the very spot which thousands seemed in need of! The most desirable distance from London! One complete, measured mile nearer than Eastbourne. Only conceive, sir, the advantage of saving a whole mile in a long journey. But Brinshore, sir, which I dare say you have in your eye. The attempts of two or three speculating people about Brinshore this last year to raise that paltry hamlet, lying as it does between a stagnant marsh, a bleak moor and the constant stench of a ridge of putrefying seaweed, can end in nothing but their own disappointment. What in the name of common sense is to *recommend* Brinshore? A most unwholesome air – roads detestable – water salty beyond example – impossible to get a good dish of tea within three miles of the place. And as for the soil it is so cold and ungrateful that it can hardly be made to yield a cabbage. Depend upon it, sir, that this is a most faithful Brinshore, not in the smallest degree exaggerated and if you have heard it differently spoken of—"

"Sir, I never heard it spoken of in my life before," said Mr Heywood. "I did not know there was such a place in the world."

"You did not! There, my dear," turning with exultation to

his wife, who had just a few minutes before seated herself on her shawl on the embankment, "you see how it is. So much for the celebrity of Brinshore! This gentleman did not know there was such a place in the world. Why, in truth, sir, I fancy we may apply to Brinshore that line of the poet Cowper in his description of the religious cottager, as opposed to Voltaire – *She*, never heard of half a mile from home."

"With all my heart, sir, apply any verses you like to it. But I want to see something applied to your leg. And I am sure by your lady's countenance that she is quite of my opinion and thinks it a pity to lose any more time. And here come my girls to speak for themselves and their mother." (Two or three genteel-looking young women, followed by as many maid servants, were now seen issuing from the house.) "I began to wonder the bustle should not have reached *them*. A thing of this kind soon makes a stir in a lonely place like ours. Now, sir, let us see how you can be best conveyed into the house."

The young ladies approached, said everything that was proper to recommend their father's offers, and in an unaffected manner calculated to make the strangers easy. And, as Mrs Parker was exceedingly anxious for relief, and her husband by this time not much less disposed for it, a very few civil scruples were enough; especially as the carriage, being now set up, was discovered to have received such injury on the fallen side as to be unfit for present use. Mr Parker was therefore carried into the house and his carriage wheeled off to a vacant barn.

CHAPTER TWO

The acquaintance, thus oddly begun, was neither short nor unimportant. For a whole fortnight the travellers were fixed at Willingden, Mr Parker's sprain proving too serious for him to move sooner. He had fallen into very good hands. The Heywoods were a thoroughly respectable family and every possible attention was paid, in the kindest and most unpretending manner, to both husband and wife. *He* was waited on and nursed, and *she* cheered and comforted with unremitting kindness. As every office of hospitality and friendliness was received as it ought, as there was not more goodwill on one side than gratitude on the other, nor any deficiency of generally pleasant manners in either, they grew to like each other exceedingly well.

Mr Parker's character and history were soon unfolded. All that he understood of himself, he readily told, for he was very open-hearted. Where he might be himself in the dark, his conversation was still giving information, to such of the Heywoods as could observe. By such he was perceived to be an enthusiast on the subject of Sanditon, a complete enthusiast. Sanditon – the success of Sanditon as a small, fashionable bathing place, was the object for which he seemed to live. A very few years ago, it had been a quiet village of no pretensions, but some natural advantages in its position and some accidental circumstances suggested to himself, and the other principal landholder, the probability of its becoming a profitable speculation. So they had engaged in it, and planned and built, and praised and puffed, and raised it to something of young renown. Mr Parker could now think of very little besides.

The facts which, in more direct communication, he laid before them were that he was about five and thirty, had been married – very happily married – seven years, and had four sweet children at home. He was of a respectable family and easy, though not large, fortune. He had no profession, having succeeded as eldest son to the property which two or three generations had been holding and accumulating before him. Of siblings, he had two brothers and one sister, all single and all independent – the eldest of the two former, Sidney, was indeed, by collateral inheritance, quite as well provided for as himself.

His object in quitting the high road to hunt for an advertising surgeon was also plainly stated. It had not proceeded from any intention of spraining his ankle or doing himself any other injury for the good of such surgeon, nor (as Mr Heywood had been apt to suppose) from any design of entering into partnership with him.

"It was merely of a wish to establish some medical man at Sanditon," Mr Parker informed them. "Having a medical man at hand would very materially promote the rise and prosperity of the place. I daresay we could expect an abundance of invalids if we had a doctor, for nothing else is wanting."

He had *strong* reason to believe that *one* family had been deterred last year from trying Sanditon on that account and probably very many more. His own sister, who was a sad invalid and whom he was very anxious to get to Sanditon this summer, could hardly be expected to hazard herself in a place where they could not have immediate medical advice.

Upon the whole, Mr Parker was evidently an amiable family man, fond of wife, children, brothers and sister and kind-hearted. His manners were liberal, gentlemanlike, easy to please, of a cheerful turn of mind, with more imagination than judgement. Mrs Parker was a gentle, amiable, sweet-tempered woman. She would have been the properest wife in the world for a man of strong understanding but not of a capacity to supply the cooler reflection which her own husband sometimes needed. Indecisive, she was often guided entirely by her husband so whether he was risking his fortune or spraining his ankle, she remained equally useless.

Sanditon was a second wife and four children to him, hardly less dear, and certainly more engrossing. He could talk of it forever. It had indeed the highest claims, not only those of birthplace, property and home, but it was his mine, his lottery, his speculation and his hobby horse, his occupation, his hope and his futurity. He was extremely desirous of drawing his good friends at Willingden thither and his endeavours in the cause were as grateful and disinterested as they were warm.

He wanted to secure the promise of a visit, to get as many of the family as his own house would contain, to follow him to Sanditon as soon as possible and, healthy as they all undeniably were, foresaw that every one of them would be benefited by the sea. He held it as certain that no person could be really well (however upheld for the present by exercise and spirits in a semblance of health) or be really in a state of secure and permanent health without spending at least six weeks by the sea every year. The sea air and sea bathing together were nearly infallible, one or the other of them being a match for every disorder of the stomach, the lungs or the blood. They were anti-spasmodic, anti-pulmonary, anti-septic, anti-bilious and anti-rheumatic. Nobody could catch cold by the sea, nobody wanted appetite by the sea, nobody wanted spirits, nobody wanted strength. Sea air was healing, softening, relaxing, fortifying and bracing, seemingly just as was wanted, sometimes one, sometimes the other. If the sea breeze failed, the sea-bath was the certain corrective and where bathing disagreed, the sea air alone was evidently designed by nature for the cure.

His eloquence, however, could not prevail. Mr and Mrs Heywood never left home. Marrying early and having a very numerous family, their movements had long been limited to one small circle; and they were older in habits than in age. Excepting two journeys to London in the year to receive his dividends, Mr Heywood went no farther than his feet or his well-tried old horse could carry him. Mrs Heywood's adventurings were only now and then to visit her neighbours in the old coach which had been new when they married and fresh-lined on their eldest son's coming of age some years ago. They had a very pretty property. It would have been enough had their family been of reasonable limits, to have allowed them a very gentlemanlike share of luxuries and change. It would have been enough for them to have indulged in a new carriage and better roads, an occasional month at Tunbridge Wells and a winter at Bath. But the maintenance, education and fitting out of fourteen children demanded a very quiet, settled, careful course of life, and obliged them to be stationary and healthy at Willingden.

What prudence had at first enjoined was now rendered pleasant by habit. They never left home and they had gratification in saying so. But very far from wishing their children to do the same, they were glad to promote *their* getting out into the world as much as possible. *They* stayed at home that their children *might* get out and, while making that home extremely comfortable, welcomed every change from it which could give useful connections or respectable acquaintance to sons or daughters. They could already boast of Freddie, who had studied law and languages and was now in the early days of carving out a diplomatic career in Europe. So when Mr and Mrs Parker ceased from soliciting a family visit and bounded their views to carrying back one daughter with them, no difficulties were started. It was general pleasure and consent.

Their invitation was to Miss Charlotte Heywood, a very pleasing young woman of two and twenty. As the eldest of the children at home, she was the one who, under her mother's directions, had been particularly useful and obliging to them and who, in chiefly attending them, knew them best.

Though not aligning to current fashions, Charlotte was

a natural beauty nonetheless. She was also credited with a quick wit and eagerness to see more of the world. Having long made peace with the fact that prospects available to brothers were denied to sisters, she would not miss an opportunity to go to a bathing place and make new friends if she could. There was only so much silliness in a day that Charlotte could recall, to pass dull hours and relate in her letters to Freddie. To laugh and be amused elsewhere was what she wished for most. Besides, she would finally have an opportunity to take the bronze, hand-held telescope, that Freddie had gifted her, out of its box in Sanditon and spy on passing boats and setting suns.

On the eve of her departure, Mr Heywood felt it his duty to caution her, as her father and the one who knew little, but enough, of the world.

"Charlotte, you believe yourself a good judge of character but there are those in the world who are best avoided. You have not met them yet and I pray you never will."

"Then I shall avoid them. You have nothing to worry about, Father. I am, as you say, a good judge of character."

"I said you *believe* yourself to be. The Parkers are respectable people and I am sure their acquaintances will be likewise but you will be out in the world without parent or brother to offer you protection. You must take care."

"Yes, Father. I will."

Mr Heywood continued with furrowed brow on a topic he was unused to but sensed he must elaborate further.

"I know we are all delighted when you read aloud a letter from Freddie but some of the scrapes he refers to are inappropriate. He should know better. We may find it amusing but a lady's reputation …"

"Father, please!" Charlotte placed her hand on his shoulder. "If you continue in this way, I will accuse you of reading silly novels. We are not all fainting creatures, locked up in towers. I have lived a sheltered life on a farm. I will go to Sanditon and, no doubt, live a sheltered life there for some months. It being a change of air and scenery is adventure enough for me. I shall make new friends. I have not the slightest intention of throwing myself in the way of a villain."

"Good, good." Mr Heywood cleared his throat, stood upright and was glad to be interrupted with a call to supper but not before he added, "Perhaps it is the poor inhabitants of Sanditon that I should be giving warning to."

Charlotte was to go, with excellent health, to bathe and be better if she could. She would receive every possible pleasure which Sanditon could be made to supply by the gratitude of those she went with and to buy new parasols, new gloves and new brooches for her sisters and herself at the library, which Mr Parker was anxiously wishing to support.

All that Mr Heywood himself could be persuaded to promise was that he would send everyone to Sanditon who asked his advice, and that nothing should ever induce him (as far as the future could be answered for) to spend even five shillings at Brinshore.

CHAPTER THREE

Every neighbourhood should have a great lady. The great lady of Sanditon was Lady Denham. In their journey from Willingden to the coast, Mr Parker gave Charlotte a more detailed account of her than had been called for before. She had been necessarily often mentioned at Willingden for being his colleague in speculation and Sanditon itself could not be talked of long without the introduction of Lady Denham. That she was a very rich old lady, who had buried two husbands, knew the value of money, was very much looked up to and had a poor cousin living with her, were facts already known. But some further particulars of her history and her character served to lighten the tediousness of a long hill, or a heavy bit of road, and to give the visiting young lady a suitable knowledge of the person with whom she might now expect to be daily associating.

Lady Denham had been a rich Miss Brereton, born to wealth but not to education. Her first husband had been a Mr Hollis, a man of considerable property in the country, of which a large share of the parish of Sanditon, with manor and mansion house, made a part. He had been an elderly man when she married him, her own age about thirty. Her motives for such a match could be little understood at the distance of forty years. She had so well nursed and pleased Mr Hollis that at his death he left her everything, all his estates, and all at her disposal. After a widowhood of some years, she had been induced to marry again. The late Sir Harry Denham, of Denham Park in the neighbourhood of Sanditon, had succeeded in removing her and her large income to his own domains. But he could not succeed in the views of permanently enriching his family which were expected of him. She had been too wary to put anything out of her own power and when, on Sir Harry's decease, she returned again to her own house at Sanditon, she was said to have made this boast to a friend: "that though she had *got* nothing but her title from the family, still she had *given* nothing for it."

For the title, it was to be supposed, she had married, finding 'Lady Denham' much more to her liking than just a 'Mrs Hollis'. Mr Parker acknowledged there being just such a degree of value for it, as to give her conduct that natural explanation.

"There is at times," said he, "a little self-importance but it is not offensive and there are moments, there are points, when her love of money is carried greatly too far. But she is a good-natured woman, a very good-natured woman. She is a very obliging, friendly neighbour, a cheerful, independent, valuable character and her faults may be entirely imputed to her want of education. She has good natural sense, but quite uncultivated. She has a fine active mind as well as a fine healthy frame for a woman of seventy, for which the sea air must take some credit, and enters into the improvement of Sanditon with a spirit truly admirable. Though now and then, a littleness *will* appear. She cannot look forward quite as I would have her and takes alarm at a trifling present expense without considering what returns it *will* make her in a year or two. That is – we think *differently*, we now and then see things *differently*, Miss Heywood. Those who tell their own story, you know, must be listened to with caution. When you see us in contact, you will judge for yourself."

Lady Denham was indeed a great lady beyond the common wants of society, for she had many thousands a year to bequeath, and three distinct sets of people to be courted by. They included her own relations, the Breretons, who might very reasonably wish for her original thirty thousand pounds among them. Secondly, the legal heirs of Mr Hollis, who must hope to be more indebted to *her* sense of justice than he had allowed them to be to *his*, and finally, those members of the Denham family whom her second husband had hoped to make a good bargain for. By all of these, or by branches of them, she had no doubt been long, and still continued to be, well attacked. Of these three divisions, Mr Parker did not hesitate to say that Mr Hollis's kindred were the *least* in favour and Sir Harry Denham's the *most*. The former, he believed, had done themselves irremediable harm by expressions of very unwise and unjustifiable resentment at the time of Mr Hollis's death. The latter had the advantage of being the remnant of a connection which she certainly valued, of having been known to her from their childhood and of being always at hand to preserve their interest by reasonable attention. Sir

Edward, the present baronet, nephew to Sir Harry, resided constantly at Denham Park. Mr Parker had little doubt that he and his sister, Miss Denham, who lived with him, would be principally remembered in her will. He sincerely hoped it. Miss Denham had a very small provision and her brother was a poor man for his rank in society.

"He is a warm friend to Sanditon," said Mr Parker, "and his hand would be as liberal as his heart, had he the power. He would be a noble coadjutor! As it is, he does what he can and is running up a tasteful little cottage *orné*, on a strip of waste ground Lady Denham has granted him. I have no doubt we shall have many a candidate for it, before the end even of *this* season."

"I did tell him," interrupted Mrs Parker, "that it would be perfect for a little bakery with a tea room at one side. He was very polite, of course, but declined, for he believes, like my husband, that it would be a commercial failure. And I am glad, for I have decided that it would have been the wrong location after all. To be near the centre of activity, where people walk and take air, is much more suitable."

"Now, now, my dear" – Mr Parker patted his wife's hand gently – "you have not a head for such things. Tea rooms will never take off and bakeries are best left to sell bread. They cannot have all sorts of people coming in and sitting about sipping tea and coffee while they work."

"But in Bath …"

"Bath is nothing but rows of wet streets and shops, where one has nothing to do but sit in out of the rain and talk nonsense. Sanditon, on the other hand, is a place of exercise and vigour. We cannot take the business from Mr

Bailey. His bake house has been making bread in Sanditon for three generations. Besides, if visitors must have refreshments, they will find a fine hearty dinner served at the hotel."

Mr Parker rotated his injured ankle with an "it improves with every mile closer to the coast" and Mrs Parker sighed and looked out the window before turning with a smile to Charlotte. Feeling compelled to say something, Charlotte leaned forward and whispered, "Well, I for one think it is a wonderful idea. Tea and cake after a long walk would be just the thing."

Mrs Parker smiled her thanks and added, "I would not mind but I met a Mr Mooney last year, who owned such a bakery in London. He told me that it is the sale of tea and coffee that make quite a sum. Unlike the coffeehouses which are boisterous and only permit men, he said that his establishment attracts very polite society. Ladies particularly love it. Then he gave me the history of the 'Bath Bun'. When I told him about Sanditon, he was enthusiastic and very much gave the impression that he had always wished to set up on the coast. He was merely looking for one that was not too far from London. Last year, he promised he would come and bring his pastry cook, to consider for himself its prospects. He has not come yet but I still hope."

Mr Parker allowed them their whisperings until he remembered that he had not finished with the Denhams and their future claim to fortune. Till within the last twelvemonth, he had considered Sir Edward as standing without a rival, as having the fairest chance of succeeding to the greater part of all that Lady Denham had to give.

There was now, however, another person's claims to be taken into account, those of the young female relation whom Lady Denham had been induced to receive into her family. She always protested against any such addition, and long and often enjoyed the repeated defeats she had given to every attempt of her relations to introduce this or that young lady as a companion at Sanditon House. Yet she had brought back with her from London last Michaelmas a Miss Brereton, who bid fair by her merits to vie in favour with Sir Edward and to secure for herself and her family that share of the accumulated property which they had certainly the best right to inherit.

Mr Parker spoke warmly of Clara Brereton, and the interest of his story increased very much with the introduction of such a character. Charlotte listened with more than amusement now – it was concern and interest. She heard her described to be lovely, amiable, gentle, unassuming, conducting herself with great good sense and evidently gaining, by her innate worth, on the affections of her patroness. Beauty, sweetness, poverty and dependence do not want the imagination of a man to operate upon. With due exceptions, woman feels for woman very promptly and compassionately. Mr Parker gave the particulars which had led to Clara's admission at Sanditon as no bad illustration of that mixture of character, that union of littleness with kindness, with good sense, with liberality which he saw in Lady Denham.

After having avoided London for many years, principally on account of these very cousins who were continually writing, inviting and tormenting her, and whom she was determined to keep at a distance, she had been obliged to go there last Michaelmas with the certainty of being detained at least a fortnight. She had gone to a hotel, living by her own account as prudently as possible to defy the reputed expensiveness of such a home, and at the end of three days called for her bill that she might judge of her state. Its amount was such as determined her on staying not another hour in the house. In anger and indignation, she prepared to leave the hotel at all hazards, yet was ignorant of where to go for better usage. Just at that moment, the cousins, the politic and lucky cousins, who seemed always to have a spy on her, introduced themselves and learning her situation, persuaded her to accept such a home for the rest of her stay as their humbler house in a very inferior part of London could offer.

She went and was delighted with her welcome. The hospitality and attention she received from everybody impressed her greatly. She found her good cousins the Breretons beyond her expectation worthy people and finally was impelled by a personal knowledge of their narrow income and pecuniary difficulties to invite one of the girls of the family to pass the winter with her. The invitation was to *one*, for six months, with the probability of another being then to take her place, but in *selecting* the one, Lady Denham had shown the good part of her character. For, passing by the actual *daughters* of the house, she had chosen Clara, a niece – more helpless and more pitiable of course than any. She was a dependent on poverty, an additional burden on an encumbered circle and one who, despite all her natural endowments and powers, was to have prepared for a situation little better than a nursery maid.

Clara had returned with her and by her good sense and merit had now, to all appearance, secured a very strong hold in Lady Denham's regard. The six months had long been over and not a syllable was breathed of any change or exchange. She was a general favourite. The influence of her steady conduct and mild, gentle temper was felt by everybody. The prejudices which had met her at first, in some quarters, were all dissipated. She was felt to be worthy of trust, to be the very companion who would guide and soften Lady Denham, whose influence would enlarge her mind and open her hand. She was as thoroughly amiable as she was lovely and since having had the advantage of their Sanditon breezes, that loveliness was complete.

CHAPTER FOUR

"And whose very snug-looking place is this?" said Charlotte as, in a sheltered dip within two miles of the sea, they passed close by a moderate-sized house. It was well fenced and planted, and rich in the garden, orchard and meadows which are the best embellishments of such a dwelling. "It seems to have as many comforts about it as Willingden."

"Ah," said Mr Parker, "this is the Manor House, the house of my forefathers, the house where I and all my siblings were born and bred, and where my own three eldest children were born. Mrs Parker and I lived here till within the last two years when our new house was finished. I am glad you are pleased with it. It is an honest old place and Hillier keeps it in very good order. I have given it up, you know, to the man who occupies the chief of my land. He gets a better house by it, and I, a rather better situation! One other hill brings us to Sanditon – modern Sanditon – a beautiful spot. Our ancestors, you know, always built in a hole. Here were we, pent down in this little contracted nook, without air or view, only one mile and three quarters from the noblest expanse of ocean between the South Foreland

and Land's End, and without the smallest advantage from it. You will not think I have made a bad exchange when we reach Trafalgar House, which by the by, I almost wish I had not named Trafalgar, for Waterloo is more the thing now. However, Waterloo is in reserve. If we have encouragement enough this year for a little crescent to be ventured on, as I trust we shall, then we will call it Waterloo Crescent and the name joined to the form of the building, which always takes, will give us the command of lodgers. In a good season we should have more applications than we could attend to."

"It was always a very comfortable house," said Mrs Parker, looking at their old residence through the back window with something like the fondness of regret. "And such a nice garden, such an excellent garden."

"Yes, my love, but *that* we may be said to carry with us. *It* supplies us, as before, with all the fruit and vegetables we want. And we have, in fact, all the comfort of an excellent kitchen garden without the constant eyesore of its formalities or the yearly nuisance of its decaying vegetation. Who can endure a cabbage bed in October?"

"Oh dear, yes. We are quite as well off for garden stuff as ever we were for if it is forgot to be brought at any time, we can always buy what we want at Sanditon House. The gardener there is glad enough to supply us. But it was a nice place for the children to run about in. So shady in summer and all those trees for climbing!"

"My dear, we shall have shade enough on the hill, and more than enough in the course of a very few years. The growth of my plantations is a general astonishment. In the meanwhile we have the canvas awning which gives us the most complete comfort within doors. And you can get a parasol at Whitby's for Mae at any time, or a large bonnet at Jebb's. And as for the boys, I must say I would rather *them* run about in the sunshine than not. I am sure we agree, my dear, in wishing our boys to be as hardy as possible."

"Yes indeed, I am sure we do. And I will get Mae a little parasol, which will make her as proud as can be. How grave she will walk about with it and fancy herself quite a little woman. Oh, I have not the smallest doubt of our being a great deal better off where we are now. If we any of us want to bathe, we have not a quarter of a mile to go. But you know," (still looking back), "one loves to look at an old friend, at a place where one has been happy. The Hilliers did not seem to feel the storms last winter at all. I remember seeing Mrs Hillier after one of those dreadful nights, when *we* had been literally rocked in our bed, and she did not seem at all aware of the wind being anything more than common."

"Yes, yes, that's likely enough," Mr Parker replied. "We have all the grandeur of the storm with less real danger because the wind, meeting with nothing to oppose or confine it around our house, simply rages and passes on. Down in this gutter, however, nothing is known of the state of the air below the tops of the trees. The inhabitants may be taken totally unawares by one of those dreadful currents, which do more mischief in a valley when they *do* arise than an open country ever experiences in the heaviest gale."

Mr Parker's blind preference for his new home amused Charlotte and Shakespeare's words came to mind:

So long as men can breathe or eyes can see,

So long lives this, and this gives life to thee.

"But, my dear love, as to garden stuff, you were saying that any accidental omission is supplied in a moment by Lady Denham's gardener. It occurs to me that we ought to go elsewhere upon such occasions, and that old Stringer has a higher claim. I encouraged him to set up, you know, and am afraid he does not do very well. That is, there has not been time enough yet. He *will* do very well beyond a doubt. But at first it is uphill work, and therefore we must give him what help we can. When any vegetables or fruit happen to be wanted – and it will not be amiss to have them often wanted, to have something or other forgotten most days – just to have a nominal supply, you know, that poor old Andrew may not lose his daily job – but in fact to buy the chief of our consumption from the Stringers."

"Very well, my love, that can be easily done. And Cook will be satisfied, which will be a great comfort, for she is always complaining of old Andrew now and says he never brings her what she wants. There now, the old house is quite left behind. What is it your brother Sidney says about its being a hospital?"

"Oh, my dear Mary, merely a joke of his. He pretends to advise me to make a hospital of it. He pretends to laugh at my improvements. Sidney says anything, you know. He has always said what he chose, of and to us all. Most families have such a member among them, I believe, Miss Heywood. There is someone in most families privileged by superior abilities or spirits to say anything."

"Yes," Charlotte agreed, "in mine, it is my older brother, Freddie. I could never say half that he has, though I may think it."

"In ours, it is Sidney. He is a very clever young man and with great powers of pleasing. He lives too much in the world to be settled. That is his only fault. He is here and there and everywhere. I wish we may get him to Sanditon. I should like to have you acquainted with him. And it would be a fine thing for the place! Such a young man as Sidney, with his neat equipage and fashionable air. You and I, Mary, know what effect it might have. Many a respectable family, many a careful mother, many a pretty daughter might it secure us to the prejudice of Eastbourne and Hastings."

Charlotte could not refrain from adding, "But how could these families learn of the existence of such a man?"

"Indeed, Miss Heywood, a very good question," said Mr Parker, taking her question seriously and moving forward in his seat. "I confess, unbeknownst to Sidney, I set the wheels in motion last year. He came to stay with us, you know, for the summer and brought some of his gentlemen friends. And I may have let it slip amongst a group of ladies whom I met at the library that there were many more, even wealthier, expected, that they were sure to be regular visitors and that, indeed, my brother had hinted at settling down. I believe it worked, for every father within miles came to call upon us the following week. It is only a matter of time before news spreads and Sanditon will be seen as a hunting ground for husbands." He slapped his knee and exclaimed, "We must have more balls."

"Oh, Tom," laughed Mary, "you should not have made such promises."

"They were not promises, Mary, merely very loose suggestions of vague possibilities. But we must really push for Sidney's return. Do you not agree, Miss Heywood, that a seaside town full of old gentlemen with aching joints and gout is no incentive to single young ladies?"

"Indeed, I do, sir!" Charlotte quipped back. "Why, I had hoped that the library in Sanditon would have full catalogues of rich gentlemen in need of wives."

"Leave it to me, Miss Heywood, and you will be tripping over such men in no time."

They were now approaching the church and the real village of Sanditon, which stood at the foot of the hill they were afterwards to ascend – a hill whose side was covered with the woods and enclosures of Sanditon House and whose height ended in an open down where the new buildings might soon be looked for. A branch only of the valley, winding more obliquely towards the sea, gave a passage to an inconsiderable stream, and formed at its mouth a third habitable division in a small cluster of fishermen's houses.

The original village contained little more than cottages but the spirit of the day had been caught, as Mr Parker observed with delight to Charlotte, and two or three of the best of them were smartened up with a white curtain and 'Lodgings to let'. Farther on, in the little green court of an old farm house, two females in elegant white were actually to be seen with their books and camp stools and in turning the corner of the baker's shop, the sound of a harp might be heard through the upper casement.

Such sights and sounds were highly blissful to Mr Parker. Not that he had any personal concern in the success of the village itself, for considering it as too remote from the beach, he had done nothing there, but it was a most valuable proof of the increasing fashion of the place altogether. If the *village* could attract, the hill might be nearly full. He anticipated an amazing season. At the same time last year (late in July) there had not been a single lodger in the village! Nor did he remember any during the whole summer, excepting one family of children who came from London for sea air after the whooping cough, and whose mother would not let them be nearer the shore for fear of their tumbling in.

"Civilisation, civilisation indeed!" cried Mr Parker, delighted. "Look, my dear Mary, look at William Heeley's windows. Blue shoes, and nankin boots! Who would have expected such a sight at a shoemaker's in old Sanditon! This is new within the month. There was no blue shoe when we passed this way a month ago. Glorious indeed! Now, for our hill, our health-breathing hill."

In ascending, they passed the lodge gates of Sanditon House and saw the top of the house itself among its groves. It was the last building of former days in that line of the parish. A little higher up, the modern began and in crossing the down, a Prospect House, a Bellevue Cottage and a Denham Place were to be looked at by Charlotte with the calmness of amused curiosity, and by Mr Parker with the eager eye which hoped to see scarcely any empty houses. More bills at the windows than he had calculated on and a smaller show of company on the hill with fewer carriages, fewer walkers. He had fancied it just the time of day for them to be all returning from their airings to dinner but the sands and the Terrace always attracted some and the tide must be flowing about half-tide now.

He longed to be on the sands, the cliffs, at his own house,

and everywhere out of his house at once. His spirits rose with the very sight of the sea and he could almost feel his ankle getting stronger already. Trafalgar House, on the most elevated spot on the down, was a light, elegant building, standing in a small lawn with a very young plantation round it, perched about a hundred yards from the brow of a steep but not very lofty cliff. It was the nearest to it of every building, excepting one short row of smart-looking houses called the Terrace, with a broad walk in front, aspiring to be the Mall of the place. In this row were the best milliner's shop, the library and where Charlotte supposed Mary would wish to set up her tea rooms. Then, a little detached from the Terrace, the hotel and billiard room. Here began the descent to the beach and to the bathing machines. This was, therefore, the favourite spot for beauty and fashion.

At Trafalgar House, rising at a little distance behind the Terrace, William could be heard telling the horses to *whoa*, and the travellers were safely set down. All was happiness and joy between Papa and Mama and their children. Charlotte, having received possession of her apartment, found diversion enough in standing at her ample Venetian window. She removed Freddie's telescope from her bag and looked over the miscellaneous foreground of unfinished buildings, waving linen and tops of houses, to the sea, dancing and sparkling in sunshine and freshness.

CHAPTER FIVE

W hen they met before dinner, Mr Parker was looking over letters.

"Not a line from Sidney!" said he. "He is an idle fellow. I sent him an account of my accident from Willingden and thought he would have vouchsafed me an answer. But perhaps it implies that he is coming himself. I trust it may. But here is a letter from my sister. *She* never fails me. Women are the only correspondents to be depended on. Now, Mary," smiling at his wife, "before I open it, what shall we guess as to the state of health of those it comes from or rather what would Sidney say if he were here? Sidney is a saucy fellow, Miss Heywood. And you must know, he will have it there is a good deal of imagination in my sister's complaints. But it really is not so, or very little. She has wretched health, as you have heard us say frequently, and is subject to a variety of very serious disorders. Indeed, I do not believe she knows what a day's health is. And at the same time, she is such an excellent, useful woman and has so much energy of character that where any good is to be done, she forces herself on exertions which, to those who do not know her, have an extraordinary appearance. But there is really no pretension about her, you know. She has only a weaker constitution and stronger mind than is often met with, either separate or together. And our youngest brother, who lives with her and who is not much above twenty, I am sorry to say is almost as great an invalid as herself. He is so delicate that he can engage in no profession. Sidney laughs at him. But it really is no joke, though Sidney often makes me laugh at them in spite of myself. Now, if he were here, I know he would be offering odds that either Diana or Arthur would appear by this letter to have been at the point of death within the last month."

Having run his eye over the letter, he shook his head and began reading.

"No chance of seeing them at Sanditon, I am sorry to say. A very troubling account of them indeed. Seriously, a very troubling account. Mary, you will be quite sorry to hear how ill they have been and are. Miss Heywood, if you will give me leave, I will read Diana's letter aloud. I like to have my friends acquainted with each other and I am afraid this is the only sort of acquaintance I shall have the means of accomplishing between you. And I can have no scruple on Diana's account for her letters show her exactly as she is, the most active, friendly, warm-hearted being in existence, and therefore must give a good impression."

He need not have worried, for having painted such a picture of his siblings, Charlotte was all amused curiosity to learn more of them.

He read aloud, "My dear Tom, we were all much grieved at your accident, and if you had not described yourself as fallen into such very good hands, I should have been with you at all hazards the day after the receipt of your letter. Although it found me suffering under a more severe attack than usual of my old grievance, spasmodic bile, and hardly able to crawl from my bed to the sofa. But how were you treated? Send me more particulars in your next. If indeed a simple sprain, as you denominate it, nothing would have been so judicious as friction, friction by the hand alone, supposing it could be applied *instantly*. Two years ago I happened to be calling on Mrs Sheldon when her coachman sprained his foot as he was cleaning the carriage and could hardly limp into the house. But by the immediate use of friction alone steadily persevered in (and I rubbed his ankle with my own hand for six hours without intermission) he was well in three days."

The image of a single lady such as Miss Parker massaging a strange and possibly startled coachman's foot for six hours brought on such a spontaneous snort from Charlotte as forced her to pretend it was a cough. Once composed, she apologised and nodded for Mr Parker to continue.

"Many thanks, my dear Tom, for the kindness with respect to us, which had so large a share in bringing on your accident. But pray never run into peril again in looking for an apothecary on our account, for had you the most experienced man in his line settled at Sanditon, it would be no recommendation to us. We have entirely done with the whole medical tribe. We have consulted physician after physician in vain, till we are quite convinced that they can do nothing for us and that we must trust to our own knowledge of our own wretched constitutions for any relief. But if you think it advisable for the interest of the *place*, to get a medical man there, I will undertake the commission with pleasure, and have no doubt of succeeding. I could soon put the necessary irons in the fire. As for getting to Sanditon myself, it is quite an impossibility. I grieve to say that I dare not attempt it, but my feelings tell me too plainly that, in my present state, the sea air would probably be the death of me. And Arthur will not leave me or I would promote his going down to you for a fortnight. But in truth, I doubt whether his nerves would be equal to the effort. He has been suffering much from a headache, and six leeches a day for ten days together relieved him so little that we thought it right to change our measures. Being convinced on examination that much of the evil lay in his gum, I persuaded him to attack the disorder there. He has accordingly had two teeth drawn from the back of his mouth, and is decidedly better, but his nerves are a good deal deranged. He can only speak in a whisper. Otherwise, I am happy to say, he is tolerably well though more languid than I like and I fear for his liver. I have heard nothing of Sidney since your being together in town, but conclude his scheme to the Isle of Wight has not taken place or we should have seen him in his way. Most sincerely do we wish you a good season at Sanditon, and though we cannot contribute to your Beau Monde in person, we are doing our utmost to send you company worth having. We believe we may safely reckon on securing you two large families, one a rich West Indian from Surrey, the other a most respectable Girls' Boarding School, or Academy, from Camberwell. I will not tell you how many people I have employed in the business – wheel within wheel – but success more than repays. Yours most affectionately."

"Well," said Mr Parker, as he finished. "Though I dare say Sidney might find something extremely entertaining in this letter and make us laugh for half an hour together, I declare *I*, by myself, can see nothing in it but what is either very pitiable or very creditable. With all their sufferings, you perceive how much they are occupied in promoting the good of others! So anxious for Sanditon! Two large families, one for Prospect House probably, the other for No. 2 Denham Place or the end house of the Terrace, with extra beds at the hotel. I told you my sister is an excellent woman, Miss Heywood."

"And I am sure she must be a very extraordinary one," said Charlotte. "I am astonished at the cheerful style of the letter considering the state of their health. Spasmodic bile, nerves, headaches, leeches and two teeth drawn at once. Frightful! Your sister Diana seems almost as ill as possible, but extracting your brother's teeth is the most distressing."

"Oh, they are so used to the operation, to every operation, and have such fortitude!"

"Your siblings know what they are about, I dare say, but their measures seem to touch on extremes. I feel that in any illness *I* should be so anxious for professional advice. Less prone to risk-filled action for myself or anybody I loved! But then, *we* have been so healthy a family that I can be no judge of what the habit of self-doctoring may do."

"Why, to own the truth," said Mrs Parker, "I do think my in-laws carry it too far sometimes. And so do you, my love, you know. You often think they would be better if they would leave themselves more alone and especially Arthur. I know you think it a great pity that Diana should give *him* such a turn for being ill."

"Well, well, my dear Mary, I grant you, it *is* unfortunate for poor Arthur that at his time of life he should be encouraged to give way to indisposition. It *is* bad that he should be fancying himself too sickly for any profession and sit down at one and twenty, on the interest of his own little fortune, without any idea of attempting to improve it or of engaging in any occupation that may be of use to himself or others. But let us talk of pleasanter things. These two large families are just what we wanted. But here is something at hand pleasanter still – Morgan with his 'dinner on table.'"

CHAPTER SIX

T he party were very soon moving after dinner. Mr
Parker could not be satisfied without an early visit
to the library and the library subscription book and
Charlotte was glad to see as much and as quickly as possible
where all was new. They were out in the very quietest part
of a watering-place day, when the important business of
dinner or of sitting after dinner was going on in almost
every inhabited lodging. Here and there might be seen
a solitary elderly man, who was forced to move early and
walk for health, but, in general, it was a thorough pause of
company. It was emptiness and tranquillity on the Terrace,
the cliffs and the sands.

The shops were deserted. The straw hats and pendant
lace seemed left to their fate both within the house and
without. The Parkers and Charlotte had almost reached
their destination when a holler from behind forced them to
turn in the direction of the hotel.

"What ho! Mr Parker! You have returned!" shouted a
portly gentleman, who was waving his hat.

Tom Parker smiled. "Indeed I have, Reverend."

"I cannot delay," cried the clergyman. "Old Mrs Clarke

in the cottage is off to her heavenly reward."

"Oh dear," said Mr Parker, searching for something more appropriate to add.

"Yes, well ... I will see you at service on Sunday."

"Of course," said Tom, raising his hand to wave off the clergyman.

"I believe it will be a great season, Mr Parker. I can feel it in my knees."

"Then it is a certainty. Thank you, Reverend. Goodbye."

Tom returned his attention to the ladies and they continued their walk.

"That, Miss Heywood, is our Reverend Hanking. You will certainly come to know him while you are here."

"He seems jovial," said Charlotte.

"That he is and very singular but, most importantly, a great friend to Sanditon."

Mrs Whitby at the library was sitting in her inner room, reading one of her own novels for want of employment. The list of subscribers was but commonplace. The Lady Denham, Miss Brereton, Mr and Mrs Parker, Sir Edward Denham and Miss Denham, whose names might be said to lead off the season, were followed by nothing better than: Mrs Mathews, Miss Mathews, Miss E. Mathews, Miss H. Mathews; Mr Richard Pratt; Lieutenant Smith R.N.; Captain Little Limehouse; Mrs Jane Fisher, Miss Fisher, Miss Scroggs; Reverend Mr Hanking; Mr Beard, Solicitor, Gray's Inn; Mrs Davis, Miss Merryweather and a Dr Hollis.

"A Dr Hollis! What a peculiar coincidence, ladies. After going to all the trouble of spraining my ankle, it appears we have a doctor currently visiting Sanditon. Lady Denham's first husband, if you remember, was Hollis."

Mr Parker could not but feel that the list was not only without distinction but less numerous than he had hoped. It was but July, however, and August and September were the months. And besides, the promised large families from Surrey and Camberwell were an ever-ready consolation.

Mrs Whitby came forward without delay from her literary recess, delighted to see Mr Parker, whose manners recommended him to everybody, and they were fully occupied in their various civilities and communications. Charlotte, meanwhile, added her name to the list as the first offering to the success of the season. She was then busy in some immediate purchases for the further good of everybody, as soon as Miss Whitby could be hurried down from her toilette, with all her glossy curls and smart trinkets, to wait on her.

The library, of course, afforded everything: all the useless things in the world that could not be done without. Among so many pretty temptations, and with so much goodwill for Mr Parker to encourage expenditure, Charlotte began to feel that she must check herself. Or rather she reflected that at two and twenty there could be no excuse for her doing otherwise and that it would not do for her to be spending all her money the very first evening. She took up a book. It happened to be a volume of *Camilla*. She had not *Camilla's* youth, and had no intention of having her distress, so she turned from the drawers of rings and brooches, repressed further enquiring after wares and paid for what she had bought.

For her particular gratification, they were then to take a

turn on the cliff. As they quitted the library, however, they were met by two ladies whose arrival made an alteration necessary: Lady Denham and Miss Brereton. They had been to Trafalgar House and been directed thence to the library. Though Lady Denham was a great deal too active to regard the walk of a mile as anything requiring rest, and talked of going home again directly, the Parkers knew that to be pressed into their house and obliged to take her tea with them would suit her best. Therefore the stroll on the cliff gave way to an immediate return home.

"No, no," said Her Ladyship. "I will not have you hurry your tea on my account. I know you like your tea late. My early hours are not to put my neighbours to inconvenience. No, no, Miss Clara and I will get back to our own tea. We came out with no other thought. We wanted just to see you and make sure of your being really come, but we get back to our own tea."

She went on, however, towards Trafalgar House and took possession of the drawing room very quietly without seeming to hear a word of Mrs Parker's orders to the servant, as they entered, to bring tea directly. Charlotte was fully consoled for the loss of her walk by finding herself in company with those whom the conversation of the morning had given her a great curiosity to see. She observed them well. Lady Denham was of middle height, stout, upright and alert in her motions, with a shrewd eye and self-satisfied air but not an unagreeable countenance. Though her manner was rather downright and abrupt, as of a person who valued herself on being free-spoken, there was a good humour and cordiality about her. She had a civility and readiness to be acquainted with Charlotte herself, and a heartiness of welcome towards her old friends, which was inspiring the goodwill, Charlotte seemed to feel. And as for Miss Brereton, her appearance so completely justified Mr Parker's praise that Charlotte thought she had never beheld a more lovely or more interesting young woman.

Elegantly tall, regularly handsome, with great delicacy of complexion and soft blue eyes, a sweetly modest and yet naturally graceful address, Charlotte could see in her only the perfect representation of whatever heroine might be most beautiful and bewitching in the volumes they had left behind on Mrs Whitby's shelves. Perhaps it might be partly owing to her having just issued from a circulating library but she could not separate the idea of a complete heroine from Clara Brereton. Her situation with Lady Denham was so very much in favour of it! She seemed placed with her on purpose to be ill-used. Such poverty and dependence joined to such beauty and merit seemed to leave no choice in the business.

These feelings were not the result of any spirit of romance in Charlotte herself. No, she was a very sensible young lady, sufficiently well read in novels to supply her imagination with amusement, but not at all unreasonably influenced by them. While she pleased herself for the first five minutes with fancying the persecution which *ought* to be the lot of the interesting Clara, especially in the form of the most barbarous conduct on Lady Denham's side, she found no reluctance to admit from subsequent observation that they appeared to be on very comfortable terms. She could see nothing worse in Lady Denham than the sort of old-fashioned formality of always calling her *Miss Clara*, nor anything objectionable in the degree of observance and attention which Clara paid. On one side it seemed protecting kindness, on the other grateful and affectionate respect.

The conversation turned entirely upon Sanditon, its present number of visitants and the chances of a good season. It was evident that Lady Denham had more anxiety, more fears of loss, than her coadjutor. She wanted to have the place fill faster and seemed to have many harassing apprehensions of the lodgings being in some instances underlet. Miss Diana Parker's two large families were not forgotten.

"Very good, very good," said Her Ladyship. "A West Indy family and a school. That sounds well. That will bring money."

"No people spend more freely, I believe, than West Indians," observed Mr Parker.

"Aye, so I have heard, and because they have full purses fancy themselves equal, maybe, to your old country families. But then, they who scatter their money so freely never think of whether they may not be doing mischief by raising the price of things. And I have heard that's very much the case with your West Indians. And if they come among us to raise the price of our necessaries of life, we shall not much thank them, Mr Parker."

"My dear madam, they can only raise the price of consumable articles by such an extraordinary demand for them and such a diffusion of money among us as must do us more good than harm. Our butchers and bakers and traders in general cannot get rich without bringing prosperity to *us*. If *they* do not gain, our rents must be insecure and in proportion to their profit must be ours eventually in the increased value of our houses."

"Oh, well! But I should not like to have butcher's meat raised, though. And I shall keep it down as long as I can. Aye, that young lady smiles, I see. I dare say she thinks me an odd sort of creature but *she* will come to care about such matters herself in time. Yes, yes, my dear, depend upon it, you will be thinking of the price of butcher's meat in time, though you may not happen to have quite such a servants' hall to feed as I have. And I do believe those are best off that have fewest servants. I am not a woman of parade as all the world knows, and if it was not for what I owe to poor Mr Hollis's memory, I should never keep up Sanditon House as I do. It is not for my own pleasure. Well, Mr Parker, and the other is a boarding school, a French boarding school, is it? No harm in that. They'll stay their six weeks. And out of such a number, who knows but some may be consumptive and want asses' milk. I have two milch asses at this present time. But perhaps the little Misses may hurt the furniture. I hope they will have a good sharp governess to look after them."

Poor Mr Parker got no more credit from Lady Denham than he had from his sister for the object which had taken him to Willingden.

"Lord! My dear sir," she cried. "How could you think of such a thing? I am very sorry you met with your accident, but upon my word, you deserved it. Going after a doctor! Why, what should we do with a doctor here? It would be only encouraging our servants and the poor to fancy themselves ill if there was a doctor at hand. Oh! pray, let us have none of the tribe at Sanditon. We go on very well as we are. There is the sea and the downs and my milch asses. And I have told Mrs Whitby that if anybody inquires for a chamber-horse, they may be supplied at a fair rate – poor Mr Hollis's chamber-horse is as good as new – and what can people want for more? Here have I lived seventy good years in the world and never took ill above twice and never saw the face of a doctor in all my life on my *own* account. And I verily believe if my poor dear Sir Harry had never seen one neither, he would have been alive now. Ten fees, one after another, did the man take who sent *him* out of the world. I beseech you, Mr Parker, no doctors here."

The tea things were brought in.

"Oh, my dear Mrs Parker – you should not indeed – why would you do so? I was just upon the point of wishing you good evening. But since you are so very neighbourly, I believe Miss Clara and I must stay."

CHAPTER SEVEN

The popularity of the Parkers brought them some visitors the very next morning. Amongst them were Sir Edward Denham and his sister, who, having been at Sanditon House, drove on to pay their compliments. With the duty of letter writing accomplished, Charlotte was settled with Mrs Parker in the drawing room in time to see them all. The Denhams were the only ones to excite particular attention. Charlotte was glad to complete her knowledge of the family by an introduction to them. She found them, the better half at least – for while single, the *gentleman* may sometimes be thought the better half of the pair – not unworthy of notice. Miss Denham was a fine young woman, but cold and reserved. She gave the idea of one who felt her consequence with pride and her poverty with discontent. She seemed gnawed by the want of a handsomer equipage than the simple gig in which they travelled, and which their groom was leading about still in her sight. Sir Edward was much her superior in air and manner – certainly handsome, but yet more to be remarked for his very good address and wish of paying attention and giving pleasure. He came into the room remarkably well, talked much – and very much to Charlotte, by whom he chanced to be placed – and she soon perceived that he had a fine countenance, a most pleasing gentleness of voice and a great deal of conversation. He was most attentive and, she thought, a most wonderful example of the men she might hope to meet at Sanditon. She liked him. She thought him agreeable and did not quarrel with the suspicion of his finding her equally so. This arose from his evidently disregarding his sister's motion to go, and persisting in his station and his discourse.

At last, from the low French windows of the drawing room which commanded the road and all the paths across the down, Charlotte and Sir Edward as they sat could not but observe Lady Denham and Miss Brereton walking by. There was instantly a slight change in Sir Edward's countenance, an anxious glance after them as they proceeded, followed by an early proposal to his sister – not merely for moving, but for walking on together to the Terrace. It altogether gave a hasty turn to Charlotte's fancy, cured her of her half-hour's fever and placed her in a more capable state of judging, when Sir Edward was gone, of *how* agreeable he had actually been. "Perhaps there was a good deal in his air and address and his title did him no harm." Her pride was soothed with a "but there is a fickleness about him that does not suit me." And she put her first experience of meeting an eligible gentleman outside her neighbourhood circle at home, as an experience nevertheless and better than none.

She was very soon in his company again. The first object of the Parkers, when their house was cleared of morning visitors, was to get out themselves. The Terrace was the attraction to all. Everybody who walked must begin with the Terrace and there, seated on one of the two green benches by the gravel walk, they found the united Denham party. But though united in the gross, they were very distinctly divided again – the two superior ladies being at one end of the bench, and Sir Edward and Miss Brereton at the other. Charlotte's first glance told her that Sir Edward's air was that of a lover. There could be no doubt of his devotion to Clara. How Clara received it was less obvious, but she was inclined to think not very favourably for though sitting thus apart with him (which probably she might not have been able to prevent) her air was calm and grave.

That the young lady at the other end of the bench was doing penance was indubitable. The difference in Miss Denham's countenance, the change from Miss Denham sitting in cold grandeur in Mrs Parker's drawing room to Miss Denham at Lady Denham's elbow, listening and talking with smiling attention or solicitous eagerness, was very striking. It was also very amusing, or very melancholy, just as satire or morality might prevail. Miss Denham's character was pretty well decided with Charlotte. Sir Edward's required longer observation. He surprised her by quitting Clara immediately on their all joining and agreeing to walk, and by addressing his attentions entirely to herself.

Stationing himself close by her, he seemed to mean to detach her as much as possible from the rest of the party and to give her the whole of his conversation. He began, in a tone of great taste and feeling, to talk of the sea and the sea shore and ran with energy through all the usual phrases employed in praise of their sublimity and descriptive of the *indescribable* emotions they excited in the mind of sensibility. The terrific grandeur of the ocean in a storm, its glass surface in a calm, its gulls and its samphire and the deep fathoms of its abysses, its quick vicissitudes, its direful deceptions, its mariners tempting it in sunshine and overwhelmed by the sudden tempest, all were eagerly and fluently touched. It was rather commonplace perhaps, but doing very well from the lips of a handsome Sir Edward – and she could not but think him a man of feeling – till he began to stagger her by the number of his quotations and the bewilderment of some of his sentences.

"Do you remember," said he, "Scott's beautiful lines on the sea? Oh! what a description they convey! They are never out of my thoughts when I walk here. That man who can read them unmoved must have the nerves of an assassin! Heaven defend me from meeting such a man unarmed."

"What description do you mean?" asked Charlotte. "I remember none at this moment, of the sea, in either of Scott's poems."

"Do you not indeed? Nor can I exactly recall the beginning at this moment. But you cannot have forgotten his description of woman – 'Oh! Woman in our hours of ease'. Delicious! Delicious! Had he written nothing more, he would have been immortal. But while we are on the subject of poetry, what think you, Miss Heywood, of Burns's lines to his Mary? Oh! there is pathos to madden one! If ever there was a man who *felt*, it was Burns. Montgomery has all the fire of poetry, Wordsworth has the true soul of it and Campbell in his pleasures of hope has touched the extreme of our sensations. But Burns – I confess my sense of his pre-eminence, Miss Heywood. If Scott *has* a fault, it is the want of passion. Tender, elegant, descriptive but *tame*. The man who cannot do justice to the attributes of woman is my contempt. Sometimes indeed a flash of feeling seems to irradiate him, as in the lines we were speaking of – 'Oh. Woman in our hours of ease'. But Burns is always on fire. His soul was the altar in which lovely woman sat enshrined, his spirit truly breathed the immortal incense which is her due."

"I have read several of Burns's poems with great delight," said Charlotte as soon as she had time to speak. "But I am not poetic enough to separate a man's poetry entirely from his character and poor Burns's known irregularities greatly interrupt my enjoyment of his lines. I have difficulty in depending on the *truth* of his feelings as a lover. I have not faith in the *sincerity* of the affections of a man of his description. He felt and he wrote and he forgot."

"Oh! no, no," exclaimed Sir Edward in an ecstasy. "He was all ardour and truth! His genius and his susceptibilities might lead him into some eccentricities but who is perfect?"

"You become less perfect," thought Charlotte, "with every moment I spend in your company." She merely looked at him as he continued his nonsense.

"It was hyper-criticism to expect from the soul of high-toned genius, the grovelling of a common mind. The sparkles of talent, elicited by impassioned feeling in the breast of man, are perhaps incompatible with some of the banal decencies of life nor can you, loveliest Miss Heywood," speaking with an air of deep sentiment, "nor can any woman be a fair judge of what a man may be propelled to say, write or do by the sovereign impulses of passion."

This was very fine, but if Charlotte understood it at all, not very moral, and being moreover by no means pleased with his extraordinary style of compliment that called her "loveliest" though she hardly knew him above an hour, she gravely answered, "I really know nothing of the matter. This is a charming day. The wind, I fancy, must be southerly."

Sir Edward smiled while looking almost beseechingly at her.

"Happy, happy wind, to engage Miss Heywood's thoughts!"

She began to think him downright silly. His choosing to walk with her, she had learnt to understand. It was done to pique Miss Brereton. She had read it, in an anxious glance or two on his side. But why he should talk so much nonsense, unless he could do no better, made no sense. He seemed very sentimental, very full of some feeling or other, and very much addicted to all the newest-fashioned words. He had not a very clear brain, she presumed, and talked a good deal by rote. The future might explain him further. But when there was a proposition for going into the library, she felt that she had had quite enough of Sir Edward for one morning and very gladly accepted Lady Denham's invitation of remaining on the Terrace with her.

The others all left them. Sir Edward did so with looks of very gallant despair in tearing himself away. The two remaining united their agreeableness – that is, Lady Denham, like a true great lady, talked only of her own concerns, and Charlotte listened. Certainly there was no strain of doubtful sentiment nor any phrase of difficult interpretation in Lady Denham's discourse. All was laid out before her. She took hold of Charlotte's arm with the ease of one who felt that any notice from her was an honour, and communicative from the influence of the same conscious importance or a natural love of talking.

She then immediately said in a tone of great satisfaction and with a look of arch sagacity, "Miss Esther wants me to invite her and her brother to spend a week with me at Sanditon House, as I did last summer. But I shan't. She has been trying to get round me every way with her praise of this and her praise of that but I saw what she was about. I saw through it all. I am not very easily taken in, my dear."

Charlotte did not doubt it but could think of nothing more harmless to say than the simple enquiry of "Sir Edward and Miss Denham?"

"Yes, my dear. *My young folks,* as I call them sometimes, for I take them very much by the hand. I had them with me last summer, about this time, for a week, from Monday to Monday, and very delighted and thankful they were. For they are very good young people, my dear. I would not have you think that I *only* notice them for poor dear Sir Harry's sake. No, no. They are very deserving themselves or, trust me, they would not be so much in my company. I am not the woman to help anybody blindfold. I always take care to know what I am about and who I have to deal with before I stir a finger. I do not think I was ever over-reached in my life. And that is a good deal for a woman to say that has been married twice. Poor dear Sir Harry, between ourselves, thought at first to have got more. But," with a bit of a sigh, "he is gone, and we must not find fault with the dead. Nobody could live happier together than us and he was a very honourable man, quite the gentleman of ancient family. And when he died, I gave Sir Edward his gold watch."

She said this with a look at her companion which implied its right to produce a great impression and seeing no rapturous astonishment in Charlotte's countenance, added quickly, "He did not bequeath it to his nephew, my dear. It was no bequest. It was not in the will. He only told me, and *that* but once, that he should wish his nephew to have his watch but it need not have been binding if I had not chosen it."

"Very kind indeed! Very handsome!" said Charlotte, absolutely forced to affect admiration.

"Yes, my dear, and it is not the *only* kind thing I have done by him. I have been a very liberal friend to Sir Edward. And poor young man, he needs it bad enough. For though I am *only* the *dowager*, my dear, and he is the *heir*, things do not stand between us in the way they commonly do between those two parties. Not a shilling do I receive from the Denham estate. Sir Edward has no payments to make *me*. He doesn't stand uppermost, believe me. It is *I* that help *him*."

Despite how coarse Charlotte found it, that a woman of rank such as Lady Denham should lay out her most intimate affairs before a stranger in such a crude way, she believed that she could not remain silent indefinitely.

"Indeed! He is a very fine young man, particularly elegant in his address."

This was said chiefly for the sake of saying something,

but Charlotte directly saw that it was laying her open to suspicion by Lady Denham's giving a shrewd glance at her and replying, "Yes, yes, he is very well to look at. And it is to be hoped that some lady of large fortune will think so, for Sir Edward *must* marry for money. He and I often talk that matter over. A handsome young fellow like him will go smirking and smiling about and paying girls compliments, but he knows he *must* marry for money. And Sir Edward is a very steady young man in the main and has got very good notions.

"Sir Edward Denham," said Charlotte, "with such personal advantages may be almost sure of getting a woman of fortune, if he chooses it."

This glorious sentiment seemed quite to remove suspicion.

"Aye, my dear, that's very sensibly said," cried Lady Denham. "And if we could but get a young heiress to Sanditon! But heiresses are monstrous scarce! I do not think we have had an heiress here or even a co-heiress since Sanditon has been a public place. Families come after families but, as far as I can learn, it is not one in a hundred of them that have any real property, landed or funded. An income perhaps, but no property. Clergymen maybe, or lawyers from town, or half-pay officers, or widows with only a jointure. And what good can such people do anybody? – except just as they take our empty houses and, between ourselves, I think they are great fools for not staying at home. Now if we could get a young heiress to be sent here for her health and if she was ordered to drink asses' milk I could supply her and, as soon as she got well, have her fall in love with Sir Edward!"

"That would be very fortunate indeed."

"And Miss Esther must marry somebody of fortune too. She must get a rich husband. Ah, young ladies that have no money are very much to be pitied! But," after a short pause, "if Miss Esther thinks to talk me into inviting them to come and stay at Sanditon House, she will find herself mistaken. Matters are altered with me since last summer, you know. I have Miss Clara with me now which makes a great difference."

She spoke this so seriously that Charlotte instantly saw in it the evidence of real penetration and prepared for some fuller remarks but it was followed only by, "I have no fancy for having my house as full as a hotel. I should not choose to have my two housemaids' time taken up all the morning in dusting out bed-rooms. They have Miss Clara's room to put to rights as well as my own every day. If they had hard places, they would want higher wages."

For objections of this nature, Charlotte was not prepared. She found it so impossible even to affect sympathy that she could say nothing. Lady Denham soon added, with great glee, "And besides all this, my dear, am I to be filling my house to the prejudice of Sanditon? If people want to be by the sea, why don't they take lodgings? Here are a great many empty houses – three on this very Terrace – no fewer than three lodging papers staring me in the face at this very moment, numbers three, four and eight. Eight, the corner house, may be too large for them, but either of the two others are nice little snug houses, very fit for a young gentleman and his sister. And so, my dear, the next time Miss Esther begins talking about the dampness of Denham Park and the good bathing always does her, I shall advise them to come and take one of these lodgings for a fortnight. Don't you think that will be very fair? Charity begins at home, you know."

Charlotte's feelings were divided between amusement and indignation – but indignation had the larger and the increasing share. She kept her countenance and she kept a civil silence. She could not carry her forbearance farther but without attempting to listen longer, and only conscious that Lady Denham was still talking on in the same way, allowed her thoughts to form themselves into such a meditation as this:

"She is thoroughly mean. I had not expected anything so bad. Mr Parker spoke too mildly of her. His judgement is evidently not to be trusted. His own good nature misleads him. He is too kind-hearted to see clearly. I must judge for myself. And their very *connection* prejudices him. But she is very, very mean. I can see no good in her. Poor Miss Brereton! And she makes everybody mean about her. This poor Sir Edward and his sister – how far nature meant them to be respectable I cannot tell – but they are *obliged* to be mean in their servility to her. And I am mean, too, and a hypocrite in giving her my attention with the appearance of agreeing with her. Thus it is, when rich people are sordid."

And with that, Charlotte turned her thoughts to her brother Freddie so that she may block out the sound of her companion and wondered, in between nodding along in response to Lady Denham, what escapades his first, long overdue, letter might hold.

CHAPTER EIGHT

The two ladies continued walking together till they were rejoined by the others, who, as they issued from the library, were followed by a young Whitby running off with five volumes under his arm to Sir Edward's gig. Sir Edward, approaching Charlotte, said, "You may perceive what has been our occupation. My sister wanted my counsel in the selection of some books. We have many leisure hours and read a great deal. I am no indiscriminate novel reader. The mere trash of the common circulating library I hold in the highest contempt. You will never hear me advocating those puerile emanations which detail nothing but discordant principles incapable of amalgamation or those vapid tissues of ordinary occurrences. You understand me, I am sure?"

"I am not quite certain that I do. But if you will describe the sort of novels which you *do* approve, I dare say it will give me a clearer idea."

"Most willingly, fair questioner. The novels which I approve are such as display human nature with grandeur. Such as show intense feeling and strong passion. Here we see the strong spark of woman's captivations elicit such fire in the soul of man as leads him, though at the risk of some aberration, from the strict line of primitive obligations to hazard all, dare all, achieve all to obtain her. Such are the works which I peruse with delight. These are the novels which enlarge the primitive capabilities of the heart and which it cannot reduce the sense, or be any dereliction of the character, of the superior man, to be conversant with."

"If I understand you aright," said Charlotte, regretting she had asked for any description, "our taste in novels is not at all the same."

And here they were obliged to part, Miss Denham being much too tired of them all to stay any longer.

The truth was that Sir Edward, whom circumstances had confined very much to one spot, had read more sentimental novels than agreed with him. His fancy had been early caught by all the impassioned and most exceptionable parts of Richardson's, and such authors as had since appeared to tread in Richardson's steps. Man's determined pursuit of woman in defiance of every opposition of feeling and convenience had occupied the greater part of his literary hours and formed his character. With a perversity of judgement which must be attributed to his not having by nature a very strong head, the graces, the spirit, the ingenuity and the perseverance of the villain of the story out-weighed all his absurdities and all his atrocities with Sir Edward. With him such conduct was genius, fire and feeling. It interested and inflamed him. And he was always more anxious for the success of the villain and mourned over his decline with more tenderness than could ever have been contemplated by the authors of such novels. Who, he wondered, would be a hero if they could choose to be a villain?

Though he owed many of his ideas to this sort of reading, it would be unjust to say that he read nothing else or that his language was not formed on a more general knowledge of modern literature. He read all the essays, letters, tours and criticisms of the day with the same ill luck which made him derive only false principles from lessons of morality and only long, complicated words that he may impress the listener.

Sir Edward's great object in life was to be seductive. With such personal advantages as he knew himself to possess, and such talents as he did also give himself credit for, he regarded it as his duty. He felt that he was formed to be a dangerous man, quite in the line of the Lovelaces. The very name of Sir Edward, he thought, carried some degree of fascination with it. To be generally gallant about the fair, to make fine speeches to every pretty girl, was but the inferior part of the character he had to play. Miss Heywood, or any other young woman with any pretensions to beauty, he was entitled (according to his own view of society) to approach with high compliment and rhapsody on the slightest acquaintance. But it was Clara alone on whom he had serious designs. It was Clara whom he meant to seduce.

Her seduction was quite determined on. Her situation in every way called for it. She was his rival in Lady Denham's favour. She was young, lovely and dependent. He had very early seen the necessity of the case, and had now been long trying with cautious attentions to make an impression on her heart and to undermine her principles. Clara saw through him and initially had not the least intention of being seduced but she bore with him patiently enough to confirm the sort of attachment which her personal charms had raised. A greater degree of discouragement indeed would not have affected Sir Edward. He was armed against the highest pitch of disdain or aversion. If she could not be won by affection, he must carry her off. He knew his business. Already had he had many musings on the subject. If he *were* constrained so to act, he must naturally wish to strike out something new, to exceed those who had gone before him. And he felt a strong curiosity to ascertain whether the neighbourhood of Timbuctoo might not afford some solitary house adapted for Clara's reception. But the expense, alas! of measures in that masterly style was ill-suited to his purse and prudence obliged him to prefer the quietest sort of ruin and disgrace for the object of his affections to the more renowned.

.

CHAPTER NINE

One day, soon after Charlotte's arrival at Sanditon, she had the pleasure of seeing, just as she ascended from the sands to the Terrace, a gentleman's carriage with post horses standing at the door of the hotel. And by the quantity of luggage being taken off, bringing, it might be hoped, some respectable family determined on a long residence.

Delighted to have such good news for Mr and Mrs Parker, who had both gone home some time before, she proceeded to Trafalgar House with as much alacrity as could remain after having contended for the last two hours with a very fine wind blowing directly on shore. But she had not reached the little lawn when she saw a lady walking nimbly behind her at no great distance and, convinced that it could be no acquaintance of her own, she resolved to hurry on and get into the house if possible before her. But the stranger's pace did not allow this to be accomplished. Charlotte was on the steps and had rung, but the door was not opened, when the other crossed the lawn – and when the servant appeared, they were just equally ready for entering the house.

The ease of the lady, her "How do you do, Morgan?" and Morgan's looks on seeing her, were a moment's astonishment, but another moment brought Mr Parker into the hall to welcome the sister he had seen from the drawing room. Charlotte was soon introduced to Miss Diana Parker. There was a great deal of surprise but still more pleasure in seeing her. Nothing could be kinder than her reception from both husband and wife. How did she come? And with whom? And they were so glad to find her equal to the journey! And that she was to belong to *them* was taken as a thing of course.

Miss Diana Parker was about four and thirty, of middling height and slender, delicate looking rather than sickly, with an agreeable face and a very animated eye. Her manners resembled her brother's in their ease and frankness, though with more decision and less mildness in her tone. She began an account of herself without delay, thanking them for their invitation but "*that* was quite out of the question for, they were both come and meant to get into lodgings and make some stay."

"You both have come! What! Arthur! This is better and better."

"Yes, we actually both came. Quite unavoidable. Nothing else to be done. You shall hear all about it. But my dear Mary, send for the children, I long to see them."

"And how has Arthur borne the journey? And why do we not see him here with you?"

"He has borne it wonderfully. He had not a wink of sleep either the night before we set out or last night at Chichester, and as this is not so common with him as with *me*, I have had a thousand fears for him. But he has kept up wonderfully. And when I left him he was directing the disposal of the luggage and helping Old Sam uncord the trunks. He would not have been unwilling himself to come with me, but there is so much wind that I did not think he could safely venture for I am *sure* there is lumbago hanging about him. So I helped him on with his great coat and told him that once he is finished with the luggage, he is to go to the Terrace to take us lodgings. Miss Heywood must have seen our carriage standing at the hotel. I knew Miss Heywood the moment I saw her before me on the down. My dear Tom, I am so glad to see you walk so well. Let me feel your ankle. That's right, all right and clean. The play of your sinews is a *very* little affected, barely perceptible. Well, now for the explanation of my being here. I told you in my letter of the two considerable families I was hoping to secure for you, the West Indians and the seminary."

Here Mr Parker drew his chair still nearer to his sister and took her hand again most affectionately as he answered, "Yes, yes, how active and how kind you have been!"

"The West Indians," she continued, "whom I look upon as the *most* desirable of the two, as the best of the good, prove to be a Mrs Griffiths and her family. I know them only through others. You must have heard me mention Miss Capper, the particular friend of *my* very particular friend Fanny Noyce. Now, Miss Capper is extremely intimate with a Mrs Darling, who is on terms of constant correspondence with Mrs Griffiths herself. Only a *short* chain, you see, between us, and not a link wanting. Mrs Griffiths meant to go to the sea for her young people's benefit, had fixed on the coast of Sussex, but was undecided as to the where, wanted something private, and wrote to ask the opinion of her friend, Mrs Darling. Miss Capper happened to be staying with Mrs Darling when Mrs Griffiths' letter arrived and was consulted on the question. *She* wrote the same day to Fanny Noyce and mentioned it to her and Fanny, all alive for *us*, instantly took up her pen and forwarded the circumstance to me, except as to *names* – which have but lately transpired. There was but *one* thing for *me* to do. I answered Fanny's letter by the same post and pressed for the recommendation of Sanditon. Fanny had feared your having no house large enough to receive such a family. But I seem to be spinning out my story to an endless length. You see how it was all managed. I had the pleasure of hearing soon afterwards, by the same simple link of connection, that Sanditon *had been* recommended by Mrs Darling, and that the West Indians were very much disposed to go thither. This was the state of the case when I wrote to you. But two days ago – yes, the day before yesterday – I heard again from Fanny Noyce, saying that *she* had heard from Miss Capper, who by a letter from Mrs Darling understood that Mrs Griffiths had expressed herself in a letter to Mrs Darling more doubtingly on the subject of Sanditon. Am I clear? I would be anything rather than not clear."

"Oh, perfectly, perfectly. Well?"

"The reason of this hesitation was her having no connections in the place, and no means of ascertaining that she should have good accommodations on arriving there and she was particularly careful and scrupulous on all those matters, more on account of a certain Miss Lambe, a young lady – probably a niece – under her care, than on her own account, or her daughters'. Miss Lambe has an immense fortune, richer than all the rest, and very delicate health. One sees clearly enough by all this the *sort* of woman Mrs Griffiths must be, as helpless and indolent as wealth and a hot climate are apt to make us. But we are not born to equal energy. What was to be done? I had a few moments' indecision, whether to offer to write to you, or to Mrs Whitby, to secure them a house but neither pleased me. I hate to employ others when I am equal to act myself and my conscience told me that this was an occasion which called for me. Here was a family of helpless invalids whom I might essentially serve. I sounded Arthur, who made no difficulties. Our plan was arranged immediately, we were off yesterday morning at six, left Chichester at the same hour today, and here we are."

"Excellent! Excellent!" cried Mr Parker. "Diana, you are unequalled in serving your friends and doing good to all the world. I know nobody like you. Mary, my love, is not she a wonderful creature? Well, and now, what house do you design to engage for them? What is the size of their family?"

"I do not at all know," replied his sister. "I have not the least idea, never heard any particulars, but I am very sure that the largest house at Sanditon cannot be *too* large. They are more likely to want a second. I shall take only one, however, and that but for a week certain. Miss Heywood, I astonish you. You hardly know what to make of me. I see by your looks that you are not used to such quick measures."

The words "Unaccountable interference! Activity run

mad!" had just passed through Charlotte's mind, but a civil answer was easy.

"I dare say I do look surprised," said she, "because these are very great exertions, and I know what invalids both you and your brother are."

"Invalids indeed. I trust there are not two people in England who have so sad a right to that title! But my dear Miss Heywood, we are sent into this world to be as extensively useful as possible, and where some degree of strength of mind is given, it is not a feeble body which will excuse us or incline us to excuse ourselves. The world is pretty much divided between the weak of mind and the strong, between those who can act and those who cannot, and it is the bounden duty of the capable to let no opportunity of being useful escape them. My brother's complaints and mine are happily not often of a nature to threaten existence *immediately*. And as long as we *can* exert ourselves to be of use to others, I am convinced that the body is the better for the refreshment the mind receives in doing its duty. While I have been travelling with this object in view, I have been perfectly well."

The entrance of the children ended this little eulogy on her own disposition and after having noticed and caressed them all, she prepared to go.

"Cannot you dine with us? Is not it possible to prevail on you to dine with us?" was then the cry. And that being absolutely negatived, it was, "And when shall we see you again? And how can we be of use to you?" Mr Parker warmly offered his assistance in taking the house for Mrs Griffiths.

"I will come to you the moment I have dined," said he, "and we will go about together."

But this was immediately declined.

"No, my dear Tom, upon no account in the world shall you stir a step on any business of mine. Your ankle wants rest. I see by the position of your foot that you have used it too much already. No, I shall go about my house-taking directly. Our dinner is not ordered till six, and by that time I hope to have completed it. It is now only half past four. As to seeing *me* again today, I cannot answer for it. Arthur will be at the hotel all the evening and delighted to see you at any time. But as soon as I get back I shall hear what he has done about our own lodgings, and probably the moment dinner is over, shall be out again on business relative to them. We hope to get into some lodgings or other and be settled after breakfast tomorrow. I have not much confidence in poor Arthur's skill for lodging-taking, but he seemed to like the commission."

"I think you are doing too much," said Mr Parker. "You will knock yourself up. You should not move again after dinner."

"No, indeed you should not," cried his wife, "for dinner is such a mere *name* with you all that it can do you no good. I know what your appetite is."

"My appetite is very much mended lately, I assure you. I have been taking some bitters of my own decocting, which have done wonders. Just at present I shall want nothing. I never eat for about a week after a journey. As for Arthur, he is only too much disposed for food. I am often obliged to check him."

"But you have not told me anything of the *other* family coming to Sanditon," said Mr Parker as he walked with her to the door of the house. "The Camberwell Seminary. Have we a good chance of *them*?"

"Oh, certain. Quite certain. I had forgotten them for the moment. But I had a letter three days ago from my friend Mrs Henry Dupuis, which assured me of Camberwell. Camberwell will be here to a certainty, and very soon. *That* good woman – I do not know her name – not being so wealthy and independent as Mrs Griffiths, can travel and choose for herself. I will tell you how I got at *her*. Mrs Henry Dupuis lives almost next door to a lady, who has a relation lately settled at Clapham, who actually attends the seminary and gives lessons on eloquence and belles-lettres to some of the girls. I got this man a hare from one of Sidney's friends; and he recommended Sanditon. Without *my* appearing however, Mrs Henry Dupuis managed it all."

CHAPTER TEN

It was not a week since Miss Diana Parker had been told by her feelings that the sea air would be the death of her and now she was at Sanditon, intending to make some stay and without the slightest recollection of having written any such thing. It was impossible for Charlotte not to suspect a good deal of fancy in such an extraordinary state of health. Disorders and recoveries, so very much out of the common way, seemed more like the amusement of eager minds in want of employment, than of actual afflictions and relief. The Parkers were, no doubt, a family of imagination and quick feelings, and while the eldest brother found vent for his excessive sensation as a projector, the sister was perhaps driven to dissipate hers in the invention of odd complaints.

The *whole* of her mental vivacity was evidently not so employed; part was laid out in a zeal for being useful. It would seem that she must either be very busy for the good of others or else extremely ill herself. Some natural delicacy of constitution in fact, with an unfortunate turn for medicine, especially quack medicine, had given her an early tendency at various times to various disorders. The rest of her sufferings were from fancy, the love of distinction and the love of the wonderful. She had a charitable heart and many amiable feelings, but a spirit of restless activity, and the glory of doing more than anybody else, had their share in every exertion of benevolence. There was, therefore, vanity in all she did, as well as in all she endured. To what extent Arthur was like his sister, Charlotte had yet to decide.

Mr and Mrs Parker spent a great part of the evening at the hotel but Charlotte had only two or three views of Miss Diana walking over the down after a house for this lady whom she had never seen, and who had never employed her. She was not made acquainted with Arthur till the following day, when, being removed into lodgings and all the party continuing quite well, their brother, his wife and Charlotte were entreated to drink tea with them.

They were in one of the Terrace houses and she found them arranged for the evening in a small neat drawing room, with a beautiful view of the sea if they had chosen it. Although it had been a very fair English summer day, not only was there no open window but the sofa and the table, and the establishment in general, was all at the other end of the room by a brisk fire. Remembering the two drawn teeth, Charlotte approached Arthur Parker with a peculiar degree of respectful compassion. She had had considerable curiosity to meet him. Having fancied him a very puny, delicate-looking young man, materially the smallest of a not very robust family, she was astonished to find him quite as tall as his brother, and a great deal stouter, broad made and lusty, and with no other look of an invalid than a sodden complexion.

Diana was evidently the chief of the family, principal mover and actor. She had been on her feet the whole morning, on Mrs Griffiths' business or their own, and was still the most alert of the company. Arthur had only superintended their final removal from the hotel, bringing two heavy boxes himself, but found the air so cold that he walked as nimbly as he could. Now he boasted much of sitting by the fire till he had cooked up a very good one. Diana, whose exercise had been too domestic to admit of calculation but who, by her own account, had not once sat down during the space of seven hours, confessed herself a little tired. She had been too successful, however, for much fatigue. Not only had she, by walking and talking down a thousand difficulties, at last secured a proper house at eight guineas per week for Mrs Griffiths, she had also opened so many treaties with cooks, housemaids, washerwomen and bathing women, that Mrs Griffiths would have little more to do on her arrival than to wave her hand and collect them around her for choice. Her concluding effort in the cause had been a few polite lines of information to Mrs Griffiths herself. Time not allowing for the circuitous train of intelligence which had been hitherto kept up, she was now regaling in the delight of opening the first trenches of an acquaintance with such a powerful discharge of unexpected obligation.

Mr and Mrs Parker and Charlotte had seen two post-chaises crossing the down to the hotel as they were setting off, a joyful sight and full of speculation. Miss Parker and Arthur had also seen something. They could distinguish from their window that there *was* an arrival at the hotel, but not its amount. Their visitors answered for two hack-chaises. Could it be the Camberwell Seminary? No, no. Had there been a third carriage, perhaps it might, but it was very generally agreed that two hack-chaises could never contain a seminary. Mr Parker was confident of another new family.

When they were all finally seated, after some removals to look at the sea and the hotel, Charlotte's place was by Arthur. He was sitting next to the fire with a degree of enjoyment which gave a good deal of merit to his civility in wishing her to take his chair. There was nothing dubious in her manner of declining it and he sat down again with much satisfaction. She drew back her chair to have all the advantage of his person as a screen, and was very thankful for every inch of back and shoulders beyond her preconceived idea. Arthur was heavy in eye as well as figure, but by no means indisposed to talk. While the other three were chiefly engaged together, he evidently felt it no penance to have a fine young woman next to him, requiring, in common politeness, some attention. His brother Tom, who felt the decided want of some motive for action, some powerful object of animation for him, observed this with considerable pleasure.

Such was the influence of youth and bloom that he began even to make a sort of apology for having a fire.

"We should not have had one at home," said he, "but the sea air is always damp. I am not afraid of anything so much as damp."

"I am so fortunate," said Charlotte, "as never to know whether the air is damp or dry. It has always some property that is wholesome and invigorating to me."

"I like the air too, as well as anybody can," replied Arthur. "I am very fond of standing at an open window when there is no wind. But, unluckily, a damp air does not like *me*. It gives me the rheumatism. You are not rheumatic, I suppose?"

"Not at all."

"That's a great blessing. But perhaps you are nervous?"

"No, I believe not. I have no idea that I am."

"I am very nervous. To say the truth, nerves are the worst part of my complaints in *my* opinion. My sister thinks me prone to nausea, but I doubt it."

"You are quite in the right to doubt it as long as you possibly can, I am sure."

"If I were nauseated," he continued, "you know, wine would disagree with me, but it always does me good. The more wine I drink in moderation, the better I am. I am always best of an evening. If you had seen me today before dinner, you would have thought me a very poor creature."

Charlotte could well believe it. She kept her countenance, however.

"As far as I can understand what nervous complaints are, I have a great idea of the effectiveness of air and exercise for them – daily, regular exercise – and I should recommend rather more of it to *you* than I suspect you are in the habit of taking."

"Oh, I am very fond of exercise myself," he replied, "and I mean to walk a great deal while I am here, if the weather is temperate. I shall be out every morning before breakfast and take several turns upon the Terrace, and you will often see me at Trafalgar House."

"But you do not call a walk to Trafalgar House much exercise surely?"

"Not as to mere distance, but the hill is so steep! Walking up that hill, in the middle of the day, would throw me into such a perspiration! You would see me all in a bath of my own perspiration by the time I got there! I am very subject to it, and there cannot be a surer sign of nervousness."

They were now advancing so deep in physics that Charlotte viewed the entrance of the servant with the tea things as a very fortunate interruption. It produced a great and immediate change. The young man's attentions were instantly lost. He took his own cocoa from the tray, which seemed provided with almost as many teapots as there were persons in company (Miss Diana drinking a sort of herb tea) and turning completely to the fire. He sat coddling and cooking it to his own satisfaction and toasting some slices of bread, brought up ready-prepared in the toast rack. Till it was all done, Charlotte heard nothing of his voice but the murmuring of a few broken sentences of self-approbation and success.

When his toils were over, however, he moved back his chair into as gallant a line as ever, and proved that he had not been working only for himself by his earnest invitation to her to take both cocoa and toast. She was already helped to tea, which surprised him, so totally self-engrossed had he been.

"I thought I should have been in time," said he, "but cocoa takes a great deal of boiling."

"I am much obliged to you," replied Charlotte. "But I *prefer* tea."

"Then I will help myself," said he. "A large dish of rather weak cocoa every evening agrees with me better than anything."

It struck her, however, as he poured out this rather weak cocoa, that it came forth in a very fine, dark-coloured stream, and at the same moment, his sister cried out, "Oh, Arthur, you get your cocoa stronger and stronger every evening," with Arthur's somewhat conscious reply of, *"Tis* rather stronger than it should be tonight," – convinced her that Arthur was by no means so fond of being starved as Diana could desire, or as he felt proper himself. He was certainly very happy to turn the conversation on dry toast and hear no more of his sister.

"I hope you will eat some of this toast," said he. "I reckon myself a very good toaster. I never burn my toasts. I never put them too near the fire at first. And yet, you see, there is not a corner but what is well browned. I hope you like dry toast."

"With a reasonable quantity of butter spread over it, very much," said Charlotte, "but not otherwise."

"No more do I," said he, exceedingly pleased. "We think quite alike there. So far from dry toast being wholesome, I think it a very bad thing for the stomach. Without a little butter to soften it, it hurts the coats of the stomach. I am sure it does. I will have the pleasure of spreading some for you directly, and afterwards I will spread some for myself. Very bad indeed for the coats of the stomach, but there is no convincing *some* people. It irritates and acts like a nutmeg grater."

He could not get command of the butter, however,

without a struggle. His sister accused him of eating a great deal too much and declared he was not to be trusted while he maintained that he only ate enough to secure the coats of his stomach, and besides, he only wanted it now for Miss Heywood.

Such a plea must prevail. He got the butter and spread away for her with an accuracy of judgement which at least delighted himself. But when her toast was done and he took his own in hand, Charlotte could hardly contain herself as she saw him watching his sister while he scrupulously scraped off almost as much butter as he put on, and then seizing an odd moment for adding a great dab just before it went into his mouth. Certainly, Mr Arthur Parker's enjoyments in invalidism were very different from his sister – by no means so spiritualised. A good deal of earthy dross hung about him. Charlotte could not but suspect him of adopting that line of life principally for the indulgence of a sluggish temper, and to be determined on having no disorders but such as called for warm rooms and good nourishment.

In one particular, however, she soon found that he had caught something from his sister.

"What!" said he. "Do you venture upon two dishes of strong green tea in one evening? What nerves you must have! How I envy you. Now, if I were to swallow only one such dish, what do you think its effect would be upon me?"

"Keep you awake perhaps all night," replied Charlotte, meaning to overthrow his attempts at surprise, by the grandeur of her own conceptions.

"Oh, if that were all!" he exclaimed. "No. It acts on me like poison and would entirely take away the use of my right side before I had swallowed it five minutes. It sounds almost incredible."

"Perhaps even unbelievable," said she.

"But it has happened to me so often that I cannot doubt it. The use of my right side is entirely taken away for several hours!"

"It sounds odd to be sure," answered Charlotte coolly, now completely convinced that she spoke to a fool, "but I dare say it would be proved to be the simplest thing in the world by those who have studied right sides and green tea scientifically and thoroughly understand all the effects of one on the other."

Soon after tea, a letter was brought to Miss Diana Parker from the hotel.

"From Mrs Henry Dupuis," said she, "some private hand."

And, having read a few lines, exclaimed aloud, "Well, this is very extraordinary! Very extraordinary indeed! That both should have the same name. Two Mrs Griffiths! This is a letter of recommendation and introduction to me of the lady from Camberwell and *her* name happens to be Griffiths too."

A few more lines, however, and the colour rushed into her cheeks and with much perturbation, she added, "The oddest thing that ever was! A Miss Lambe too! A young West Indian of large fortune. But it *cannot* be the same. Impossible that it should be the same."

She read the letter aloud for comfort. It was merely to introduce the bearer, Mrs Griffiths from Camberwell, and the three young ladies under her care, to Miss Diana

Parker's notice. Mrs Griffiths, being a stranger at Sanditon, was anxious for a respectable introduction. Mrs Henry Dupuis, therefore, at the instance of the intermediate friend, provided her with this letter, knowing that she could not do her dear Diana a greater kindness than by giving her the means of being useful. "Mrs Griffiths' chief solicitude would be for the accommodation and comfort of one of the young ladies under her care, a Miss Lambe, a young West Indian of large fortune in delicate health."

It was very strange! Very remarkable! Very extraordinary! But they were all agreed in determining it to be *impossible* that there should not be two families. Such a totally distinct set of people as were concerned in the reports of each made that matter quite certain. There *must* be two families. Impossible to be otherwise. "Impossible" and "impossible" was repeated over and over again with great fervour. An accidental resemblance of names and circumstances, however striking at first, involved nothing really incredible and so it was settled.

Diana herself derived an immediate advantage to counter-balance her perplexity. She must put her shawl over her shoulders and be running about again. Tired as she was, she must instantly repair to the hotel to investigate the truth and offer her services.

CHAPTER ELEVEN

I t would not do. Not all that the whole Parker race could say among themselves could produce a happier *catastrophé* than that the family from Surrey and the family from Camberwell were one and the same. The rich West Indians and the young ladies' seminary had all entered Sanditon in those two hack-chaises. The Mrs Griffiths who, in her friend Mrs Darling's hands, had wavered as to coming and been unequal to the journey, was the very same Mrs Griffiths whose plans were at the same period (under another representation) perfectly decided, and who was without fears or difficulties.

All that had appeared strange in the reports of the two might very fairly be placed to the account of the vanity, the ignorance, or the blunders of the many engaged in the cause by the vigilance and caution of Miss Diana Parker. *Her* intimate friends must be meddlesome like herself and the subject had supplied letters and extracts and messages enough to make everything appear what it was not. Diana probably felt a little awkward on being first obliged to admit her mistake. A long journey from Hampshire taken for nothing, a brother disappointed, an expensive house on her hands for a week, must have been some of her immediate reflections and much worse than all the rest must have been the sensation of being less clear-sighted and infallible than she had believed herself.

No part of it, however, seemed to trouble her for long. There were so many to share in the shame and the blame that probably, when she had divided out their proper portions to Mrs Darling, Miss Capper, Fanny Noyce, Mrs Henry Dupuis and Mrs Henry Dupuis's neighbour, there might be a mere trifle of reproach remaining for herself. At any rate, she was seen all the following morning walking about after lodgings with Mrs Griffiths as alert as ever.

Mrs Griffiths was a very well-behaved, genteel kind of woman, who supported herself by receiving such great girls and young ladies as wanted either masters for finishing their education or a home for beginning their displays. She had several more under her care than the three who were now come to Sanditon, but the others all happened to be absent. Of these three, and indeed of all, Miss Lambe was beyond comparison the most important and precious, as she paid in proportion to her fortune. She was about seventeen, of mixed race, chilly and tender, had a maid of her own, was to have the best room in the lodgings, and was always of the first consequence in every plan of Mrs Griffiths.

The other girls, two Misses Beaufort, were just such young ladies as may be met with, in at least one family out of three, throughout the kingdom. They had tolerable complexions, showy figures, an upright decided carriage and an assured look. They were very accomplished and very ignorant, their time being divided between such pursuits as might attract admiration, and those labours and expedients of dexterous ingenuity by which they could dress in a style much beyond what they ought to have afforded. They were some of the first in every change of fashion. And the object of all was to captivate some man of much better fortune than their own.

Mrs Griffiths had preferred a small, retired place like Sanditon on Miss Lambe's account. The Misses Beaufort, though preferring anything to smallness and retirement, having in the course of the spring been involved in the expense of six new dresses each, were constrained to be satisfied with Sanditon till their circumstances were retrieved. There, with the hire of a harp for one and the purchase of some drawing paper for the other, and all the finery they could already command, they meant to be very economical, very elegant and very secluded. Miss Beaufort expected praise and celebrity from all who walked within the sound of her instrument while Miss Letitia anticipated curiosity and rapture in all who came near her while she sketched. To both, they intended to be the most stylish girls in the place. The particular introduction of Mrs Griffiths to Miss Diana Parker secured them immediately an acquaintance with the Trafalgar House family and with the Denhams, and the Misses Beaufort were soon satisfied with "the circle in which they moved in Sanditon," to use a proper phrase, for everybody must now "move in a circle".

Lady Denham had other motives for calling on Mrs Griffiths besides attention to the Parkers. In Miss Lambe, here was the very young lady, sickly and rich, whom she had been asking for and she made the acquaintance for

Sir Edward's sake and the sake of her milch asses. How it might answer with regard to the baronet remained to be proved, but as to the animals, she soon found that all her calculations of profit would be vain. Mrs Griffiths would not allow Miss Lambe to have the smallest symptom of a decline or any complaint which asses' milk could possibly relieve. Miss Lambe was "under the constant care of an experienced physician," and his prescriptions must be their rule. And except in favour of some tonic pills, which a cousin of her own had a property in, Mrs Griffiths never deviated from the strict medicinal page.

The corner house of the Terrace was the one in which Miss Diana Parker had the pleasure of settling her new friends. It commanded in front the favourite lounge of all the visitors at Sanditon and, on one side, whatever might be going on at the hotel. There could not have been a more favourable spot for the seclusion of the Misses Beaufort. They missed nothing. And accordingly, long before they had suited themselves with an instrument or with drawing paper, they had, by the frequency of their appearance at the low windows upstairs, in order to close the blinds, or open the blinds, to arrange a flower pot on the balcony, or look at nothing through a telescope, attracted many an eye upwards and made many a gazer gaze again.

A little novelty has a great effect in so small a place. The Misses Beaufort, who would have been nothing at Brighton, could not move here without notice. And even Mr Arthur Parker, though little disposed for unnecessary exertion, always quit the Terrace on his way to his brother's by this corner house, for the sake of a glimpse of the Misses

Beaufort, though it was half a quarter of a mile round about and added two steps to the ascent of the hill.

CHAPTER TWELVE

Charlotte had been ten days at Sanditon without seeing Sanditon House, every attempt at calling on Lady Denham having been defeated by meeting with her beforehand. But now it was to be more resolutely undertaken, at a more early hour, that nothing might be neglected of attention to Lady Denham or amusement to Charlotte.

"And if you should find a favourable opening, my love," said Mr Parker, who did not mean to go with them, "I think you had better mention the poor Mullinses' situation and sound Her Ladyship as to a subscription for them. I am not fond of charitable subscriptions in a place of this kind. It is a sort of tax upon all that come. Yet as their distress is very great and I almost promised the poor woman yesterday to get something done for her, I believe we must set a subscription on foot, and, therefore, the sooner the better. Lady Denham's name at the head of the list will be a very necessary beginning. You will not dislike speaking to her about it, Mary?"

"I will do whatever you wish me," replied his wife, "but you would do it so much better yourself. I shall not know what to say."

"My dear Mary," he cried. "It is impossible you can be really at a loss. Nothing can be more simple. You have only to state the present afflicted situation of the family, their earnest application to me, and my being willing to promote a little subscription for their relief, provided it meet with her approbation."

"The easiest thing in the world," cried Miss Diana Parker, who happened to be calling on them at the moment. "All said and done in less time than you have been talking of it now. And while you are on the subject of subscriptions, Mary, I will thank you to mention a very melancholy case to Lady Denham which has been represented to me in the most affecting terms. There is a poor woman in Worcestershire, whom some friends of mine are exceedingly interested about, and I have undertaken to collect whatever I can for her. If you would mention the circumstance to Lady Denham! Lady Denham *can* give, if she is properly attacked. And I look upon her to be the sort of person who, when once she is prevailed on to undraw her purse, would as readily give ten guineas as five. And therefore, if you find her in a giving mood, you might as well speak in favour of another charity which I and a few more have very much at heart – the establishment of a Charitable Repository at Burton on Trent. And then there is the family of the poor man who was hung last assizes at York, though we really *have* raised the sum we wanted for putting them all out, yet if you *can* get a guinea from her on their behalf, it may as well be done."

"My dear Diana!" exclaimed Mrs Parker. "I could no more mention these things to Lady Denham than I could fly."

"Where's the difficulty? I wish I could go with you

myself. But in five minutes I must be at Mrs Griffiths' to encourage Miss Lambe in taking her first dip. She is so frightened, poor thing, that I promised to come and keep up her spirits, and go in the machine with her if she wished it. And as soon as that is over, I must hurry home, for a reluctant Arthur is to have leeches at one o'clock which will be a three hours' business. Therefore I really have not a moment to spare. Besides that, between ourselves, I ought to be in bed myself at this present time, for I am hardly able to stand and when the leeches have done, I dare say we shall both go to our rooms for the rest of the day."

"I am sorry to hear it, indeed. But Arthur will come to us, in the evening, if he has adequately rested?"

"If Arthur takes my advice, he will stay in bed, for if he remains up by himself he will certainly eat and drink more than he ought. But you see, Mary, how impossible it is for me to go with you to Lady Denham's."

"Upon second thoughts, Mary," said her husband, "I will not trouble you to speak about the Mullinses. I will take an opportunity of seeing Lady Denham myself. I know how little it suits you to be pressing matters upon a mind at all unwilling."

His application thus withdrawn, his sister could say no more in support of hers, which was his object, as he felt all their impropriety, and all the certainty of their ill effect upon his own better claim. Mrs Parker was delighted at this release and set off very happily on this walk to Sanditon House.

It was a close, misty morning and, when they reached the brow of the hill, they could not for some time make out what sort of carriage it was which they saw coming up. It appeared at different moments to be everything from a gig to a phaeton, from one horse to four, and just as they were concluding in favour of a tandem, little Mae's eyes distinguished the coachman and she eagerly called out, "It is Uncle Sidney, Mama. It is indeed." And so it proved.

Mr Sidney Parker, driving his servant in a very neat carriage, was soon opposite to them, and they all stopped for a few minutes. The manners of the Parkers were always pleasant among themselves and it was a very friendly meeting between Sidney and his sister-in-law, who was most kindly taking it for granted that he was on his way to Trafalgar House. This he declined, however. He was "just come from Eastbourne proposing to spend two or three days, as it might happen, at Sanditon" but the hotel must be his quarters. He was expecting to be joined there by a friend or two.

The rest was common enquiries and remarks, with kind notice of little Mae, and a very well-bred bow and proper address to Miss Heywood on her being named to him. And they parted to meet again within a few hours. Sidney Parker was about seven or eight and twenty, very good-looking, with a decided air of ease and fashion and a lively countenance. They had not been more than a few moments in his company when Charlotte decided that, of all the Parker siblings, here was the most favoured in both looks and manners. In looks, he resembled Diana but without the furrowed brow that elder siblings often wore. His energy belied an enthusiasm that rested somewhere short of Tom's but with more easiness built in and there was a distinctive playfulness about his eyes. This adventure afforded agreeable discussion for some time. Mrs Parker entered into all her husband's joy on the occasion and exulted in the credit which Sidney's arrival would give to the place and Charlotte, on behalf of single young ladies everywhere, agreed that it was a very good thing entirely.

The road to Sanditon House was a broad, handsome, planted approach between fields. It led, at the end of a quarter of a mile, through second gates into grounds which, though not extensive, had all the beauty and respectability which an abundance of very fine timber could give. These entrance gates were so much in a corner of the grounds or paddock, so near to one of its boundaries, that an outside fence was at first almost pressing on the road, till an angle *here* and a curve *there* threw them to a better distance. The fence was a proper park paling in excellent condition, with clusters of fine elms or rows of old thorns following its line almost everywhere.

Almost must be stipulated, for there were vacant spaces, and through one of these, Charlotte, as soon as they entered the enclosure, caught a glimpse over the pales of something white and womanish in the field on the other side. It was something which immediately brought Miss Brereton into her head and, stepping to the pales, she saw indeed and very decidedly, Miss Brereton seated not far before her at the foot of the bank, which sloped down from the outside of the paling. Miss Brereton was seated, apparently very composedly, and Sir Edward Denham by her side.

They were sitting so near each other and appeared so closely engaged in gentle conversation that Charlotte instantly felt she had nothing to do but to step back again and say not a word. Privacy was certainly their object. It could not but strike her rather unfavourably with regard to Clara. Why would a lady who gave the impression of publicly shunning the attentions of a man, be now meeting him in secret? But Charlotte felt she must withhold judgement. On consideration, Clara's was a situation which was compromised and dependent and, therefore, must not be judged with severity.

She was glad to perceive that nothing had been discerned by Mrs Parker. If Charlotte had not been considerably the taller of the two, Miss Brereton's white ribbons might not have fallen within the ken of *her* more observant eyes. Among other points of moralising reflection which the sight of this tête-à-tête produced, Charlotte could not but think of the extreme difficulty which secret lovers must have in finding a proper spot for their stolen interviews. Here perhaps they had thought themselves so perfectly secure from observation, the whole field open before them, a steep bank and pales never crossed by the foot of man at their back. Yet here she had seen them. They were really ill-used.

The house was large and handsome. Two servants appeared to admit them and everything had a suitable air of property and order. Lady Denham valued herself upon her liberal establishment and had great enjoyment in the order and importance of her style of living. They were shown into the usual sitting room, well proportioned and well furnished, though it was furniture rather originally good and extremely well kept than new or showy. And as Lady Denham was not there, Charlotte had leisure to look about her and to be told by Mrs Parker that the whole-length portrait of a stately gentleman which, placed over the mantelpiece, caught the eye immediately, was the picture of Sir Harry Denham. And one amongst many miniatures in another part of the room, little conspicuous, represented Mr Hollis, poor Mr Hollis! It was impossible not to feel him ill-used – to be obliged to stand back in his own house and see the best place by the fire constantly occupied by Sir Harry Denham.

A sound of rustling skirt brought Lady Denham, who was quick in getting the formalities out of the way. In the short time it took the visitors to take their seats, the weather and absence of Clara were already spoken about and dealt with and suddenly the subject turned to Charlotte herself. With a keen eye, Lady Denham commenced questioning:

"Your friend is very quiet, Mary, but I can tell that little escapes her notice."

Then turning to Charlotte and questioning her on topics more suited to their first meeting.

"You come from a large, genteel farming family, I believe, Miss Heywood."

"Yes, ma'am."

"Of course, farming so close to the coast must be a laborious and unprofitable business as we also know hereabouts. And your parents or siblings, will they be following you to Sanditon shortly?"

"No, ma'am." Charlotte smiled at the thought of her family of sixteen together with a servant or two entirely filling up Sanditon's hotel and the cost of such a crazy scheme.

"You smile; why would not they, or some few, join you? There are rooms enough available in the hotel or in leasable properties. We could secure them for you for a good price."

Charlotte attempted to hide another smile that Lady Denham, who had called visitors to bathing places 'foolish' and had refused to pay for a hotel in London, now expected others, much poorer than herself, to do so.

"It would not suit them, ma'am. I fear my parents never leave home and with the exception of my older brother Freddie, who is always either on the continent or in London, they are busy with the other twelve."

"Fourteen children in all! What a miracle that your mother is still with you – a dangerous and expensive business. If you think of your friends, Miss Heywood, you will press for at least one or two of the more grown-up siblings to come. They might add just the right busyness to our otherwise dull set. That brother of yours in London, what is he about?"

"He studied law, Your Ladyship, and speaks several languages. He spends much time overseas in a diplomatic role to European gentry. He is currently in London assisting them with their affairs here."

"Indeed! It would be more fortuitous to our land if he paid more heed to our own gentry instead of swaggering his way around the courts of Bavaria and who knows where else."

Here Mary felt obliged to deflect her host. "I am happy to report, Lady Denham, that my brother-in-law, Sidney, is just come and will be joined by a number of friends in the coming days."

"Well, that is something, I suppose. Though, if he had made Esther an offer as he should have, perhaps he would live hereabouts and his coming and going would not always be a surprise for us."

This was a new interest for Charlotte. Had an understanding existed between Sidney Parker and Esther Denham? Had the young lady been slighted? But looking at Mary, whose head was decidedly bowed, her gaze fixed on the floor, it was evident that this subject was one that made her uncomfortable and had not required a response. Lady Denham, recollecting that she had not yet finished with Charlotte, began again.

"So that makes you the oldest of thirteen at home. It is good that you have come. Enslaved, as you are, to the care of your younger siblings, you might never find a husband."

"I believe Your Ladyship has given this more thought than I, when …"

"But perhaps that was your intention in joining the Parkers," Lady Denham finished with a grin, "two wealthy, eligible brothers and the opportunity to be flung in amongst others."

Charlotte flushed. "I am not so calculating as you credit me, Your Ladyship."

Again Mary felt she must politely come to her friend's defence. "I am afraid you are mistaken a little, Lady Denham, for it is we who insisted in kidnapping Charlotte. I became so attached to her during our fortnight at Willingden that I was most insistent she be my companion." Mary placed her hand on Charlotte's and smiled warmly as Mae instinctively nestled into her on the other side. "And I am so grateful every day that I did."

"Hmmm. Well, as you are expecting so much company,

perhaps you can advise Tom to host a dinner party at Trafalgar House. I do believe it is our duty to provide entertainment for our visitors, particularly Miss Lambe."

"What a wonderful idea, Lady Denham, but I believe we would not have adequate room to host such a large gathering of visitors. We have not space for above twelve at the dinner table and I'm afraid we would be very crowded in our drawing room."

"Nonsense. If you are very careful who you invite, you shall manage perfectly. Let the Reverend Hanking fend for himself. He has a tendency to turn up wherever there is company. Mrs Griffiths, the two Misses Beaufort and Miss Lambe, who must be seated next to Sir Edward, of course. Then there is Miss Denham, Mr Sidney Parker, two of his friends, Miss Diana and Arthur Parker, Tom, yourself and I. That is fourteen. I'm sure you can manage fourteen."

Charlotte noticed that she and Miss Brereton had been placed in the same category as Reverend Hanking by being omitted and that they, too, must fend for themselves.

Mary, visibly unhappy with the suggestion, just succeeded in saying, "I must speak with my husband, Lady Denham. I think he would not wish to offend many of the other visitors to Sanditon as well as the shop owners and Mrs Whitby at the library for example ... and of course Miss Heywood and Miss Brereton."

At the moment her name was mentioned, the door opened and Clara entered the room. She sat next to Lady Denham, joining in the conversation in a relaxed and easy manner. She apologised that she had not joined them earlier but she had mislaid a pair of gloves and was obliged to speak with the housekeeper.

Charlotte wondered at Miss Brereton's lie and the risk she took of losing her wealthy relatives' favour so that she may spend time alone with Sir Edward. Could she love Sir Edward? Was it possible that any young lady, in the possession of even the smallest amount of reason, could love him? She stared at Clara as she pondered the answer, concluding that, despite all her beauty and attributes, Miss Clara Brereton must pay the heavy price of sinking in Charlotte Heywood's good opinion.

CHAPTER THIRTEEN

On their walk home and with Mae busy zig-zagging collecting wildflowers along the path, there was much for Mary and Charlotte to talk over. It started with an apology from Mary. "Tom and I often forget how difficult it is, for a newcomer, to remain composed when Lady Denham speaks. She is not very refined, her manners are not perhaps what a great lady's should be, but she means no harm."

"I generally consider conversation requires two participants, with listening and engagement necessary on both sides. And dare I say it, respectfully too," laughed Charlotte. "I do not think Lady Denham views conversation in this way."

"Oh but I am sorry that I had not prepared you better. You had met her before so I did not think she would be so direct in her questioning."

"Or impertinent?"

"I am sorry, Charlotte."

Again Charlotte laughed. "You have nothing to apologise for, Mary. I am sure that once I become accustomed to any rudeness in her speech, I may actually come to like her directness. Anything is better than falsehood and flattery."

"Well, that is a forgiving statement and I will agree with you. Lady Denham can be quite mean in her ways but you always know where you stand with her. That is a virtue, I am sure."

Both ladies linked arms and talked of more general things until Charlotte recollected what had been said of Sidney and Esther and in this found an eager communicant in Mary. "Lady Denham had hoped that Sidney would make Miss Denham an offer. She even threw them together a great deal last summer when he came visiting with friends but nothing came of it. They had always been well acquainted – the Denhams and Parkers – so I can see where the idea sprang from. Tom spoke of it once or twice and even had a word with Sidney to encourage him, especially when he knew that it would please Lady Denham, but Sidney quit for London and with the exception of seeing him briefly during our recent trip to London, this is our first time having him back to Sanditon since."

"And Miss Denham, was she heartbroken? Had she been expecting it too?"

"Esther and I have never been confidantes and, therefore, I cannot say but she did seem very out of sorts when we met for some time after. I thought, at one time, she blamed us for Sidney leaving or that she wrongly believed we may have discouraged him. But she is reserved and never spoke a word of the affair to me."

"But fortune would not be a deterrent for Mr Parker, if he did indeed love her."

"No, it would not have been. My husband believes he is too fond of his independence."

"And yet, if Lady Denham is so keen to see Miss Denham married and it is well within her power to secure her financially, so that she may make a good match, why has she not settled something on her?"

"I also cannot think why but as Tom would say, when the subject is money, Lady Denham would chop off her own nose if she thought it could spare her a halfpenny. She complains of those dependents who surround her and yet she seems to like having them powerless and running about her, all the same."

Just then Mae returned to the pair and pushed all the flowers into her mother's hands before turning and running excitedly in the direction of a gentleman walking towards them, shouting "Sidney, Sidney" all the way until he picked her up and swung her around thrice.

"Ladies," Sidney bowed, "may I escort you home? Tom left on business just now and I thought it wise to depart before Diana learnt of my arrival. No doubt I would be subject to scrutiny and a physical examination before she'd believe me well enough to walk out."

They laughed.

"And who might you be bringing to Sanditon this summer, Sidney?"

"Why, the same fellow you met last year, in my company – Captain Russell."

"Just one? Oh Sidney, you gave the impression that there were several of you and I have told Lady Denham as much."

"Well, had I known the level of excitement it would stir up in Lady Denham, I should have brought twenty. Perhaps she seeks husband number three."

"Sidney!"

"Another friend, an acquaintance of Captain Russell's, said he may join us too, but I cannot be certain."

"Very well," said Mary, "you are forgiven. But be sure to join us for dinner tonight. We expect Diana and Arthur too."

The remainder of the journey was spent in cheerful chat while the mind of Charlotte was occupied with wondering how disappointed Miss Denham might have been, how ashamed or humiliated, if their company had expected an engagement. But surely she would not have been so hurt if she had not also longed for it. She must have loved him too. Poor Miss Denham!

That evening all was noise, fuss and laughter in the dining room of Trafalgar House. Tom, buoyed up by the support and company of his three siblings returned home, was even more social than usual. Mary was pleased at being asked by Diana about the most minute details of her children's health and diet while Arthur laughed constantly and Sidney declared every scheme of Tom's as 'damned foolish' to peals of laughter.

Charlotte was unaccustomed to such revelry at dinner time, especially amongst adults. With Freddie away and her father spending long hours on the farm, she was mostly left to assist her mother at mealtimes, settling the children and ensuring they ate and behaved. Mealtimes at Willingden involved coaxing, scolding and sulking.

Therefore, such enquiries and inquisitiveness on display now were new to Charlotte. She was surprised at how Tom laid out details of even the most private of his financial investments, how Arthur revealed the most alarming and embarrassing of ailments before them, how Diana asked Mary whether she ate oats for breakfast as she had recommended to aid regularity in her digestion. Only Sidney sat back and spoke less of himself than the others. But when he did speak, he held everyone's attention for his wit and enjoyment. Charlotte, though out of her familiar setting, could rarely recall a mealtime as enjoyable and relaxed – the only change in tone being the occasional misgiving by Diana who might look up in a shot and scold Arthur.

"Put that potato down, Arthur!" Then a moment later, "Arthur, that is the fourth potato you have eaten this evening."

"Diana, I declare it is not. Really? I do not believe that I have had above two."

"Four," said Diana firmly, "and with butter on each. You know it does not agree with you."

"You are quite right, sister," Arthur answered, popping the dripping potato into his mouth, "and that will be my very last one tonight."

Then Tom called across to Mary at the other end of the table. "My dear, I have been thinking it over all afternoon and I believe I have the answer to Lady Denham's request that we host dinner here for a very select few."

The entire company were all ears.

"We will arrange for an evening event to be held at

the hotel. Let us call it an assembly. Some few of us may have dinner first and, afterwards, let us open the evening to all shopkeepers, visitors to Sanditon and the like, with some light refreshments at eleven. There will be music, of course."

"But husband, Lady Denham wished for a small gathering, that she may get to know Miss Lambe better. She is not usually in favour of dancing. Will she not be displeased?"

"A dinner here is quite out of the question, if we cannot accommodate the many good people who make up Sanditon society. What of our boisterous Reverend Hanking and Mrs Whitby? What of Jebb, Heeley and the tradespeople who do so much to promote our bathing place and put it on the map? So many would be offended at not being invited, we had best not risk it. No, I believe an inexpensive evening at the hotel, with the best and most lively of Sanditon's citizens, will do wonders for the morale of our community and offer our visitors and those considering visiting a bit of excitement."

"Lady Denham will not be pleased."

"Indeed, why would she object – when it is costing her nothing, enabling her to scrutinise poor Miss Lambe and saving her a dinner at home?"

"It is a great idea," added Sidney, raising his glass, "and I will only have to fall up the stairs to reach my bed."

"And I shall be able to dance." Arthur clapped his hands.

"But do not overexert yourself, Arthur," added Diana. "Too much revelry makes you quite flushed and brings on palpitations. Remember last New Year's Eve at the Halpins'.

We had to lay you across three chairs."

The following morning, Tom returned in jubilant mood from Sanditon House. Not only did Lady Denham approve his plan but she believed it to be her own and gave instructions as to how Mary should organise the seating. Once a date for the following week was agreed with the hotel and their best rooms engaged, all were excited and turned their thoughts to preparations.

The week passed quickly. Charlotte's days were filled with accompanying Mary to the hotel. Mary had exceptional taste and attended to even the most minute of particulars. She did not trust herself, however, so Charlotte's only means of assisting was to reassure Mary that she was making excellent choices.

When she was not assisting Mary, Charlotte enjoyed solitary walks along the cliffs or on the shore. Occasionally, she met Miss Denham who also enjoyed walks and solitude and, although politely joining her, Miss Denham remained guarded. In Charlotte's opinion, whatever had happened between herself and Sidney Parker last year had caused this constant sullen mood. She had heard that Esther Denham had once been a great conversationalist and social butterfly but nothing of that remained now. Disappointment must have taken the colour from her days. But, in Charlotte's inexperienced mind, there was no excuse, one year on, for Esther Denham not to rally her own spirits. Charlotte herself, one of fourteen children, could hardly expect to make a great match. She would very likely wed one of the gentleman farmers in a neighbouring village and while luxuries would not be expected, her needs and comfort would most likely be assured. It was a good thing, in her mind, not to look for much in life. Her brother Freddie may dream, travel and do as he wished but not she. And here was Miss Denham all melancholy and self-pity – while Charlotte convinced herself that, if their roles were reversed, she would have overcome her disappointment by now.

One afternoon, as both Charlotte and Miss Denham accidentally met and then strolled along the cliffs together, they saw far beneath them on the sands a group of gentlemen. It seemed to prompt a change in Miss Denham and she commenced a lively discussion.

"I have been disappointed, Miss Heywood. I dare say you may have heard something of it?" she said, looking at the outlines of Sidney, Tom and Arthur Parker with Captain Russell who had arrived at the hotel two nights before.

"Yes, a little," replied Charlotte.

"Then you know of whom I speak and that he is here amongst us as if nothing passed last summer." Here she paused, inhaled deeply and continued in a quivering voice, "It was a short but sweet time and now how bitter I have turned. I confess I am surprised to see him. And so unchanged."

Charlotte looked over to where Sidney, the broadest of the men, waved his arms, engaged in earnest conversation with his companions.

"I am sorry."

"There is no need for sympathy. I have learnt my lesson. At the first opportunity, I will wed, so do not feel sorry for me. Come, let us keep walking. I will not be blinded by feelings again. I shall marry for wealth."

Charlotte did not feel there was anything she could say. Miss Denham was not seeking her advice and, inexperienced in such matters, she had none to give. They strolled along for the remainder of their walk mostly in silence.

On returning to Trafalgar House, Charlotte discovered a letter had arrived from her brother Fred. With no one at home to interrupt her, she remained in the parlour and relaxed into a comfortable chair with the light of the sun shining in from the window. With delight, despite it being shorter than she would have liked, she commenced reading.

64 Sloane Street,
London.

My dearest Lottie,

What a strange creature you are. Living a life of pretence! We had believed you to be the quiet, reserved daughter of a farming family and the sister of many but how wrong we were. All the while, you were waiting to overturn a carriage so that you might imprison its occupants and force yourself upon them when they say they must return home to their bathing place. What sort of adventures can a young woman be having in this Sanditon? The town built on sand, according to its name. It sounds like a strange business to me. Be careful not to disappear into the shifting sands yourself. Always carry an umbrella lest you must use it to hoist yourself onto a rock or hook yourself onto a passing curricle. And are you having adventures, Lottie, my dear? I so look forward to your response for instead of telling me whose cows are calving or how many chickens the fox caught, I will be hearing of dances and elopements and what not.

On my side, I remain for now in London. Our plan to return to Moravia has been put off by Count Von Lamberg who is having too much fun in town. He has now decided to see more of England and we are making plans which change every other day. The rest of the party must do as he bids but being of European nobility themselves and with little else to be worrying them excepting occasional letters from their fretting mothers, they are content enough.

Is there any possibility of your getting to London when the season begins here? I know it would never be something you considered at home but perhaps, you will now that you have attached yourself mercenarily to the pleasant, pliable Parkers. You must remain on with them a little longer (sprain your ankle if you must, it is all the rage) and encourage them to take themselves to town for the winter.

Wishing you sunny days by the sea,
Freddie

CHAPTER FOURTEEN

At Diana Parker's suggestion, Mrs Griffiths, Miss Jemima Lambe and the Misses Beaufort called to Trafalgar House on the morning of the assembly. It would enable her to finally introduce them to Mrs Mary Parker, hostess for the evening, and her young friend, Miss Heywood. Diana in her enthusiasm, however, had hardly allowed them their tea before she began hastening their visitors back out the door again. There was much to be done for the evening and she had promised Reverend Hanking that they would call on him too. A school, she informed Mrs Griffiths, should always count a clergyman amongst its instructors. So although it had been a short visit, it was long enough for Charlotte to form an opinion of their guests.

There was nothing in the Misses Beaufort that could interest her. They put on airs, spoke more eloquently than was necessary and pretended to show interest in their host and her children – all the while taking in every ornament, piece of furnishing and what the other ladies wore, that they may ridicule it later.

Miss Lambe, however, was different. She had a natural elegance, spoke softly and emitted a playfulness through her large eyes. She and Charlotte spoke a little together when the opportunity arose and a laugh shared over Morgan's walking about with something stuck to his shoe convinced Charlotte that Miss Lambe was worth getting to know better.

Within several hours, they were all reunited again, in their finery, at Sanditon's only hotel. Soon it emerged that Lady Denham's suggested seating arrangement for dinner was flawed or, rather, persons took it upon themselves to change it. The Reverend Hanking, whom Tom Parker insisted on inviting, was adamant that he sit next to Mrs Griffiths who in turn insisted on sitting on one side of Miss Lambe. Lady Denham insisted that Sir Edward sit on the other. Mary was obliged to make changes on the spot to accommodate them all. This meant that Miss Lambe was one person away from Lady Denham; that was one person more than she had planned on, but, Her Ladyship concluded, sacrificing her own curiosity for the sake of her nephew was a noble act indeed. The distance, however, did not stop her from making an occasional comment to the heiress, loud but not always appropriate.

"You speak very good English all things considered and your hair is more elegant than I had expected. Am I not right?"

Though the comment drew the attention of more than its intended recipient, a brief silence during which nobody spoke, followed by a hurried return to their own conversations, showed that all were embarrassed by her rudeness. Frustrated and bored at not being of more use to her nephew, she turned to Miss Brereton on her other side just as the hotel owner and his daughters were bringing the food.

"My dear, this is all wrong. We already know everything there is to know of one another. Would you kindly swap seats with that army man?"

Clara, embarrassed, did as she was told and as everyone had heard her speak, Captain Russell was already making his way from the end of the table. Mary was mortified at Lady Denham's dissatisfaction with her seating arrangements and memorised the current set-up so that she may not make the same mistake again. Meanwhile, the captain sat next to Lady Denham and did not leave it again until his income, place as second brother and lack of fortune or prospects were discussed with the great lady and, with a sigh, she at last dismissed him as nobody worth knowing.

Charlotte, amused by the moving of persons about her, was glad not to be asked to move herself. She had just commenced a friendly argument with Sidney Parker on the remaining few men who continued to wear powdered wigs – she in defence and he opposed.

"I suppose it was the fashion of their youth and we must allow them to feel young for as long as they wish," she argued.

"But what a fashion!"

"It gives them extra work and cost but if it grieves them not, what harm does it do to you or me?"

"You have never been sea bathing, I suspect, when the powdered wig floated past? There is no fright quite like it, Miss Heywood. I was obliged to ensure that there was not a body attached to it."

"And was there not?" laughed Charlotte.

"No. However, there was a bald, unclad gentleman near the shore waving at me and shouting to ask if I would do him the honour of returning the offensive item to him."

During the meal, opportunities of making observations could not fail to occur and Charlotte delighted in each one of them. The captain was speaking earnestly to a now obviously uninterested Lady Denham. Tom Parker was in animated conversation with Sanditon's shop owners at the other end of the table. Sir Edward spoke a great deal to the silent Miss Lambe while stealing an occasional sheepish look in the direction of Miss Brereton. Miss Lambe, Charlotte concluded, was sweet and perhaps mischievous. Whenever Sir Edward looked away, she smiled over at Charlotte and pretended to cover a yawn.

The Reverend Hanking, however, struck her as one of the more interesting persons. He was large, robust and a fixture in every sense of the word. To Lady Denham's disgust he had the living in her parish for life, due to a service unknown which he had rendered the late Sir Harry. She had tried to find a way to uproot him but was unsuccessful,

"Until he dies, I die or I have him killed, I shall not be rid of him."

Charlotte did not wonder that Lady Denham, who wished to be presiding over all interactions, resented his being there and the attention he stole from herself. His presence in a room, Charlotte believed, would always be felt, even when he was silent – a groan, a sigh, a cough, a quick movement, a jump up or a loud cry of indignation showed that he truly was larger than life. But he appeared delighted with Mrs Griffith whom he had, just the day before, discovered to be a widow. They vigorously discussed the importance and responsibility of educating young ladies – both claiming expertise in the area. Meanwhile Mary and Miss Denham spoke politely to the persons on either side of them, ate little and seemed to wish the dinner over. Mrs Whitby and Mr Jebb complained of bad roads while Mr Heeley and his wife spoke only to each other. The loudest part of the table came from where the Misses Beaufort sat as they laughed loudly whenever spoken to.

"Ah Plato, Plato," thought Charlotte to herself, "they that have the least wit are the greatest blabbers."

With Captain Russell now at the other end of the table, looking back longingly at his former seat, the responsibility of drawing forth useless laughter from the sisters fell to the lot of Arthur Parker. They imagined their giggling pleased onlookers. Their mother had said it showed them to be very agreeable and good-humoured – qualities that any young lady seeking a husband should display. Despite being the recipient of several frowns from Mrs Griffith, Arthur believed himself to be funnier than he was and even said aloud, "It is a very good thing that I came tonight to liven up this dull party."

When the clock struck nine, the table was cleared away to make room for a space to dance. Diana Parker almost ran to Charlotte. "My dear Miss Heywood, I was quite in the horrors that I had not the opportunity to tell you how splendid you look, does she not, Mary?"

"Yes, I have been telling her all evening that she is an angel."

"Absolutely! Who needs silks, feathers and jewels when one is naturally favoured? And your dress is just as it should be ... simple and modest."

Charlotte thanked her for her kindness but could not help feeling, as she looked at the excellent taste of Miss Brereton, the showy figures of the Misses Beaufort and the feminine finery of Miss Denham, that Diana's compliment hinted at her being plain by comparison. It was evident that her finest dress, purchased only the year before and more than adequate for the assembly at Willingden, was not in equal company here.

Soon the room filled up with many of the families of Sanditon, old and new, all looking and acting their best. The shyer amongst them, Charlotte assumed to be the visitors, some of whose names must have been those on the library subscription list. Tom Parker raised a glass and made a toast to the health of all friends of Sanditon. Then he quickly proceeded to bow or shake hands with the more reserved present, showing his good manners in making strangers feel welcome and introducing persons to others, that no one was left alone and staring into their glass. Tom Parker, who earlier in the day had insisted that the piano belonging to the hotel owner be moved into this room, now called that some young lady should play the piano and a small dance be started. A local fiddler, who had also been engaged, took up a chair beside the piano and joined in for jigs and the more lively tunes. This request led to a decided change in Miss Lambe's countenance and she spoke more assertively than she had all evening.

"I would be honoured to play for you."

Tom clapped his hands in delight and organised as many as he could into couples while Mary apologised to Miss Lambe that she had not brought a greater collection of music sheets. Miss Lambe smiled her happiest smile of the evening.

"Oh, do not worry. I love to play and miss the instrument so much. I know so many by heart. You will have to force me to stop."

Charlotte was surprised to find her hand taken by Sidney and led to the set.

"My word, Mr Parker, but I was brought up to believe gentlemen asked ladies for the honour of their hand for the forthcoming dance, rather than kidnap them."

"In company such as this, if I did not steal you, I might have been left with a scolding sister or cross dowager."

"And instead you find yourself dancing with a wig-approving farm girl."

"It was the best, I am afraid, of a very bad lot."

Charlotte feigned indignation and the dance continued with great energy and mirth from all those who took part and nowhere more so than from Diana Parker who lectured Arthur for dancing but declared the exercise worked wonders for the pains in her lower back. Miss Denham, still cold in her manners, was escorted to the floor by Captain Russell and, despite appearing dissatisfied, remained his partner for the second dance also. Everyone commented that they made an elegant pair. With Miss Lambe at the piano, Sir Edward excused himself of the duty of her seduction and instead danced with Miss Brereton. For the first time all evening he appeared more relaxed and content

– more like his former self. This substitution and apparent enjoyment incensed Lady Denham. She announced to the room that Miss Lambe had best share the instrument with other ladies or she may be considered immodest and in need of constant praise. Miss Lambe jumped up suddenly, to be replaced at once by Miss Whitby who was eagerly awaiting an opportunity to exhibit her skills. Miss Lambe apologised to Charlotte and Mary who were nearest, saying she had quite forgotten herself and that she was disappointed that there was not yet an instrument secured for her use at the Terrace. Mary quickly promised that she may come to her home at any time and practise.

"Really?" Miss Lambe clapped her hands. "But I do not think Mrs Griffiths will permit it. She is under strict instructions to ensure I am chaperoned at all times and as she also must tend to the Misses Beaufort, I'm afraid it would be impossible."

"Not at all," cried Charlotte, linking her arm and leading her up to Mrs Griffiths. "Mrs Griffiths, could you possibly spare Miss Lambe every other day to attend to piano practice at Trafalgar House? It is Mrs Parker's greatest wish that the instrument should be used more often and, I fear, I am a dreadful pianist. I will happily collect Miss Lambe on each occasion and chaperone her throughout. You may be sure that I am of good and responsible character. I believe Mrs Parker will vouch for me."

"No, I am afraid we could not impose, Miss Heywood," said Mrs Griffiths.

"Now, now, Mrs Griffiths," interrupted Reverend Hanking, "were we not, just now, discussing that the greatest way to praise the Lord was in song? 'Awake, my soul, and with the sun thy daily stage of duty run'. Would the Almighty have blessed mankind with a love and skill for music, if not to adore Him?"

"The good Lord has blessed mankind with many things – not all good and pure, however, I acknowledge that you are right in this instance."

Mary, who had joined them, added, "Please, Mrs Griffiths, Miss Heywood is most responsible and would set an excellent example for Miss Lambe. I, too, will be at home most days so you need not worry that they will be disturbed or be interrupted by company. We are very quiet in our ways."

Charlotte nodded, though she felt that if Tom Parker had his way, every person who set foot in Sanditon would walk through his house several times each day.

"Oh, Mrs Parker, please do not think for a moment that I am implying otherwise. Your home, your character and the very society we find ourselves associating with" – looking briefly at Reverend Hanking – "is most respectable and desirable. I absolutely approve Miss Lambe availing of your kindness and can only express my sincerest gratitude."

Jemima Lambe squeezed Charlotte's hand with delight.

"Tell me, Mrs Parker," said Mrs Griffiths, "do you feel there will ever be a place at Sanditon for ladies to sit, eat buns and drink tea?"

Mary almost hopped.

"Why, Mrs Griffiths, it is a dear wish of mine. Have you been to a tea room before?"

"Yes, frequently, when we were at Bath. They are the

most fashionable places for ladies and are always so busy, especially when the weather is unpredictable."

"Now, Charlotte," said Mary, clapping her hands, "you see, it would be a success. I know it would be. And perhaps old Stringer can supply us. He has the most wonderful berries and fruit for pies, tarts and buns."

"A teahouse," interrupted Reverend Hanking, "is just the thing we need. If you ladies would join me sitting over here, I would be happy to tell you of all the delicacies I have sampled in the *salons* of Paris, Vienna and Rome. They have been quite the thing in the Orient for centuries."

"Why, Reverend Hanking," exclaimed Mrs Griffiths, "I had not known you to be so well travelled."

"I was quite the seasoned traveller, Mrs Griffiths. It goes a long way to explaining why I have not *yet* settled down."

This last comment was said with emphasis and directed only at Mrs Griffiths, who giggled, like one of the Misses Beaufort, on hearing it.

The assembly continued throughout the night in the liveliest fashion, when at last Sir Edward, under the watchful eye of his aunt, requested Miss Lambe's hand for the next dance.

"Impossible, I am afraid," answered Mrs Griffiths, her tone changing immediately. "We thank you most decidedly but must absolutely draw the line at dancing. I am afraid that Miss Lambe is of a weakly constitution and cannot dance. Her doctor would not approve."

"We need not dance a jig. This dance is Kelsterne Gardens, a fine, slow, genteel dance."

"I apologise, Sir Edward, this is a direct instruction from her guardians."

And before he had reached his infuriated aunt, Lady Denham had announced that her carriage had best be called and the night's festivities come to a close. This meant a hurried ending for all, as Lady Denham and Miss Brereton were to see the Denham siblings home. The Reverend Hanking, warning of unpredictable weather, insisted on escorting Mrs Griffiths and her charges back to the Terrace and seemed annoyed when Captain Russell joined him in this noble quest. Meanwhile Diana, who in enjoying a medicinal glass of sherry, had tripped over a foot rest, declared that Arthur had best take her home at once for unknown damage may have occurred to her ligaments. Within ten minutes, the room was emptied of all but Charlotte and Tom, Mary and Sidney Parker.

"If I had known Sanditon were to provide such diversion," announced Sidney, "I would have come sooner."

"Well, perhaps it is best that you did not, Sidney," said Mary, "for up to a few weeks ago, Tom and I were busy overturning carriages, spraining ankles and kidnapping young ladies from the comforts of Willingden. The wrong Willingden at that."

"Well, I am truly glad you did," he smirked, playing with the tassels at the end of the table cloth as Charlotte blushed and looked away, "for it is far more agreeable to spend an evening scolded by Miss Heywood than by Lady Denham."

"Be that as it may, Sidney, and despite all the scolding,

I must declare the night a success," Tom said. "I can feel it in my bones, just as Reverend Hanking feels it in his knees, that this season is one we are unlikely to forget."

CHAPTER FIFTEEN

Buoyed up with happy remembrances of the night before – acknowledged hopes of friendship with Miss Jemima Lambe and unacknowledged hopes with regard to Sidney Parker – Charlotte sat down the following morning, to write to her brother in London.

Trafalgar House
Sanditon
Sussex

Dearest Freddie,

You rogue! You rascal! Where is my second letter? Despite my confidence in the speed of the London postal service and my brother's hand, I find I have not yet received it. Perhaps you have so much to tell me of the baron from Liechtenstein, the Austrian viscount and the Italian prince that you are writing yet. How do idle young men spend their time? But do remember I am a lady of delicate sensibilities and perhaps had best not know.

I am very content with Sanditon. The Parkers are very good to me, though some of their family are bordering on the ridiculous. Diana, the eldest sibling, an invalid by her own account, is the most determined and organised lady I have ever met. Such vigour, such energy! And although I have never seen her eat more than a small carrot in all the times we've dined together (swearing that fasting makes her strong) she declares she is in decline and could be taken by her maker in an instant. As for her obsession with quack medicine, she is a law unto herself.

Arthur, the youngest sibling, is also a terrible invalid. But again, I cannot see how that is. They speak of it a great deal but his appetite and spirits vouch for a hearty young man who is nothing more than bored and idle. If he were to occupy himself with some line of work, stop pulling out his teeth and remove himself from his sister's influence, he would thrive. But alas, he is under her thumb.

Sidney, the second brother, is a very agreeable gentlemanly type of gentleman. He lives in London too but I have forgotten where. He has brought his friend, Captain Russell, who is quite a miserable, complaining fellow when he is not the most jovial man in the world. He swings high and low.

Then there are those who I have mentioned to you before – the frightening Lady Denham and her poor dependent Miss Clara Brereton (a beautiful creature, I believe you would call her) and her niece and nephew, the cold and reserved Miss Denham and the silly, theatrical Sir Edward. I believe that there may be secret feelings between Miss Brereton and Sir Edward but with Lady Denham announcing that the heiress Miss Lambe "will do" for him, I believe that is an end to that.

Which leads me to Miss Jemima Lambe, my newest friend, a wonderfully sweet-natured girl who is controlled in every aspect of her life. Imagine you or I being told that we are not to dance! She will be very rich when she comes of age but that is not why she is my friend – I found that I may sneak her away from the sharp-eyed Mrs Griffiths (the lady who runs the Camberwell school she attends) and bring her here to play piano, drink tea and hopefully laugh a great deal. Perhaps I will even get her to dance around the drawing room with the Parker children when nobody is looking! She said that her guardians, the Chesters, are horrible people. Mrs Chester dislikes everything about Jemima and cannot bear to be in the same room. Mr Chester is only interested in shooting and drinking. But they have their eyes on her riches. The Misses Beaufort are her fellow students but so silly that I will not waste ink on them. Finally, there is the Reverend Hanking, whose hair always sticks out

*at the back, and who shuffles in a heavy way,
shouts when he speaks and often mishears what
is said to him. Last night, when he was speaking
to Diana Parker on the subject of sea bathing,
I asked him whether he, himself, enjoyed the
<u>pursuit</u>, to which he answered that no, he never
wears a bathing suit. You can imagine how I tried
to keep in my mirth, and when quizzed by the
curious Sidney Parker as to why there were tears
running down my face, I was obliged to tell him
the truth. "Well," he said, "you, unlike me, have
at least been spared the sight." And we laughed
some more. But I believe that Reverend Hanking
has his bushy eyebrows fixed on Mrs Griffiths
and she appears to be encouraging him. I should
say at this point that she is a widow.*

*My next letter will keep you abreast of all
developments but, Freddie, I had better receive a
letter from you soon or I will keep you in suspense,
especially with regard to the love affair of the
vicar! I have no intention of travelling to London
when I finish with Sanditon, though I need a new
dress badly. If you have nothing better to do you
may send me some blue silk.*

*Your fond sister,
Lottie*

It was such a fine morning that Charlotte decided to
post her letter immediately and extend her walk on the

return journey home. With a ready smile for everyone she met, a "How d'you do?" and a look of admiration from a pair of gentlemen walking along the Terrace, Charlotte felt very content and satisfied with herself indeed. Having heard of a private little beach simply called The Cove on the other side of the cliff walk, just west of the main beach, Charlotte, despite her fatigue after the late night, decided that it was her destination.

So rarely alone in a house full of children at Willingden, Charlotte had ample time to contemplate her new freedom and leisure. Yes, she played with the Parker children but only when it suited her. This idea of having time to herself was thrilling. At the top of the cliff walk she could see the expanse of sea spread out in all directions around her. It was boundless, unlimited by horizon or sky, and it felt magnificent. It reminded her of the awe she felt when staring up at the night sky – an infinite number of stars in an endless black sky. If she ever doubted that a God existed, she would just have to look up and feel herself as a speck in the universe.

Climbing down a very rickety wooden stairs to the beach below, her sense of adventure was heightened when she discovered she was alone. A quick look around and she removed her slippers and stockings and allowed her feet to sink into the warm sand as she trod towards the lapping waves and retreated fast, laughing aloud. There was no feeling quite like this feeling and she recalled her father's shock to discover that people actually visited the sea for leisure.

"My word, there's nothing as strange as folk, paying good money to look at water."

After twenty minutes spent in this way and not wanting

to return yet to Trafalgar House, Charlotte laid out her shawl on the sand as she had seen some mothers with young children do on the main beach and sat herself down. She shook off the sand between her toes and rolled up and secured her stockings. The lolling of the waves and the sun reflecting on the surface like silver ribbons were hypnotic and soon she decided to lie back on her shawl, close her eyes and listen to the sounds. The sun on her face reminded her of home, when she would hide in the meadow for hours on a Sunday, surrounded by high grass and wild flowers, and listen to the bees and birds. Here it was a more soothing and habitual sound of waves gently crashing to shore and no insects but the wide-winged gulls announcing their presence. With such comforting sounds and such heat from the sun, Charlotte was soon closing her eyes and fell fast asleep.

"Miss Heywood! Miss Heywood! Is it you? We are coming to help you."

Charlotte sat up suddenly. She had been asleep. She did not know for how long but when she looked around she saw Mrs Griffiths and her companion, Miss Lambe, making their way down the wooden stairs to join her.

"No, I am quite well, I assure you," said Charlotte, reaching for her bonnet.

Soon she saw Sidney Parker making his way from the rocks towards them. How long had he been there?

"No, you cannot be. A lady does not lie down on a beach in the middle of the day, prostate like a, like a ..."

"Like a starfish," added Sidney.

"Yes, exactly, like a starfish. Are you quite sure that you

have not fainted or been set upon? Truly, you look very shaken. Your hair is a mess. Did you fall? Have you hit your head on a rock?"

Charlotte realised that in Mrs Griffiths' eyes, it would be preferable that she had been attacked by pirates than fallen asleep in this unkempt way of her own free will, and, wishing to appear a responsible chaperone for Miss Lambe, she said, "Well, perhaps I was a little faint as I strolled along. It was a very late evening and I have not yet had breakfast."

"Oh, my word, well, we must get you home at once."

"Please, Mrs Griffiths, if it is permissible to you, I will escort Miss Heywood back to my brother's house. I have a strong arm and will ensure she gets there safely. And look, I have an apple here which will give her ample sustenance until she has breakfasted."

"Why, thank you, Mr Parker, I do not see anything improper in you returning your brother's guest home. In fact, we are going in the opposite direction."

Miss Lambe smiled. "Dear Charlotte, are you sure you are well? I am so looking forward to our meeting tomorrow; please be sure you are well or send word."

As Sidney reassured Mrs Griffiths, Charlotte whispered her response.

"There is absolutely nothing wrong with me. I fell asleep."

Jemima hid a giggle and ushered Mrs Griffiths along.

"Had we best not hurry, Mrs Griffiths? The Reverend Hanking is due to instruct the Misses Beaufort in theology."

"Yes, yes, indeed, good girl, we had better hurry. Best not keep the good reverend waiting."

Sidney and Charlotte began the ascent up the stairs.

"You may let go of my arm now, Mr Parker, you know as well as I do that I am quite well. How long, may I ask, were you sitting on the rocks?"

"Long enough. And no, I will not release your arm. I find that I drank a little too much last night and it is I who is shaken. You must carry me back. If you let go of my arm, I may collapse, or worse, fall over the cliff."

"Well, I had better not let that happen for I did not pack a mourning dress."

"Then it is settled," and Sidney held onto her arm tighter.

They spoke of the sea, of travel and of Sidney's life-long delight in collecting 'treasures' he found washed up on the shore. He removed something from his pocket, and opened up his palm to display what looked like a small, transparent stone.

"It is very pretty. Is it a gem?"

"It is to me."

"Then what is it, if not a gem? I have not seen such a pebble before."

"That is because it is, in fact, a fragment of glass – cleaned, cut, sanded-down to its current blunt, yet dainty size by the mighty sea."

"I would never have guessed. And you collect such things?"

"Yes, not so much for themselves but for the beauty of the stories they tell me."

"And what story does this tiny piece of polished glass tell you?"

Sidney closed his palm and held his fist to his ear, frowning as if straining to listen. "It tells me that I am the first person to hold it in eight months. The last man was a Portuguese sailor who drank of its contents to nurse his broken and homesick heart before the bottle slipped from his hands into the sea. It crashed against rocks and finally finds itself here. Do you find it a sad story, Miss Heywood?"

"I find it a great pity that the sailor's hands were so slippery and had they not been, our friend here, this piece of glass, might be enjoying himself beneath a palm tree in warmer climes at present."

"You find me sentimental, Miss Heywood, and my pastime silly?"

"On the contrary, objects do contain something of the life of their owners. My brother Freddie has gifted me a small telescope and it is my most precious belonging. That he purchased it in Vienna, picked it out with me in mind, inscribed his name and mine and handed it to me with such emotion that brought tears to both our eyes, means it is everything to me. It represents his travels and our being separated from each other. If I bring it close, I feel him nearby. I wonder if a piece of a person's soul, or 'story' as you say, enters the object?"

"Yes, I believe it does."

By now they were back at the steps of Trafalgar House.

"Mr Parker," said Charlotte, just as they were parting ways, "earlier at the beach, when I was alone, you did not see me remove, you did not see … my stockings? It would be most improper if you had."

Sidney grinned, turned and walked away. "Indeed it would, Miss Heywood. Indeed it would."

CHAPTER SIXTEEN

One morning while visiting the Terrace, Charlotte had requested of Mrs Griffiths that she may take Miss Lambe occasionally with her to the library when on her way to or from Trafalgar House.

"Books, don't you find, Mrs Griffiths, are an excellent interest for a young lady?" asked Charlotte.

"I am afraid they are not always so. Some novels are exceedingly immoral and influence girls in unimaginable ways. Do you not agree, Reverend?"

Reverend Hanking was almost a daily fixture with the Camberwell School.

"Call me a libertine if you will, Mrs Griffiths, but I have always found books were an excellent diversion for a young lady."

"Oh, indeed, Mr Hanking, I am surprised. Are you not a follower of James Fordyces and his *Sermons For Young Women*?"

"Not if I can help it, madam."

"Well, perhaps, when guided by tutors or parents as to quality reading material, it can be educational and improve the mind."

"Oh, yes, indeed," said Charlotte, "we always kept a good bookcase at home, full of books on all manner of subjects. All very interesting."

"That, Miss Heywood," responded Mrs Griffiths, "is because you come from a family who value such things. Miss Lambe's guardians, the Chesters, have other areas of interest. Hunting, mostly. They spend much of their time in the country. Their plans for Miss Lambe, to the best of my knowledge, do not involve extensive learning. A commitment, or not, to reading is entirely a family matter, I suppose."

"Murder, I hear," said Reverend Hanking, "is also a family matter. An inordinate number of them are committed within family circles. I really do believe, Mrs Griffiths, that you are too hard on the girl. Allow her to read, for has not God given her two eyes in her head and an excellent education, which you have enabled? Let her read of wildflowers and cities. It will open her mind. How can she ever hope to attain your level of excellence and refinement without them?"

Mrs Griffiths, embarrassed, could no longer put up a defence but in order to appear in control said, "Miss Heywood, she must only visit the library in your company. You are not to delay or allow her to speak alone with anyone. On these conditions, she may join you. There are to be no rendez-vous or entanglements with gentlemen."

"Good heavens, Mrs Griffiths, would that it were so easy to become entangled. I should have been a daily visitor to the library in my youth," said Mr Hanking. Then, clearing his throat on seeing Mrs Griffiths' frown, he added, "I jest, of course, madam. But I must point out that there is a greater chance of my bulldog, Hector, reading Gibbons' *The Decline and Fall of the Roman Empire* than of anything untoward occurring at Mrs Whitby's library. Next to church, there is no more superior building in the land for guiding one's thoughts to higher and greater things."

Excited with this victory, Jemima and Charlotte decided to set off immediately for the library.

"We will find Sir Edward Denham there, of course," announced Charlotte.

"How can you know?"

"Because he longs to be thought of as an intellectual and I also happen to know that a very sordid novel arrives this morning, in which he declared himself interested. He cannot help himself."

"You know people so well."

"Oh, I cannot boast of any such thing, but I have found that most people are predictable."

"Am I predictable?"

"Yes."

"How so?"

"You are the dearest girl, who trusts easily and wishes to please everyone. You will be a great favourite wherever you go."

"That is very good to hear. Although I must confess that I would like to surprise everyone and not do something that is expected of me and instead be something I am not."

"Then we will have you hold Mrs Whitby hostage, throw books at Sir Edward's head and run off with the post boy."

"Perfect," laughed Jemima. "That is exactly what I wish for."

When they arrived at the library, they were pleased to find that they were not alone. Inside was Sir Edward, as Charlotte predicted, and in the company of Sidney Parker. Just as the gentlemen approached them, the door opened again and Miss Brereton joined their circle.

As Sir Edward commenced with lengthy exclamations of delight and praise, Charlotte had a moment to compare the young ladies beside her. Here was the exquisitely beautiful Clara Brereton standing next to a young lady who, while not quite her equal in beauty, held everything that Clara Brereton must dream of – wealth and security. She was also curious as to where Sir Edward would focus his attention, now that his aunt was not present. She was not obliged to wait long in suspense.

"Dear Miss Brereton, I am so glad you are here. I wish to buy my sister a pair of gloves. There are some very colourful ones in a cabinet over there. As you know her so well, perhaps you would do me the honour of assisting in choosing a pair."

Clara acceded and was whisked away by Sir Edward whose indifference to Miss Lambe was as excessive now as his interest had been at the dance a few nights before. Charlotte could not help but find the interaction amusing and secretly delighted at how furious it would have made Lady Denham to see it.

Following some general conversation, Charlotte found herself looking out at the view of the sea from the window. Jemima stood beside her but sneaked over to a nearby bookshelf when Sidney approached. "You approve of Sanditon, Miss Heywood?"

"I approve of the sea."

"And not of Sanditon?"

"Yes, Sanditon is most enjoyable."

"Because of the people you have met here?"

"Yes," Charlotte smiled, "some more so than others."

"I am intrigued. I do hope I have made it on to the 'acceptable' list."

"It is early days yet, Mr Parker. I will be sure to let you know before I leave."

"Which I hope will not be for some time … to give Sanditon a chance to grow on you, of course, and its inhabitants to prove they are worthy of your approval. You are not homesick?"

"No, sir, I know my family are well and that I will be back amongst them before too long so I am savouring my time away. It is what my parents would wish. Besides, I write to my brother Frederick and his letters keep me company."

"One cannot be lonely when one has family."

Charlotte smiled and was just about to turn and rejoin Jemima, when Sidney stopped her with, "You are a great favourite with my family, Miss Heywood."

"That is very kind of you to say, sir."

"They like you … a great deal. I hope … I do hope … that I, that *we* shall see more of you …"

Jemima now approached Charlotte, holding a book for her attention.

Sidney quickly finished his sentence, " … more of you at Sanditon in future years."

"Thank you, Mr Parker," said Charlotte turning suddenly to Jemima and looking at the title of the book several times before making it out. Her head was full of curiosity as to the manner in which she had just been spoken to. Was Sidney Parker informing her that she was of interest to him? That he was wishing to know her better? That his family's approval for a choice of wife mattered to him? She could not tell. The warm feeling it gave her inside and the fixed smile she carried all day, however, meant many sweet hours on its contemplation.

CHAPTER SEVENTEEN

The following morning Sidney Parker came unannounced to breakfast at Trafalgar House.

"My word, but you keep late hours here. I have been up and strolling about since six o'clock."

"We keep the hours of aristocracy here, Sidney, in readiness for the great wealth which is our due when Sanditon is established as the greatest seaside town in England," said Tom.

"That is remarkable, I suppose," replied Sidney, "considering it is now but a village."

"Patience, my dear Sidney, patience. And what have you planned for today?"

Charlotte laughed at this demonstration of brotherly affection and was curious to hear of Sidney's plans when a knock came to the door and moments later they were joined by Arthur.

"Goodness!" said Mary. "Is every Parker to join us this morning? I would have prepared more tea, had I known."

"That is something that can be remedied in a moment," and Tom asked Morgan to bring more tea.

Arthur looked eagerly around the table. "I have just

informed Diana that I was going for a lengthy walk to stretch my legs. She has only permitted me one slice of dry bread for breakfast and very weak tea without milk or sugar. No ham, no eggs, no jam!"

"Well, help yourself, dear fellow. There is nothing wrong with a man who owns a good appetite. That will be the fortifying Sanditon sea air for you – always works up an appetite," said Tom good-humouredly.

Sidney returned once again to finish his sentence on his plans for the day. "In fact, I have nothing planned and wondered if I may be at the disposal of the ladies. They, perhaps, wish to be accompanied somewhere."

"As it so happens, Sidney, Miss Heywood and I intend to call upon Lady Denham this morning and then Charlotte must walk to the Terrace and collect Miss Lambe. She is to play piano here this afternoon. We would love you to join us."

"Well, I will come too," said Arthur, "though it is generally known that Lady Denham serves nothing with her tea. Will you come too, Tom?"

"No, I am afraid not, you may send my apologies. I must meet the builders today. If they keep building as they do, they will soon be putting up houses on the sea-floor."

As the morning was pleasant, the party walked to Sanditon House by means of the shortest route – a natural, narrow path through a large meadow. When wet, it was muddy and impassable for anyone intending to be presentable at the other end, but today it was perfect. The narrowness of the path ensured that the group of four could not walk abreast and as soon as Charlotte stayed back behind the other three, Sidney fell back to walk by her side.

"You are a very closely tied family, Mr Parker, it is lovely to witness."

"Are you not close to yours, Miss Heywood?"

"Oh, indeed I am, in proximity and affection. I have so many siblings, one cannot ever be in a room without at least three or four others. Freddie and I, however, are the closest in age and friendship."

"Then you understand that with siblings, it sometimes feels like we are still children when we are together."

Charlotte nodded and Sidney continued, "It is a strange love – that of a sibling. Is there a hurt greater, loyalty stronger, grief deeper than what you feel for them? It is as if God created you to go through life together, mixing up parts of you into each other so you can never be truly separated from them. You must always feel for them," Sidney smiled.

"Exactly! I shared in all Freddie's pain when he struggled to tell my parents that he wished to give up the farm in order to travel and study law. Being the eldest, he was to inherit our small estate but farming did not suit him and he did not suit it."

"Were your parents greatly disappointed?"

"Yes, very much so at first. They felt it was his duty. But then my next brother, Thomas, loves the land and works so hard that it did not seem fair to force it upon the son who had no interest. Fortunately, we have a distant cousin in London, a solicitor himself, who on hearing Freddie wished to study law, vouched to support him. This included an allowance to travel abroad. Now Thomas is to inherit the farm and Freddie looks set for a career in diplomacy. Everyone is happy."

"You are fortunate to come from such an understanding family. We too never fell out over such things. Tom being the eldest inherited the estate and Manor House and being the one most in love with Sanditon, that was as it should be. We had an unwed uncle who favoured me and I inherited a house in London and the means to one day purchase an estate if I wish. And Arthur and Diana have their own considerable inheritance, which I believe they have hardly touched – Diana due to frugality and Arthur because he has not yet found out what to do with it."

"Then you do not guide him?"

"I never felt it my duty and besides Diana does enough guiding for us all. I have myself to think of and have yet to decide where I will permanently live." He stole a sideways glance at Charlotte and quickly looked away again. "I had always thought it best to wait until I am wed to make such a decision."

Charlotte had no idea how to follow up on this and Sidney remained silent. Eventually Charlotte felt it best to make light of the topic so they could return again to friendly chat and not have this awkwardness between them.

"I believe you will have to fight your brother Tom on that point. He is determined that you remain a bachelor so he may advertise Sanditon as a husband hunting ground. He is convinced that mothers and daughters will come in their hundreds."

Sidney laughed but he would not be snapped out of his contemplative mood. "Well, he had better move fast for I may get married sooner than he thinks."

Charlotte was grateful that Mary and Arthur turned

around just then and, as they had now reached the entrance and the path became the driveway, they walked all together again until they reached the steps of Sanditon House.

CHAPTER EIGHTEEN

T he group were led into Lady Denham's study where Her Ladyship sat at her desk writing, while Miss Denham sat in a chair at one end reading and Miss Brereton embroidered.

"You will have to have tea in here this morning. I am busy writing invites to a dinner party that will be held here in a couple of weeks."

"How wonderful, Lady Denham ... we would be ..." said Mary.

Lady Denham cut her off.

"Of course, I would not have to go to this trouble and expense if the event the other evening at the hotel was a success. But I do not blame you, Mary, it was my own fault for allowing myself to be influenced."

Mary began to apologise and Sidney looked visibly annoyed that she felt she must.

"Lady Denham, the seating arrangements were a ..."

"... A great mistake. The point of the matter, Mrs Parker, is that I had not had my way."

"Which was," said Sidney boldly, "to convince Miss Lambe that she should marry and that Sir Edward was the very man for the job."

Lady Denham's chin rose higher. "Yes, Mr Sidney Parker, if you must put it like that. It was precisely its purpose. And you may hold your smirk, Miss Heywood, one such as you has absolutely nothing to smirk about."

"I was not laughing, Your Ladyship. Please forgive me if I gave that impression."

Despite the ladies all sitting on a pair of sofas facing each other and the gentlemen pretending to read the titles of books on the shelf, Lady Denham ruled the room and allowed no interference. She had something to say and they must listen.

"You are twenty-two years of age, I believe, Miss Heywood, and one of fourteen children from a middle-sized farm. You have no wealth, no connections, no title and only a fresh-faced prettiness to recommend yourself. Do you not give marriage any thought?"

Charlotte was startled by Lady Denham's hostile tone of voice and hardly knew how best to react or respond. In front of a large group such as this, many of whom she respected and believed she cared for, she began to wish she had not come. All were silent, then both Mary and Sidney started to say something at once.

"Silence in my house! I may say as I wish under my own roof and I have not finished. Miss Heywood would do well to heed my advice. Look here at Miss Clara and Esther; neither have any more than you but see how they dress. See how they carry themselves and when they walk into a room, all eyes are on them. Men do not marry just with their heads and hearts – there are other inducements."

Mary stood up. "Please, Lady Denham, say no more.

You have mortified my friend and, therefore, mortified me. I apologise again if you were disappointed but it was my fault, not Miss Heywood's."

"If you would let me finish, you will see that I mean well and to guide your friend. She will thank me in the long run. Sit down, Mrs Parker. Please."

Charlotte, though red-faced and close to tears, kept her head held high and looked directly at Lady Denham that she may not appear intimidated as the older lady continued in a calmer voice. "You must pretend that you are something that you are not, Miss Heywood. You must make men wish to have you as a wife. If you do not think of yourself as a magnificent prize, then men will not either. Be smart and use all your beauty and charms to the best of your ability. The Misses Beaufort seem to have that instinct and they are at least five years younger than you. Mark my words, they will both be married within the year and married well."

Lady Denham raised her hands as if to point to all about her in the room. "Do you think I would have all this and a title too, if I had not been sharp? Naivety is not a quality worth having, Miss Heywood, but you were clever enough to ingratiate yourself to Miss Lambe. Perhaps you are a sly one after all."

"Enough! Lady Denham," interjected Sidney suddenly. "May we speak of something else?" Then smiling, "If you ladies leave us in no doubt as to your arts and inducements, then we gentlemen will know when we are being worked upon."

"Indeed, Mr Parker?" Lady Denham, turned on him.

"We were all led to believe, last summer, that you could not be worked upon."

Such an exhibit of bad manners must result in silence. Most of the ladies looked at the floor. Sidney moved over to the window and kept his back to the room. Only Arthur broke the silence by humming a tune as he looked over the titles of books which lay on the table beside him. It was obvious to all that Lady Denham had awoken in abominable humour and as she was never herself at fault, someone must be in receipt of her scorn. Today, it was Charlotte's turn.

The tea arrived and Charlotte heard little else of what was said, still sinking in embarrassment and wondering how she looked and acted. She had never doubted that she was all that she should be in manners – a gentleman's daughter – until now. Her morning was ruined, perhaps her whole day. Miss Denham and Clara were extra attentive to her. She supposed this kindness may be due to the fact that they too knew what it was to be publicly humiliated by Lady Denham. But in this company and in front of Sidney Parker, in particular, she could not but feel the sting of Lady Denham's words and perhaps even the truth of them. At twenty-two, most of her friends and cousins had already married, and she had not ever been approached or made an offer. She had always assumed she had not yet the chance, had not mixed enough in society, but now she wondered if she attended a ball every night of the week for a whole year, would she always be overlooked. The walk home was largely silent and Mary held closely to Charlotte's arm and tried to cheer her up but nothing, even Arthur's attempts at humour and Sidney's sympathetic glances, could alter her mood.

That afternoon, Charlotte remained in the privacy of her room, hugging Freddie's telescope, and allowed the great relief that only the uninterrupted outpouring of tears can give. In the stillness that followed, she contemplated again, those thoughts that had earlier caused her agonies. She had never given thought to marriage in the way other young ladies did. She had not whispered and giggled about it. She had never undertaken the playful looks and cunning glances that the Misses Beaufort seemed expert in. She knew she wanted to marry one day and that, in fact, she must marry so that she may not be a burden to her family. She had danced with enough young men but had never formed an attachment nor been the target of one. Her parents were practical people who believed that all their children would wed in time, for marry they must. They had never made any efforts to encourage it, however, nor with such a quantity of offspring, saved enough to make a moderate financial provision for each, which would tempt gentlemen to step forward.

Now, the subject burned just below her ribcage. She was not quality marriage material and although she felt Sidney Parker liked her well enough, perhaps she was misreading his words and all their playfulness was similar to her horse-play with Freddie. Perhaps she was just another sisterly type person in his life and if he were to choose a wife, he would choose one with wealth and beauty. If Esther Denham, with all her good breeding, beauty and connections, was not good enough for him, how could she believe herself to fare any better?

Charlotte determined, just prior to coming downstairs

and setting off to collect Jemima Lambe, that she would no longer be the simple, dismissible country girl she had been until now. She would be taken seriously. Henceforth she would be seen as the refined, discerning, intelligent, pretty young woman she knew herself to be. She must refrain from rolling down hills with the Parker children or lying prostate on the sand or indulging in casual chit-chat with all and sundry that she met on her walks. She would be a lady of decorum and elegance. She would set herself higher than even she felt herself to be. Lady Denham would not have the satisfaction of judging her before company again.

When Charlotte reached the bottom of the stairs, she found Sidney Parker sitting on the bench in the hallway.

"Oh, I believe your brother has not returned yet and Mary has taken the children to the rock pool," said Charlotte.

"I was not looking for them actually, Miss Heywood," said Sidney, turning the rim of his hat in his hand. "I was wondering if I may escort you to the Terrace for your meeting with Miss Lambe."

Charlotte smiled, "It is only around the corner, Mr Parker. I shall be well able to make the journey without fainting or bumping into highwaymen."

"Ah, yes, but we can never be sure."

"I doubt that I will be of interest to them. As Lady Denham revealed, I have little to tempt them."

"That is the true reason that I wish to accompany you. Come, let us walk and talk. You are not to listen to her. She was very wrong in what she said."

Charlotte grabbed her shawl and they walked slowly

down the hill in the direction of the Terrace.

"Perhaps, but it would not have hurt, if there was not some truth in it."

"It was total nonsense. That old lady is mean-spirited and twists those around her until they become like her too. It is cruel to witness. If you had known Esther Denham as a girl. She was the kindest, sweetest creature. It is only a matter of time before the same becomes of Miss Brereton."

Charlotte remained silent. He must have known Esther most intimately once. If anyone could have known Esther Denham as sweet and kind, it must have been Sidney Parker.

They arrived at the Terrace and found Miss Lambe smiling from the window, arising and apparently getting ready to depart.

"I will leave you now, Miss Heywood, and may I offer you one piece of advice."

Charlotte wondered if everyone she met this week was wishing to offer her advice.

He continued, "If anything, as a result of Lady Denham's words, be more yourself, not less."

Charlotte was unsure of his meaning. "Be more uncouth?"

"Yes, no ..."

"Remain ignorant of my own charms?"

"No."

"Then I should learn them and if I do not have any, I must invent them."

"No. You are acceptable just as you are. You do not need to improve yourself."

"Acceptable?"

"Adequate, sufficient, satisfactory …" he added.

"Sir, please, not another word. Lady Denham's insults have all the appearance of compliments next to your words."

"Miss Heywood, you are misinterpreting my meaning."

"Your meaning is very clear, Mr Parker."

"Miss Heywood, do not change. Do not change because there are no improvements for you to make."

And before Charlotte could look at his features, to see whether he was sincere or jesting, Sidney Parker had turned and walked fast in the direction of the sea. The door opened at that moment and Jemima, greatly overdressed for the occasion, beamed with delight.

"Shall we, Miss Lambe?" asked Charlotte as she linked arms with her friend and they began their walk to Trafalgar House.

"Yes, Miss Heywood, I believe we shall."

CHAPTER NINETEEN

T he days trickled by in the pleasant manner that
routine, friendship and fine weather can combine
to make. The library subscription list was never
as full as Tom Parker would have wished but he did own
that Sanditon was beginning to have a greater hum about
it. The hotel took additional bookings, more lodgings were
taken and Lady Denham's list of invitations to her dinner
party was getting so great that she decided instead to turn
it into a ball. The expense of a full six-course meal would
be replaced with a buffet of cold meats. Musicians were
inexpensive and if she pushed it out by another two weeks,
when vegetables were plentiful and, therefore, cheaper,
she could truly congratulate herself.

Charlotte and Miss Lambe had become great friends.
Jemima, being several years younger than Charlotte,
was in some respects like a sister and Charlotte felt all
the responsibility of guiding her charge. In manners,
deportment and conduct she required no instruction but
where Charlotte found her lacking was in judgement.
Miss Lambe's world had been too guarded, her exposure
to company limited. Charlotte, therefore, enjoyed

demonstrating her superiority in discernment, perception and comprehending the intentions of others.

"My dear friend," said Charlotte one day after she witnessed Jemima laugh at Sir Edward's jokes while they were visiting the library, "do not encourage the man. You will mislead him into believing himself intelligent when we all know that there is more sense to be got from the glove-stand over there."

"Oh," answered Jemima, "I had not intended to encourage him. I merely wished to be polite."

"Well, Sir Edward is the kind of man who, if a lady returns his smile, begins planning their honeymoon."

"Oh, do not say so."

"I am afraid it is so. And what is worse, he will speak in such elaborate nonsense that one will not even realise one is being lured. It is as if he has eaten many volumes of dictionaries, poetry and silly novels. Then when he opens his mouth, one never knows what nonsense will come out. He does not seem to know himself."

Miss Lambe laughed. "You are so witty, Miss Heywood, and I dare say correct. I will be very serious and silent around him from now on. I have no intention of encouraging him. You must guide me on this subject, Charlotte, please."

On another occasion, Jemima commented on how considerate she found Diana Parker and her brother Arthur. "There was no detail, no enquiry insignificant when they noticed I had coughed. They were so attentive to my comfort. Diana recommended several spoons of honey, while Arthur brought two cushions to place behind my back and insisted that I move closer to the fire. Now you cannot find fault with that."

"There you have me. Indeed, where health matters are concerned, there is no one to compare with Diana Parker. I have no doubt she delighted in hearing you cough, that she might enjoy the sound of her own advice and credit herself for curing you. And poor Arthur is but her echo – a weak man with a fondness for toast."

Jemima seemed disappointed.

"Oh, dear Jemima, do not look sad. I do not mean any harm by it. They are well-meaning but please allow me to say, they are also ridiculous, with the latter trait often winning out the day. I will say no more of it but allow me to intercede if I ever find them pulling out your teeth to rectify a headache."

Jemima smiled. "I am rather fond of my teeth."

"Good. then we are agreed. No teeth pulling."

Mary had wondered if the Misses Beaufort were jealous of Charlotte and Jemima's friendship and perhaps felt left out. When she made enquiries of Mrs Griffiths, however, she learnt that they were as acquainted with Miss Lambe as they wished to be and felt that Miss Heywood offered them no assistance in society. It was lack of interest, therefore, rather than jealousy that they felt.

Charlotte found another benefit in befriending Miss Lambe. With the finest clothes and her own maid, Sarah, to assist with her hair and toilette, Jemima was always immaculately styled. Charlotte felt that her own decision to transform herself into a more becoming lady could not have come at a better time. If she wished to walk out and be seen with Jemima, she must at least make the effort to appear her best. She wore her hair up every day now, spent additional time readying herself in the morning, altered her dresses to imitate current fashions and purchased some becoming ornaments for her hair. She would never again have someone like Sidney Parker laugh while removing a piece of grass from her unruly hair or have Lady Denham stare at her, up and down. The old Charlotte belonged in Willingden; the new Charlotte would mingle in society and do herself proud. She would never be made feel ashamed of herself again.

Mary and Diana were the first to compliment her on her loveliness of appearance, although Diana recommended the addition of a neck ruff to prevent a sore throat. Mary ran to her room and returned with a turquoise and pearl brooch which she begged Charlotte to keep as a token of friendship. And one morning, Mary informed Charlotte that her husband had said that there was a marked improvement in Charlotte's complexion of late which he put down to brisk walks in the sea air.

But the one compliment that delighted and mortified her most was the one that involved Sidney Parker. One morning, as Charlotte approached the door of the breakfast room, she heard Mary say to Sidney that "Miss Heywood looks very fine these days, do you not think so, Sidney?" To which he hesitated and then replied, "Yes, she does, I suppose, but then I have always thought her pretty." Suddenly the door opened. Tom Parker, who had just at that moment decided to take a plan from his study to show his brother, almost crashed into Charlotte. Both jumped appropriate to their level of surprise.

"My word, Miss Heywood, there is no need to be lurking about out here. The eggs are getting cold."

Charlotte apologised and said she was securing her bootlaces and joined the smirking pair at the table.

"Miss Heywood, I was only saying to Sidney how fate works in mysterious ways. Was I not, Sidney?"

"Indeed you were and gave me the oft told tale of how the gods intervened to throw Tom Parker your way, and now you are wed."

"Oh, Sidney, but Charlotte does not know it so forgive me for repeating it again."

Sidney nodded and smiled. Charlotte looked at Mary attentively.

"Charlotte, I cannot recall if I informed you before, that I am from the town of Tunbridge." Mary waited eagerly for a response which Charlotte felt it best to give her.

"No, I do not believe you did."

"My father was a solicitor there."

Again, Charlotte felt she must respond. "How interesting."

"And so you see, it is impossible that I would ever have met Tom. But I did, for I attended a dinner that I was not supposed to attend and Tom visited a friend that he had not intended to visit."

"Oh, really? That is very strange."

"Yes, is it not wonderful?"

Charlotte was underwhelmed but nodded nevertheless as she could see Sidney's amusement as he searched her face for a reaction.

"My sister, who was to attend the dinner at the Hugheses' with my mother, took ill and so I went in her place. Tom, meanwhile, was supposed to be at home at Sanditon but had taken a notion to visit his friend from college, Geoffrey Hughes, that very weekend instead of the following one."

"How remarkable."

"Yes, and we were put sitting next to each other as old Mrs Hughes felt cold and wished to sit nearer the fire, so I took her place."

"And here you are," interrupted Sidney, slapping the table and obviously knowing there were many more parts to be told but wishing to spare Charlotte and himself the deluge of particulars, "the happiest Mrs Parker in the world."

Mary beamed, Sidney excused himself and Charlotte was free to recall again what he had said before she entered the room – Sidney Parker thought her pretty.

Even Miss Brereton commented the next time she called to visit with Lady Denham. "You wear your hair in such a lovely style, Miss Heywood. It is very becoming."

Charlotte smiled while Lady Denham continued talking to Mary.

"Do you enjoy sea bathing, Miss Brereton? I cannot believe that I have waited this long already to try it."

"Yes, very much, but I do not often get the opportunity."

"Miss Lambe and I intend to bathe tomorrow. Mrs Griffiths allows me to accompany her. But with it so close to the ball, perhaps you would prefer to wait until another time. "

"No, on the contrary. The exercise would be very refreshing."

With that, the ladies fixed on a time and location to meet and a feeling of adventure and excitement stole over Charlotte for the morrow.

CHAPTER TWENTY

T he weather remained warm and the sun shone uninterrupted on the day selected for sea bathing. Charlotte packed a light bag with an extra chemise, shawl and stockings – just in case, she told herself, a great wave came and ruined some of her other clothes. Then just before leaving her room, she added a pair of light slippers, some extra towelling, a comb, an additional clasp for her hair (in the event the one she was wearing was swept out to sea) and finally another light shawl in case one of her companions forgot to pack one. Only when she was obliged to unpack and pack again, so that her parasol may fit inside, did she make her way down the stairs.

Charlotte decided a light breakfast would be best and joined Mary, who laughed at her baggage.

"My dear Charlotte, you would hardly need as large a bag if you were sailing out to conquer the Americas."

"I like to be prepared. Perhaps the other ladies will forget something."

"I am sure they will not. They have both bathed here before. You have not. They will know what they need. Still, it is a good idea, once you do not mind carrying it."

"Yes, I believe so." Charlotte smiled back. "I am quite the mule today."

"It is a pity but Arthur was here earlier. He would have carried it for you."

"It matters not. It is not heavy, but thank you."

After a few moments, Mary put down her teacup. "I am very proud of myself, Charlotte, for I have spoken again to Tom over breakfast about my bakery and tea room. Arthur agreed that it was a wonderful idea. I reminded Tom of my contacts in London, what Mrs Griffiths and Reverend Hanking said, how successful they are in other seaside destinations and other matters, such as where I imagine it to be. He praised me for my constant commitment to Sanditon and agrees that he will consider it at a future phase in Sanditon's development."

"That is wonderful, Mary. Do you believe that it will be this season?"

"Oh no, nor next year's for the focus is on the crescent and creating a green. But I do very much hope it will be not too long after. Tom says it would require considerable personal investment to get it up and running and he has not the time for it now. He also feels that the owners at the hotel would feel it a very disloyal thing to go into direct competition with them in providing food to visitors."

"That is a pity for I do not see it as competition. Surely it would give visitors more variety. The tea rooms would be for leisure and delicacies while out and about and the hotel can still provide hearty meals."

Mary looked sheepish. "Yes, I was thinking so myself."

Charlotte knew it was useless to encourage Mary to

challenge her husband once more so she tried diplomacy instead. "You do know, Mary, that I believe your idea is genius. I also believe you would be the very woman to make it a success for you have such great skills in bringing people together and have such exemplary taste in decor and interiors."

"You are too kind, Charlotte. I do so wish to provide a lovely, social place for people to go." Mary now had tears in her eyes.

"Well, then, you should start planning now, all the little and big details, so if anything should happen to speed up Tom's plans, you will be ready."

"Oh, and I would enjoy that so much. The planning would make me happy. I am so excited, even speaking of it. I will do exactly as you say. I have a new journal which is just the thing. I will enjoy thinking over the selection of cakes we will offer. Thank you for encouraging me, Charlotte."

"That is a wonderful idea and I shall expect you to show me your ideas next week. Now I must set out and not keep the ladies waiting."

Charlotte made her way to the main gates of Sanditon House, where she and Miss Brereton had agreed to meet. Just as Clara arrived, a gentleman they did not recognise rode past. On seeing them, he slowed to a trot, smiled and tipped his cap. "Good morning, ladies."

"Good morning, sir."

"Such a fine gentleman," said Clara, "such an air and so well dressed. Do you not agree, Miss Heywood? I wonder who he is."

"Perhaps he is another of Mr Sidney Parker's friends

come to seduce the unmarried daughters and take them off their mothers' hands."

"Indeed, perhaps he is," laughed Miss Brereton.

They made their way to the appointed spot where Miss Lambe had arrived before them. And with Miss Lambe was another lady whom at first Charlotte assumed was Sarah but turned to reveal herself as Mrs Griffiths. They had hoped she would not come but supposed she had merely wished to see Miss Lambe arrive safely to the beach.

"Oh, how do you do, Miss Heywood? Miss Lambe and I are so excited for this morning's adventure. A little bit of sea bathing will set me up for the day, I am sure."

Charlotte hid her disappointment with a smile and stole a look at Miss Lambe who was making a face of apology behind Mrs Griffiths.

A number of other ladies arrived to partake in the sport and hastened to the bathing machines. It was then that Charlotte realised that there were only two left, which Mrs Griffiths hurriedly secured for their use.

"I know it is preferable that we have one each but perhaps it is best this way. I will share with Miss Lambe and you, Miss Heywood, may share with Miss Brereton. We are lucky, in fact – the attendant tells me that these are two new bathing machines that have not been used before. Such is the business of late, that they have had to increase. Mr Parker will be delighted to hear it."

Just as they were about to alight the steps, they could hear Reverend Hanking approach from behind.

"Ladies, ladies, I just came to wish you well, especially Miss Heywood on her maiden voyage. Remember propriety and modesty above all things. I will not detain you. Farewell!"

Once he left, the excitement rose within Charlotte at this new adventure. The bathing machines were but enclosed wooden carts led by a horse, with a canvas overhang sheltering the steps, for privacy, as persons descended into the water.

"Nothing but your chemise, ladies," said the attendant as she assisted them up the steps. "Knock on the door when ready and I'll help ye in."

Mrs Griffiths and Miss Lambe, quicker in their defrocking, were first to set out from the shore. By the time Charlotte descended the steps she could see them not far from her, making faces or squealing aloud at the coldness of the water. They laughed in turn as Charlotte shrieked and quickly submerged herself to get it over with. Mary had advised her that this was best and as Charlotte arose again, spitting out the strange tasting, salty water and noticing that her body felt pleasantly buoyant, she looked back to see if Miss Brereton was joining her.

"Is all well, Miss Brereton? You really must come out and join me. The water is exceptionally warm," she joked.

"One moment. I am almost ready."

But suddenly their young horse, who was also on his maiden voyage, was startled by a seagull flying very close and dashed off further into the swell. The attendant, who was next to Charlotte, shouted at him to come back but the frightened horse managed to break from the carriage and race back to shore. The carriage, which had been pulled out into deeper water by the horse before he escaped, now went over on its side. Charlotte looked on in horror as it began to sink beneath the surface and fill with water. Miss Brereton was trapped. The attendant, who was struck by the horse as she tried to stop him, stood holding her head. Charlotte, unable to swim, tried to wade further towards the carriage but was soon getting out of her depth while Mrs Griffiths and Miss Lambe screamed and shouted for assistance.

Charlotte tried once more to wade out to the now almost fully submerged carriage but it was useless. Just as she lost her footing and flapped her arms in an attempt to stay up, she felt a strong arm around her waist pulling her back. Thinking at first it was her attendant, she was shocked to see it was Sidney Parker. When he had her securely back beside Mrs Griffiths, she was free to observe the scene before her. Arthur was already at the overturned bathing machine and dived to try to release the back door. He arose gasping for air and Sidney dived, immediately followed by Arthur again. Sidney now rose to get air and dived again. Arthur had not yet returned to the surface. Sidney rose once more, gasping, and dived again. After what felt like an age, Arthur rose to the surface, dragging Miss Brereton along behind him, and started swimming to the shore. He was then joined by Sidney who assisted his brother in getting her back onto the beach.

A sizeable crowd, suitably appalled, had already gathered and, curious to look upon a beautiful, dead lady, congregated around her. Reverend Hanking, who was amongst them, began mumbling her last rites.

"Stand back! Stand back at once! I am a doctor," came

a voice from the crowd. The gentleman whom Charlotte had met earlier on horseback stepped forward and bent to kneel by the patient.

Charlotte, Mrs Griffiths and Miss Lambe were by now standing on the shoreline watching on helplessly. For all her changes of clothing, Charlotte had nothing but her wet chemise to cover her, as her large bag and all her clothing remained in the carriage, under water. Some ladies nearby threw their shawls over the ladies and the attendant brought Mrs Griffiths' belongings to her.

Meanwhile, all were mesmerised by the workings of the doctor. He checked Miss Brereton's pulse and breath.

"There is a pulse but I cannot detect breath," and quickly he got to work pumping her chest and breathing into her mouth.

Sir Edward, who had now arrived at the scene and was visibly distraught, shouted, "Good God! What is that man doing? Step away from her at once. Take your hands off that lady."

But the doctor continued until a spasm of coughs came over Miss Brereton and water emerged from her mouth. The doctor turned her on her side and covered her with a large blanket given to him by one of the onlookers.

"She is alive but she must be brought home immediately. Her recovery is not certain. I will go with her. Someone, show me the way."

"She lives at Sanditon House," said Sidney, still finding his breath.

"I see," said the doctor, looking up.

"Sir Edward," Sidney continued, "you have your gig. You must bring them."

"Of course," said Sir Edward, relieved to be of use.

"And we will bring the other ladies home," said Arthur. "And what is your name, Doctor, that we may know to whom we owe so much?"

The doctor, carrying Miss Brereton in his arms, was now following Sir Edward. He looked over his shoulder and said, "Dr Hollis, at your service."

CHAPTER TWENTY-ONE

"**A**Dr Hollis? What an extraordinary coincidence."

Tom Parker was just receiving an account of the alarming event from Sidney who had escorted Charlotte home while Arthur had done so with the other two ladies.

"Yes, Tom. Mary, please take Miss Heywood upstairs at once and perhaps she will need something for the shock. Do you drink brandy, Miss Heywood, or wine?"

Charlotte, shaking and with teeth chattering, looked back at him but said nothing. Stunned by all that had occurred, she was fixed to the spot, as if in a dream. She heard voices but could not tell from whom they came. Tom continued.

"I did see his name on the library subscription log but forgot about it again. Is it not strange that he is Hollis? That is the name of Lady Denham's first husband, you know Miss Heywood, a man of fortune and the original proprietor of Sanditon House."

"Charlotte, your lips are quite blue. Please come upstairs," whispered Mary.

Charlotte approached Sidney, who still stood, shaking

and cold, at the door as if to leave immediately. "Thank you, Mr Parker, for saving me."

"Do not mention it." He looked away while Charlotte seemed rooted to the spot until Mary pulled her gently by the hand towards the staircase.

"Sidney," said Tom, "I will return with you to the hotel at once and find out a little more of this Dr Hollis and why we have seen little of him these past few weeks. Such a man, at such a time. Surely Lady Denham cannot deny now that a doctor is wanted."

Mary escorted Charlotte upstairs, treating her with all the kindness and soothing talk that she would one of her own children, if they had fallen from a tree or banged their head. Changed, wrapped up and having sipped a large cup of cocoa to which she was convinced Mary had added some brandy, Charlotte, warm at last, fell into a deep sleep.

When she returned downstairs for dinner, still a little dazed from her midday sleep and the activity of the morning, Charlotte asked if the Parkers had heard anything about the health of Miss Brereton.

"Yes, we got word from Sanditon House," answered Mary. "She does well but not as well as the doctor hoped. He fears that much water got into her lungs which is a very dangerous thing but bed rest and observation will be the remedy for now."

"And I have made my enquiries at the hotel, Miss Heywood. This Dr Hollis, it appears, is a very wealthy gentleman from London. Such is his wealth from business that he rarely practises medicine with the exception of a few very select clients who attend his practice at Harley

Street. One of whom, a member of the aristocracy, required his services recently and he was obliged to return to London. He had only just returned again to Sanditon yesterday and a good thing for us and Miss Brereton, in particular, that he did."

"Indeed," answered Charlotte.

"Yes, yes. What a good thing for Sanditon and does it not prove my point, Mary? He could not have returned at a better time nor saved a more precious life to Lady Denham, if I had paid him to do so. There was little else to be discovered at the hotel but I was informed that the doctor said that he once had family in these parts but it was a very long time ago. You see, he must be related to Mr Hollis and, therefore, by marriage to Lady Denham. I wonder if she has made the connection yet?"

"Of course she has, husband. Very little escapes Lady Denham's notice."

"True. Well, I left my card for him, with an invitation to dinner tomorrow evening, so we will discover more then. In the meantime, I will visit Sanditon House in the morning and see how things be. Will you join me, Mary, Miss Heywood?"

"No, Tom, I believe Miss Heywood needs at least another day of rest and I would feel it improper to impose upon them so soon after the accident. They will think I seek gossip."

"But Diana has been twice already."

"That is because your sister would not see her enquiries as meddlesome, Tom."

"A heart of gold. Diana always goes where she feels she may be of greatest assistance."

"Or how it may appear to others. But I do suppose the

ball will be cancelled now. I was so looking forward to it."

"Yes, my dear, with such a near tragedy to happen and Miss Brereton is not out of danger yet, it is unlikely to go ahead. A great shame. We must arrange something ourselves later in the summer so visitors to Sanditon will not be too disappointed."

But the Parkers need not have worried, for when Tom arrived home the following morning after his visit to Sanditon House he brought the news that the ball was going ahead. Apparently, Lady Denham had already purchased all her meats and fuels for the fire.

"Why," she declared, "would I have the servants eating the finest cuts by a roaring fire downstairs while I sat up here eating a bowl of gruel by candlelight? The ball will go ahead, without the presence of my dear cousin, but it will go ahead."

As for her meeting with Dr Hollis, she knew at once who he was and stated to Tom that while she owed him a great service, he had better not be looking at her silverware or fine rooms. The Hollis line had estranged themselves in their behaviour to her following her dear Mr Hollis's death. Although this Dr Hollis was but a boy at the time and a distant cousin, she felt no obligation whatsoever. She even went so far as to say he may send her the bill for his services, that she may not feel that she owed him anything. Dr Hollis naturally refused to accept payment. Lady Denham relented that he may visit the patient regularly, to oversee Miss Brereton's full recovery but he would be chaperoned by Nelly, the chambermaid, and must not make a nuisance of himself.

To this information yet more was added. Diana Parker had set out to learn all there was to know of Dr Hollis and brought all intelligence, at once, to Trafalgar House. She started by assuring them all that there was more information yet to come.

"I have written to my great friend Mrs Eagleston back in Hampshire, whose sister is married to a leading doctor in London. I think she perhaps mentioned Harley Street or else it was the home for bewildered women but he is sure to know of this Dr Hollis. They move in such tight circles, these medical men."

"But what, Diana, have you discovered from your enquiries here at Sanditon?" asked Tom.

"A not insignificant amount, actually," she replied. "He advocates tea for the morning and cocoa for the evening. He likes a good breakfast himself and, in my opinion, in accordance with my sources, eats a great too many eggs first thing. He favours a light lunch and a good dinner."

"Excellent! He is joining us for dinner tomorrow evening. But what else of the man? What of his wealth? His personality? His background and family?"

"Of this, I am afraid, I have discovered little. He is believed to be generally wealthy, for his boots were handmade in Italy. Do not ask how I have learnt this. He is courteous in his manner and is a great favourite with the staff at the hotel. Although he apparently once claimed to the stable boy that he too is from a large family, he has never yet posted a correspondence with the exception of one letter to his solicitor, a Mr Travis, in London."

"Dear God, Diana, your methods of extracting

information are quite devious. I should never wish you to investigate me."

"And I have it, practically from the horse's mouth, that Sir Edward Denham loathes the man. He is convinced that he has only come to Sanditon to work on Lady Denham and oust them all out of their inheritance."

"Well, we know what Lady Denham feels about the Hollis family and doctors in general, so I feel Sir Edward has nothing to worry about."

"The most telling thing of all, however," Diana continued, "is that the doctor denounces the use of tonics and powders and there I must draw the line. A doctor who condemns fumigations, gargles and proven tonics will never receive so much as a shilling from me. I must away now. Sidney, Captain Russell and Arthur are planning to dine with the Denhams tomorrow evening but you can depend upon me to be here, to form an opinion of this doctor."

The following afternoon, Tom decided it was best that he meet with Dr Hollis at the hotel first, introduce himself and bring his guest back to dinner with him. But when the gentleman did not return in time for dinner, Mary declared her husband must have encountered some difficulty along the way. Almost one hour later, when Mary had apologised to her cook that her fare was surely spoilt, a jubilant Tom entered the house with his arm around Dr Hollis. Mary's anger and Charlotte's feelings about the rudeness of such an unnecessary delay vanished with the doctor's apology and introduction.

"Dear Mrs Parker, please accept my sincere apologies. This is a disgraceful time to make an appearance and we have kept you waiting. The delay was entirely my fault. As your husband arrived early, I suggested we raise a toast to Sanditon and its success and, well, we got talking of his plans and there you have us."

"Not at all, Dr Hollis, we had hardly noticed. But please, when we sit down to eat, do not think we always serve such dried beef, and we shall forget the whole thing."

"I shall be so busy admiring the softness of your potatoes and the buttery carrots, that I will not even notice the beef."

Charlotte marvelled at the friendship that was already struck up between Tom and Dr Hollis. In such a short time, they seemed to know much of the other, shared many jokes and had all the appearance of two old school friends reunited again after many years' absence.

"What is your opinion on gallstones, Doctor?" asked Diana, who was more cautious in her judgement.

"A terrible nuisance ... too much bile, in my experience. I do hope you do not suffer yourself, Miss Parker."

"No, sir, I do not. But do you recommend surgery?"

Dr Hollis paused, drank from his glass, paused again and then answered. "Gallstones may lead to infection and, therefore, often require surgery."

Diana sat forward in her chair.

"And what of drinking oil and certain herbs to flush them out?"

Dr Hollis looked at her keenly.

"I have heard of it but have not recommended it myself ..."

Diana gave a kind of snort and folded her arms.

"I have not recommended it myself ... as yet," continued

the doctor, "for I believe that prevention is better than cure."

Diana slapped her hand on the table.

"As do I, Dr Hollis, as do I. Mary, Tom, am I not forever saying that prevention is better than cure? How extraordinary to find a doctor, whose very livelihood depends upon illness and disease, recommending the same thing."

With Diana won over, the party continued with good-will from all quarters.

"You are, like me, Miss Heywood, a new-comer to Sanditon?" asked Dr Hollis.

"Yes, sir."

"And how do you find the library? Are its shelves well stocked?"

Here Charlotte recalled her first meeting with Sir Edward and all the nonsense that she was obliged to listen to. The library, in her opinion, must own some of the blame.

"It is very well stocked, Doctor. So well stocked, indeed, that whether one was of superior mind or soft in the head, one may find reading to suit all tastes."

The doctor laughed aloud. "Miss Heywood, you speak from experience." Then in a whisper, "You have evidently met all kinds of persons since your arrival. Plenty of soft in the head persons about, I dare say. I applaud your discernment. You fall into the superior of mind category."

Charlotte nodded in acceptance of his compliment and ruminated on a new agitation. She was struck by a sensation she had not felt before – of being drawn by something appealing and indescribable in the gentleman before her.

Dr Hollis was not overly handsome in a traditional sense but there was that attention to his appearance that was striking. It was debonair and considered, giving a certainty of his confidence that she found alluring. He held himself in a relaxed manner that convinced Charlotte that when he entered a room, all eyes would be on him. The men, jealous, and the ladies, giddy and curious. Everyone would sense that this man 'was something' and, more importantly, was on his way to becoming more. Even now, in the dining room, as the servants entered and left, their heads turned to admire him. And when he spoke, he was always courteous and eloquent but fully attentive to others – the most engaging person she had ever encountered. All in all, Charlotte, though not for a moment thinking that he could be in any way attracted to herself, found herself wishing she had tied her hair in a better style and wore her second-best dress instead of this plain one.

Just as they moved onto the sweet pudding, Charlotte realised that neither she, Diana nor Mary, and she fully doubted Tom, had enquired after Miss Brereton.

"I do hope there is an improvement in Miss Brereton's health, Dr Hollis. She is out of danger, we are told."

"Yes, she is, but I fear both her nerves and her lungs suffered terribly. It will be some time before she is downstairs again."

"If her legs are sound," said Tom, "you should encourage her to walk in the garden, Doctor. Surely the sea breeze which can be felt from the east side of the garden at Sanditon House would do her the world of good."

"I fear not at present, or at least, I would not recommend

it … but perhaps there is something in what you say and I can advise that her bedroom window remains open, a little, at night."

"Yes, that is just the thing. The sea breeze will work its magic on her at night, fortifying her for the morning, and when she is stronger, she will be bathing again in no time. I must say, we were fortunate that you were about, Doctor. The death of a young lady due to a swimming accident would be detrimental to the reputation of Sanditon. It would be in the papers in no time. The subject of mischievous talk up and down the coast. We would never hear the end of it from our competitors in Bournemouth or Sidmouth."

A short silence followed and then Mary added, "Truly, we are grateful. You have saved a young woman's life, a friend of ours and the very nearest companion to Lady Denham. A tragedy has been avoided."

"Yes, and who would inherit Lady Denham's fortune then?" asked Tom. "The Denhams to be sure but now that Miss Brereton is …"

"Tom!" interrupted Mary. "Please! Let us not dwell on such low subjects. She is safe now and that is enough. And we have the doctor to thank for it."

"Thank you, Mrs Parker. We doctors must act with a lack of self-interest, in a way that protects and saves lives. 'Primum non nocere' is the Latin for 'first, do no harm.' It is how we are trained."

"First, do no harm," repeated Tom. "What a noble principle to live by."

Charlotte, fascinated by the doctor's values, wished to probe further.

"Dr Hollis, your principles are a credit to you and you, in turn, are a credit to your profession. It seems that where values and occupation meet, there lives a person contented with their lot. You strive to make the world a better place, to be of service to others, to walk amongst the sick without a thought for yourself. Did you always wish to take up the profession?"

"Yes, there is nothing else I have ever wanted to be. I cannot watch others suffer and the only way I can bear it is to assist them as I can or remain with them in their final moments, when no more can be done. But, I have not told you this Tom, I am drawn more and more away from my beloved profession by business."

"How so?"

"Last year, I inherited a great deal, much more than I deserve, from an uncle on my mother's side. Coming from a very large family myself, I have no idea why he favoured me over others, but he did and, alas, I am now burdened with the responsibility of being in trade with a house in London. I am obliged to reduce my practice and may perhaps eventually give it up."

"Oh, no," said Charlotte, "you must not do that. Surely, when a person finds their purpose in life – to relieve the suffering of others – it is like a mission, they will sacrifice anything for it."

Dr Hollis smiled, and with more spirit added, "How impassioned you are, Miss Heywood. And you are quite correct. It is a profession I will not give up without a fight and perhaps, instead, I will found a hospital that I may help even more unfortunates. Though the businesses and investments require a great deal of my time, and I confess, bring me much wealth, it is emptiness when one is not called upon by a higher force to undertake it. Money has no soul."

"Indeed, it does not, my dear fellow, but I rather like it all the same. One can never have enough."

"There we will have to disagree, Mr Parker," said Dr Hollis, as Mary signalled to Charlotte and Diana that it was time to remove themselves to the drawing room and the gentlemen stood, "to have enough, a home, some comforts, this is enough and to this perhaps add domestic happiness, and as I look around here, sir, I see you are already blessed in all these things."

Diana, satisfied that she had seen enough of Dr Hollis to decide on his character, announced she must return at once to Arthur and bade them all farewell.

Charlotte had just time to close the door of the drawing room and sit opposite Mary when her friend broke into praise of their new acquaintance.

"The doctor is so agreeable and the more time one spends with him, the handsomer he becomes."

"Superior. That is the word he makes me think of," said Charlotte. "There is something of the highest order about him. I wonder if he will be in attendance at the ball?"

"Why, I forgot to ask him, Charlotte. I will do so as soon as they join us. He seems to be a great favourite with Tom. What if he were to sell his businesses in London and come to live in Sanditon? He can be our resident doctor. He may settle down. There must be some divine reason for his being here, just as he is. It is too great a coincidence."

"I believe you give fate too much credit, Mary."

"Fate works in mysterious ways, my dear Charlotte. We must delay his departure, if at all we can. I will speak with Tom."

Mary's excitement and curiosity continued to grow, until the gentlemen joined them. Dr Hollis sat next to Charlotte while Mary put several questions directly to him.

Yes, he intended to stay at least several more weeks. No, he had no immediate plans to sell his businesses in London, and yes, he would be attending Lady Denham's ball.

CHAPTER TWENTY-TWO

Just before noon the following day, Charlotte passed on all her opinions of Dr Hollis to Jemima as they walked about the library.

"I never thought I should meet with such a man – so noble in his profession, so generous with his time, so clever in all he says."

"So charming, wealthy and unmarried?"

"Perhaps," laughed Charlotte, "perhaps those traits too."

A small bell at the door announced the arrival of another person into the room and it was none other than Dr Hollis. Seeing Charlotte, he immediately approached her and saluted both ladies.

"I beg your pardon, Miss Heywood, but I believe this is our fourth meeting in two days. If I did not know better, I would suggest that you are following me about."

"Indeed, sir, it is you who follow me, for I was here first."

"So it would seem to the common onlooker. Perhaps, however, you deduced from our conversation at dinner last night that I, having a soft head, would seek out those books for such persons which you claimed were held here at this library. Knowing that I would come today, you set out before me to give the impression of having arrived first. In truth, it was a very cunning plan. Do you admit it?"

"The only thing I admit is your having a soft head. As you are a doctor and have diagnosed yourself as such, who am I to dispute it?"

Just then Tom Parker, passing the window, caught Dr Hollis's eye and he quickly excused himself. Charlotte was sorry that their conversation had ended so abruptly but as Miss Lambe pointed out, he was sure to seek her out again at Lady Denham's ball.

Returning home for luncheon, Charlotte was met on the stairs by Mary who was taking refreshments to the nursery. Mary said with a grin, "Come along, Charlotte. We have a gentleman come to join us. I will be with you shortly."

It must be Sidney or Arthur, thought Charlotte. Then another idea struck her – perhaps it was Dr Hollis come home with Tom. Mr Parker was hospitable to a fault and he thought nothing of having friends call by at any hour.

Charlotte stole a look at her reflection in the hall mirror before entering the parlour to find Sidney sitting next to Tom and rising on her entering. A small pang of disappointment did not go unnoticed by Charlotte and she determined to cheer herself up. After all, the ball was approaching and there was so much diversion to look forward to. She placed her copy of Cowper's poems, which she had brought with her, on the table and chatted cheerfully of the morning and the ball.

A knock at the door indicated a tenant had arrived to meet with Tom so Sidney and Charlotte were left, for a short time, alone.

"I am sure Mary will be rejoining us soon. She is with the children," said Charlotte, looking to the door.

Following a short pause, Sidney said, "You are here long enough now, Miss Heywood. Tell me, do you still like Sanditon?"

"Yes, very much."

In a gentler tone and playing with his serviette, Sidney said, "Are you quite recovered from the sea bathing incident? It must have come as a great shock."

"I am as recovered as you are yourself. We women are quite strong, you know, and even in a crisis have been known to be the stronger sex."

"You need only point to my sister Diana to win that argument. But now I have run out of questions. I have asked about your health and your opinion of Sanditon and I know how you feel about powdered wigs. Perhaps it is time for you to ask me questions."

Charlotte smiled. "I do not wish to interrogate you, sir. I trust that anything I need to know of a person is revealed in time."

"But do we have time, Miss Heywood, to get to know each other better?"

Charlotte continued to butter and rebutter her slice of toast. She did not wish to misconstrue his meaning yet she was very aware that each week he postponed his departure, and his attendance, unexpectedly, at meal times was being remarked upon by her hosts. She did not look up but knew his gaze was on her. It would be impossible for her to approach any closer to his meaning.

"Time is irrelevant, Mr Parker, where some people are

concerned." And then in an attempt to lighten the subject, "What is your favourite colour?"

"It was yellow, but now it is blue."

Was he referring to her eyes?

"Who is your favourite poet?"

Sidney stole a look at her book. "Cowper."

"Do you prefer city or country?"

"Country."

"Dinner or breakfast."

"Breakfast."

"What is your favourite memory of childhood?" Charlotte was convinced he could not allude to her in his response and she felt she would tease him a little longer, if it was within her power to do so.

Sidney leaned forward. "Ah, Miss Heywood, that is unfair. Now you speak of the past and it pleases me better to speak of the present."

"And it pleases me better if you answer the question."

"Very well, my favourite memory from childhood is fishing at the river at the back of the Manor House with Tom. But as Tom was too impatient if he did not catch a fish at once, it quickly turned to swimming, climbing trees in the orchard and floating boats we'd made from sticks and leaves. That is my favourite memory. I would like to take you to the Manor House, Miss Heywood, someday."

Charlotte looked up and saw an earnestness in his brown eyes.

"Miss Heywood, will you promise me the first two dances this evening?"

Caught by his sudden change of topic and the eagerness of

his tone, Charlotte hesitated for a few moments, as Dr Hollis flashed before her mind, and answered, "Yes, sir. I thank you."

Her hesitation, caused by the momentary wish that another man might approach her for the same honour, did not go unnoticed by Sidney.

"You are sure you are not already engaged for the first two?"

"No, absolutely not. I am completely free and thank you for the asking."

Just then Mary joined them.

"Sidney, you will not believe who we had to dinner last night. I am sure Tom has told you. The doctor, Dr Hollis, and what a gentleman he is. So handsome, so wealthy, such a catch for any young lady. I do hope his stay is long. Was he not excellent company, Charlotte?"

"Oh, I see!" Sidney answered, then looked over at Charlotte. "Yes, Tom did mention what a fine fellow he was. I will leave you now and look forward to seeing you both at Sanditon House this evening."

The ladies wished him good day. Sidney bowed and left. Charlotte looked as his head passed the window, wondering at the sinking feeling, just below her ribcage. She had somehow disappointed him and in doing so, disappointed herself. But it was soon replaced with anger. How dare a person, who only last week called her "adequate, acceptable and sufficient", make her feel ashamed? She may dance with whomever she chose and if Dr Hollis or any other gentleman present should think her delightful, well, she would not discourage them.

CHAPTER TWENTY-THREE

I f the success of a ball is measured by the giddiness of those attending in the hours leading up to it, then the ball at Sanditon House surely outshone Versailles' best efforts. Sanditon was humming with excitement. Few walked the Terrace, most rushed about and it was noticed that all the pretty shoes in William Heeley's windows were sold. In almost every house, there were ribbons that still required dying and drying, shoes polishing and cravats finding, but the energy of the day was playful and the hours flew by. Before Charlotte knew it, Mary was shooing her upstairs for her own maid, Sylvia, to begin on Charlotte's hair. Handing herself over entirely to Sylvia, whose grandmother was French, and despite never having met her, Sylvia boasted of inheriting a natural flair for style. Charlotte, therefore, was free to look at her own reflection with satisfaction and daydream of the night to come, while Sylvia pulled the comb through her hair with a great frown.

As Sylvia's frowns gave way to sighs of satisfaction, Charlotte contemplated the lovely reflection she saw in the mirror. She was not standing up at The Crown at Hailsham this evening, swinging to country jigs with half a dozen brothers, neighbours and cousins. She would be standing up as a fine, eligible lady in the country house of a deceased baron's widow. People would whisper of her – that she wais pretty, elegant and a fine conversationalist – a wit, some might say, but in the best of taste. Yes, it was true that she was not wealthy, nor likely to be in the future, but she was a gentleman's daughter from a well-educated family – which must stand for something. When she considered her fine penmanship, flair for languages, sketching abilities and indirect connection with European aristocracy through Freddie, she had as much in her favour as any young lady who sewed or played an instrument. As for her husband-to-be when she dreamed of him, she could not fix on whether he was tall and broad like Sidney Parker or alluring and self-assured like Dr Hollis. As she remembered how principled the doctor had been, how very great a man he was, she could not help but think that to be his wife would be something very special. But then she thought of Sidney and his arm around her waist as he pulled her to safety. He had not the charm of the doctor. In fact, he could insult when his intention was to compliment, but his heart was good, she was sure of that, and she felt he would never willingly deceive. But if she were to receive the attention of both men at this evening's ball, which would she favour? She would have to wait and see.

Lady Denham greeted all the guests on arrival with both her niece and nephew by her side. "No expense has been spared, Tom, as you can see. The fires are lit, the candles are burning and the tables are laden with food. You look splendid, my dear Mrs Parker," as Lady Denham kissed

Mary on the cheek, "but a new dress, really! Look how I
still fit in my blue silk! It is the best dress I ever had made.
It has lasted longer than my marriages. All it needs is a
change of lace about the neck and there we are, as good as
new. And your friend, Miss Heywood, looks well," she said,
looking briefly in Charlotte's direction. "She has heeded my
advice."

Charlotte curtsied her acknowledgement and turned to
Miss Denham. "We will miss Miss Brereton this evening."

"Indeed we will but ..." and Charlotte waited as Esther's
eyes were fixed to something or someone behind Charlotte.
She could not help but turn to see what had transfixed
Miss Denham to discover it was the entrance of Dr Hollis.
Charlotte's own heart skipped a beat at his appearance and
Esther, flushed, returned to their conversation yet seemed
in a hurry to finish it. "A great loss to this evening's ball."
And Esther commenced acknowledging the next guest so
Charlotte was obliged to move on, and as she passed Sir
Edward, who just then also seemed to spy the doctor, she
heard him mutter, "the blasted impertinence of the fellow."

Tom Parker offered Charlotte his free arm, and with an
absolute contentedness she had rarely displayed before,
she entered the ballroom with her hosts. Indeed, she
could not fault Lady Denham tonight – everything had the
appearance of comfort and generosity. There was light and
heat, music and crowds, food and laughter even already and
Charlotte felt that this would be a memorable ball.

She was joined at once by Jemima Lambe, which meant
that Mrs Griffiths and Reverend Hanking were also with
them within a minute. The Misses Beaufort, as reflected in

Mrs Griffiths' opinion and purse, required less supervision and could be heard laughing loudly in amongst a group of soldiers, currently on leave. Tom moved about the room to chat and laugh with everyone he could and Mary recommended that they find a nice seat by the fire.

As Jemima and Charlotte caught up on all that had happened since they last met, Charlotte noticed a line of gentlemen hovering nearby. Then as the conductor announced that dancing would commence in ten minutes, the first man approached Miss Lambe to ask her for a dance, but Mrs Griffiths responded in the negative. Another man approached, perhaps believing himself better than his predecessor, and tried, but again, as Miss Lambe's head lowered, Mrs Griffiths made her apologies. It was only on the attempt by a third man that Mrs Griffiths announced, loud enough for the entire group of men to hear, that Miss Lambe was of a sickly and delicate constitution and dancing was absolutely and completely out of the question. As for those who chose to commence a conversation with her anyway, they soon found Mrs Griffiths positioning herself between them. Eventually, the bewildered gentleman gave up and took himself off to the card room or looked about for another rich lady to approach. It was on the subject of such restrictions that Mrs Griffiths and Reverend Hanking found themselves, at last, unable to reconcile.

"I do believe, my dear Mrs Griffiths, you are too harsh with Miss Lambe."

"On the contrary, Reverend, I am too liberal."

"How on earth so? You will not let her dance nor speak to young gentlemen. How is such a lady to enjoy herself at a ball? What, eh, am I not correct, Miss Lambe?"

Jemima smiled at the reverend but did not respond.

"I am surprised at you, Reverend, a man of the cloth demonstrating a relaxed approach to moral guidance in young ladies."

"Ah, Cynthia, we both know where I stand on that issue and the great respect I hold for you and your school – possibly the most proper of all young ladies' schools – but this is a ball and a dance should not be out of the question."

"I am afraid under this circumstance it is. Miss Lambe's guardians, the Chesters, requested that she be taken to a very quiet bathing place, where the opportunities to dance and make new acquaintance would be limited. They expressly said she is not to" (and Mrs Griffiths whispered this part) "make new gentlemen friends."

"One does not become wed to the first man one dances with," answered the reverend, "however, let us see if we can disprove it this evening. Cynthia, will you step up for the first two dances with me?"

Mrs Griffiths almost spilled her glass of punch at such a statement. She stuttered and blushed and hushed the reverend – what was he thinking, saying such things in the company of Miss Lambe and Miss Heywood?

"Time will tell if I jest, Mrs Griffiths, now please stand up with me."

Mrs Griffiths turned to Miss Lambe and said, "I do not wish to embarrass Reverend Hanking and, therefore, will dance these first two dances. Jemima, under no circumstances are you to dance or speak with strangers. I will return shortly. Miss Heywood, I depend upon you."

And before Charlotte had an opportunity to object and state that she herself was engaged for the first two dances, Mrs Griffiths was whisked away by her partner and the music for the first dance commenced.

Just then she saw Sidney Parker smiling as he made his way through the crowd to meet her. He had just left Captain Russell who approached Miss Denham as Tom Parker led his wife to the floor.

"Miss Heywood, you have not forgot your promise?" asked Sidney, now with her.

"No, Mr Parker, but I find myself …"

"You find yourself free to dance at once," said Jemima. "Please take her immediately, Mr Parker, or she will be charged with standing guard over me all night. I am quite well, Miss Heywood. I will not move but sit here quietly, staring into the fire and watching you dance."

Charlotte thought with horror of the possibility of meeting Mrs Griffiths on the dance floor.

"No, Jemima, I cannot. If Mrs Griffiths thinks I have abandoned you, she may refuse permission for you to continue your visits to Trafalgar House."

"Miss Denham!" called out Jemima. "Miss Denham, as you are passing, would you mind sitting with me a while? There is so much about Sanditon I would wish to know from you."

And with a glare, Jemima pushed Charlotte towards Sidney as Miss Denham, who had obviously decided to decline dancing, sat down with her by the fire. Charlotte was free to dance.

Sidney took all this strange to-do in his stride. "Miss

Heywood, you were not attempting to get out of your promise, I hope."

"No, not at all. It is very pretty here this evening. So many candles."

"Yes, I am sure Lady Denham has been in darkness all week to save them for this evening."

Charlotte laughed. Then Sidney placed his hand on her waist and the memory of his doing so, firmly and quickly when in danger at sea, came back to mind and she blushed.

"What is it, Miss Heywood, that made you smile just now?"

"I cannot say."

"Tell me at once."

"Indeed, I cannot."

"Then I will tell you what I was thinking. Just now, as I placed my hand around your waist for this dance, I recalled how I did so the other day, under different circumstances, and it made me glad that I had been of use."

"To save a life is definitely of use. And my life is of great use to me, so I thank you."

Sidney smiled and whispered, "And just now as I placed my hand around your waist, it felt familiar and I liked it very much."

Charlotte could not speak. What he had said had taken her breath away. But even if she could, she would not answer. It was too bold a comment for her. How could she say that she too enjoyed the feeling of his hand firmly around her waist? She blushed but smiled, so that he may not feel discouraged.

"I have had reason to think of late, Miss Heywood, of

what Mary said about fate. That had she and my brother not overturned their carriage exactly where they did, had Tom not sprained his ankle and required to stay with your family, had I not returned to Sanditon, unplanned, just when I did, we would not be here now, enjoying this dance."

He tried to look at her face which she was busily attempting to hide from him.

A delicious silence ensued only to be broken by Miss Lambe who swung past them with her partner, Arthur Parker.

"Oh, Charlotte," said Jemima, "what fun I am having. I am quite crying with laughter."

"Jemima, you promised to remain seated until I returned to you."

"I did not promise. Miss Denham left me."

"Is there a problem?" asked Arthur as he danced in and out. "I arrived late and could not believe my luck that Miss Lambe was unengaged. But if there is a problem, you must let me know. There will be no sitting down while Arthur Parker is in the room."

As the dance finished, all returned to their seats where Diana Parker and Mrs Griffiths sat waiting. Reverend Hanking had been sent on an errand to fetch drinks that he may not get in the way.

"Arthur!" cried Diana. "I could not believe my eyes. You will bring on a seizure."

"Miss Lambe," added Mrs Griffiths, "how utterly irresponsible of you. I forbade you to dance this evening. What would your guardians say?"

"Diana," said Arthur, "I was merely acquainting Miss

Lambe with the Sanditon style of dancing. A very old, informal type of dance, you know, Mrs Griffiths."

"I should have known, Arthur, that you would not dance, had not you felt compelled to," Diana responded. "Miss Lambe, you really should not have encouraged him."

"I beg your pardon, Miss Parker," said Mrs Griffiths. "It was your brother who took liberties in this instance."

"I do not believe it was so," answered Diana, "for if you had not been swinging the reverend about like a cricket bat, you may have chaperoned your charge as you are being paid to do."

At this point, Reverend Hanking returned. Observing the tension between the two ladies he nestled down, very neatly, between them, uttering, "Let slip the dogs of war!" and attempted to restore civility to proceedings.

While the older persons were thus engaged, Arthur availed of the opportunity to escort Miss Lambe to the punch bowl, leaving Sidney and Charlotte quite alone, standing a little separate from all others. After talking, however, of the weather and the ball, their conversation began to flag, and so little was said at last that Charlotte expected Sidney to go at any moment. He did not, however, and seemed in no hurry to do so. At last, with a little smile, he said, "Miss Heywood, there is something I would like to ask you."

Charlotte was puzzled.

"Yes, sir?"

"I would prefer not to ask in such a public place."

"I see."

"But I must, for who knows when I will get the

opportunity to do so in private? Are your affections engaged at present?"

Charlotte was startled. "Sir … I …"

"I am sorry but I must know. You force me to speak more frankly than I wish. Are your affections engaged at present? Yes or no?"

"They are not, sir."

"Excellent and may I ask …"

Before he could finish his sentence, Arthur and Jemima had returned, soon to be joined by others, and it was impossible to speak alone again. Sidney, with a look of frustration, excused himself and Charlotte, unsure of her own heart, felt all the confusion of wondering if she was exasperated by the interruption or grateful for it.

CHAPTER TWENTY-FOUR

I n seeking out Mary, for she had promised to sit with her for supper once she had danced several more dances, Charlotte wondered where Dr Hollis may be. She had seen him arrive but had not laid eyes on him since. The disappointment that this thought lent her was soon replaced with satisfaction as Tom brought Dr Hollis with him to their table.

"I do declare, Doctor," said Charlotte, "you have not danced yet this evening. Surely all eligible bachelors are obliged to dance."

"He plays a very good hand," Tom answered in his defence, "a very fine card player."

"I am shy in company, Miss Heywood, so I often retreat to the card room for the first half of the evening until my nerves have been settled by vingt-et-un and port."

"For shame, I do not believe you," said Mary. "A man of the world, of business, of medicine, who meets people all day, cannot be shy. Perhaps you are not avoiding the ladies but their mothers."

"There may be some truth in that," laughed the doctor. "Either way, I am now at ease and can face off even the most calculating mother, so I am determined to dance after supper. If Miss Heywood would do me the honour?"

Charlotte had danced with several gentlemen that evening and with the exception of Sir Edward, who complained incessantly how Miss Lambe had refused to dance with him, how his aunt would be furious and whether there was anything Charlotte could do to help him along, she had enjoyed each and every dance. Those dances with Sidney Parker had been particularly fun and she felt closer to him and confident that there would be less formality between them in future – for a couple could not dance so intimately as they had done and be indifferent to each other afterwards. But now as she stood before Dr Hollis, an internal struggle ensued which left her with all the bad feelings that accompany inconstancy. And yet, she reminded herself, she was not being inconstant. There was no understanding yet with Sidney Parker and if he did not ever finish his sentences, there might never be. Right now, she could not deny that she was equally looking forward to dancing with Dr Hollis. His appeal grew with every moment she spent in his company. It was his presence, whatever invisible pull it held, that was mesmerising. And when he made it apparent, through a look or a touch, that the attraction was mutual, Charlotte's vanity could not ignore it.

Miss Denham, who was walking past, stopped behind Charlotte's chair.

"Oh, Miss Heywood, I was looking everywhere for you. We must continue our conversation."

Which conversation she was referring to, Charlotte had no idea. She turned in her chair but Esther was looking past her to the doctor.

"Good evening, Dr Hollis. I do hope you are enjoying the ball. You have not yet been to dance, I am sure."

"I am rectifying that appalling state of affairs, almost this moment, with Miss Heywood. I hope my dancing abilities exceed your expectations."

"Oh," said Miss Denham, "how fortunate for Miss Heywood. Well, I do hope she will not tire you so that other young ladies are denied the pleasure of standing up with you." Esther turned from them and left to join another group.

Charlotte felt all the awkwardness of his not asking Esther to dance when it was obvious that this had been Miss Denham's intention. But men, her mother often told her, could be incredibly stupid. Charlotte decided, instead, to vastly enjoy the compliment paid to her rather than regretting another's bruised pride.

Just then they were joined by Sidney Parker, who again asked Charlotte if she wished to dance. In telling him that she was already engaged to the doctor, she noticed a change in his countenance.

He looked over to the doctor and said, "Indeed, the doctor is a lucky man."

"Quite," replied Dr Hollis. "Why do you not dance with Miss Denham? I believe she is looking for a partner right now."

Sidney looked over in the direction of Esther, who now sat by Lady Denham near the fire, but instead of joining her, he quickly bowed and said "excuse me" and departed in the opposite direction.

"That is a great pity that Sidney Parker would not dance

with Miss Denham," said the doctor. "Fortune, or lack of it, seems to matter a great deal to some men. Thank goodness such matters elude me."

"That is where you are wrong, Doctor," said Tom who they had not realised was standing nearby. "My brother means no disrespect. He and Miss Denham are old friends. Besides, Miss Denham may yet be the richest of all. The rumour that Miss Brereton is to receive everything is quite the fabrication. Lady Denham thinks too much of titles. I have it from an excellent authority – Lady Denham herself – that Miss Brereton will receive no more than a piece of jewellery."

"Really! I am surprised," said the doctor, "and disappointed, of course, for Miss Brereton's sake. It is a cruel thing to bring one in and get one used to living in comfort, only to leave one penniless and destitute later. But let us dwell on pleasanter things."

With a broad smile, he put out his hand to take Charlotte's and escorted her to the floor for their dance and remained close to her for much of the night. Sidney Parker looked over on occasion but never approached and this gave Charlotte, unused to the attentions of two men at once, a decided feeling of power. She believed herself flattered by the doctor's attention and was very tempted to encourage him but deep down Charlotte knew that it was Sidney she cared for most.

"Let this," she told herself, "teach Sidney a lesson and force his hand or he risks losing such a prize."

During one absence, when Dr Hollis had offered to find Charlotte a piece of melon which he had seen earlier, as she had never tasted one before, Tom Parker sat her down in a fatherly fashion.

"And how do you find Sanditon now, Miss Heywood?"

"What," wondered Charlotte, "is everyone's obsession with my opinions on Sanditon?" But she responded promptly. "Absolutely delightful, Mr Parker. I am so very glad that you brought me here."

"We are so very glad that you came. You are very much liked by all who meet you and your companionship is highly rated by my wife."

"It is I who benefit from her friendship."

"No, Miss Heywood. Mary feels more relaxed, more confident, more like her old self again, now that you are around. Please stay with us for as long as possible and if we go to London for some share of the season, you must come with us. Unless, of course, our friend Dr Hollis moves quickly."

Charlotte blushed. "No, Mr Parker. Please do not say such things. I only know him a few days."

"But you find him agreeable?"

"Yes, absolutely."

"And principled."

"I have met none more principled than he. The betterment of his fellow man, is for what he lives."

"Then you respect him and trust him."

"Sir," laughed Charlotte, "we may be living in fast times compared to yesteryear but I cannot possibly know him fully in a few short days."

Tom kept looking at her as if expecting an answer and Charlotte felt obliged to give it to him. "However, I am known to be an excellent judge of character. Everything I have seen and heard of, and from, the doctor, thus far, shows him to be a good man, a superior man even, worthy of the respect and gratitude of others."

"That, Miss Heywood, is enough. One cannot ask for higher praise than that."

The doctor just then returned with a small plate containing a variety of citrus fruits, berries and nuts and, most importantly, a small slice of melon. Tom Parker slapped him on the back, sending several blueberries flying from the plate, and said he must away to meet another but they would talk again soon. A secret look passed between the men and the doctor took this opportunity.

"Sir, I would appreciate it, if I may have your permission to visit Trafalgar House again tomorrow or the day after."

"Surely," thought Charlotte, "Tom will have his brother's interests at heart. Surely, Sidney has confided in Tom, if he has serious intentions with regard to me."

Tom looked down at Charlotte, who sat with her head dipped, too embarrassed, and said, "Why, certainly, sir. Nothing would make Mary and me happier. Please feel free to call upon us at any time. We must have you to dinner again soon."

"This, however much I have not sought it," thought Charlotte, "is a compliment, I am sure. I do not think I am in any real danger and perhaps some good shall come of it, for it will make Sidney Parker speak up at last."

CHAPTER TWENTY-FIVE

The night was almost coming to an end and Charlotte was exhilarated at how it had gone. She had spent a splendid evening feeling quite the most spectacular person present. No one compared to her, in her own opinion. She had been at her prettiest, friendliest and wittiest – with the two most handsome men in the room vying for her attention.

Sidney Parker stood now with his two brothers and Captain Russell by the hearth. He stole a look or two in Charlotte's direction which made her sense that he was ever watching her, jealous of those who were near her. Miss Denham stared at her a great deal too and at the first opportunity, when the doctor had gone to secure them some drinks, Miss Denham sat down beside Charlotte and began, "Miss Heywood, you appear to be very pleased with yourself and why would you not? Dr Hollis is such an attractive and wealthy young man. I believe you are the envy of every woman in the room."

"I am sure you are mistaken, Miss Denham."

"But let me warn you, now, while I have the opportunity. Not all men are honourable. I was once like you. There he stands by the hearth. Do you know of whom I speak?"

"Yes, I believe so." Charlotte looked at Sidney. "But please, say no more. I do not wish to extract your confidence."

Miss Denham did not appear to hear her plea, or chose to ignore it.

"Last summer, we were in love and he made me a promise. But he has not kept that promise."

Charlotte felt a stab of pain below her ribcage; she had not known this before. Yes, she knew that people had hoped that they would become attached to each other, but it had never been said that it was imminent or even likely. She had never thought of them as intimate, of promises being made and broken. All talk, all behaviour indicated differently.

"He stands there with his friends like nothing has happened. They are part of a very fashionable set in London. I believe that he may even have a mistress! There is talk! He can afford a mistress and yet cannot marry me."

Charlotte was struck dumb.

"Miss Heywood." Esther placed her hand on Charlotte's "I was like you once and I am like you still – pretty and almost penniless. You must marry for money. I will never let my heart rule over me again. I am determined to marry well and so should you."

Charlotte could listen no more. When the doctor returned with their drinks, she left him in the company of Miss Denham, stating she needed air for she was developing a headache. Both offered to accompany her but she refused, saying she was tired and would rather be alone; a few minutes by an open window would revive her.

Charlotte reached the side door and stepped outside

into a narrow courtyard. She stood still, attempting to slow her breath and racing thoughts. Sidney Parker was not the kind of man that would play with a woman's feelings, break his promises and humiliate her in such a fashion. Of this, she was sure. And yet Esther was so angry and if it had been, even a little, like she portrayed him, then it was little wonder. But Sidney Parker was sufficiently wealthy to marry without care of a dowry, if he had loved. If he had given his word, and broken it, then he was not an honourable man. Perhaps it was beneath him to marry without securing a fortune. It made no sense. There must be a mistake. And he definitely would not be the kind of gentleman who kept a mistress in town.

But Charlotte was unfortunate in choosing where she stood, for Arthur Parker was just inside the door, positioned there by Diana with strict instructions not to leave until his colour had been reduced by the cool summer evening air. Alone for a few minutes, while Diana looked for Mary, he was soon joined again by his brothers and their familiar voices reached Charlotte. She could not move now.

"How do, Arthur? You are very red about the face."

"That is the colour of excitement."

"Over-excitement, I would say."

"Is Miss Lambe not the most beautiful creature?"

"I thought you liked the Misses Beaufort."

"The Misses Beaufort are nothing to Miss Lambe."

"Speaking of lovely ladies, how goes 'The Duchess', Sidney?" asked Tom.

"Remarkably well."

"She must be missing you now. You are a long time from London."

"Good Lord," thought Charlotte, "they are speaking of his mistress."

"I wrote to her yesterday and stated that I will return the first opportunity I get."

"Then what is delaying you?"

"I am not at liberty to say," Sidney laughed.

"How is my face now?" asked Arthur. "Is it sufficiently settled? Come let us return to our group. An inspired idea has just struck me."

Charlotte waited another few minutes and returned to the room but before she could return to the doctor and Miss Denham, Mary Parker took her by the hand.

"Charlotte, come at once. Arthur has had the most wonderful idea. We are all to go to the old Manor House so that I may show you the walled garden. Oh, it is so beautiful and I miss it so much. He has also invited Mrs Griffiths and her charges. We must arrange a picnic."

Charlotte looked around at the smiling group and pretended a smile herself but inside her heart was breaking. She must feel no more for Sidney Parker. Was she not as Miss Denham was the summer before – his play thing? He would break her heart, if he had not done so already, and then return to his mistress. The words "he has deceived me" sat as a stone in her heart as she repeated them over and over again for the rest of the evening and much of the night.

CHAPTER TWENTY-SIX

C harlotte decided, after an ill night of sleep, that she must avoid Sidney Parker at all cost and ensure that their conversations in the future were kept short and formal. He must be under no illusion that she felt anything for him. Although it may sting his pride, and may require her to act as if she felt less than she did, she consoled herself that he would soon return to London and seek his comfort there. In order to ensure that she saw and thought of him as little as possible that day, she decided that she would pay Miss Brereton a visit, before returning with Miss Lambe to Trafalgar House and locking themselves into the front room to play piano. As for the morrow, when they were all to go to the Manor House to visit the walled garden, she decided that she would attach herself to Mary and show excessive interest in all her plants. Engaging herself too much with Miss Denham would do her spirits no good whatsoever but between Mary and Miss Lambe, she was sure to be safe.

These thoughts gave her comfort despite her sunken spirits and she approached the breakfast room with resolve and optimism only to find Sidney Parker yet again sitting opposite her seat.

"Good morning, Miss Heywood. I thought I would see how all the revellers were holding up. You slept well?"

"Yes, I thank you."

"But I can see that you did not. Lady Denham will be very pleased to hear that there are casualties in every house in Sanditon."

Sidney looked and smiled as he said it but Charlotte did not return his good humour and instead gave considerable attention to the toast which sat on her plate.

Tom continued chatting to Mary about pieces of news in the newspaper which he held aloft. Sidney leaned across the table and whispered in a concerned voice. "Are you not well, Miss Heywood?"

Charlotte looked up at his face, his face drawn, his eyes questioning, and could hardly bear to lie.

"No, sir, I am very well." But as the tears arose in her eyes, she stood up suddenly, excused herself and rushed from the table, back to her bedroom where she lay on the bed and cried and cried. This was going to be much more difficult than she had thought. Perhaps it would be better if she made an excuse and cut her own visit short. There was no guarantee that Sidney would leave soon and she could not go on like this, day in, day out.

At Sanditon House, Charlotte found Clara Brereton extremely flushed and excitable. Clara wished most particularly for details of who would make up the excursion and also about how Sir Edward got on with Miss Lambe. "He has forgot me already. He has not sent word or enquired. I hear he goes well with Miss Lambe."

This was the proof Charlotte needed to confirm that

Miss Brereton, in believing herself in love with Sir Edward, had less sense than she had originally credited her with.

The patient's nerves, she concluded, must have been greatly affected by the accident. On pressing Clara for details of the treatment she was following, she was informed that the doctor, who called on her almost daily, still insisted that bed rest at this time was essential. Charlotte wondered whether the doctor's remedies would be the same for the farm labourers as they were was for the young delicate charge of a wealthy relative. She believed that some employment would be better than this idleness and encouraged Clara but to little avail.

"I will ask Nelly to bring me my needlework but really I cannot seem to concentrate on anything these days. I am all a-flutter."

Charlotte promised to visit again with a basket of whatever produce she may gather from the Manor House and take her walking once she was permitted to do so. Charlotte, rather than being comforted by this visit, left Miss Brereton more concerned than when she had arrived.

The day of the visit to the old Manor House had arrived. Mary was to go in their own carriage with Arthur, Diana, her children and Tom. Sidney was to take Charlotte, Miss Lambe and Mrs Griffiths, with the intention of returning for the Reverend Hanking and the Misses Beaufort.

On the morning in question, Charlotte looked out her window to witness Tom and Sidney arguing. Tom shrugged his shoulders and turned and Sidney called back but Tom did not turn around and so Sidney walked away. At breakfast, Tom was his usual jovial self but, halfway through, made apologies that he would not be able to join their party that day. His reasons were many and Mary was very disappointed.

"Oh, Tom. This is terrible. Should we cancel?"

"Not at all, my dear. I am so very sorry, but you will make a wonderful day of it. The sun is out and I hear that the garden is heaving. You may never get such an opportunity again."

"But without you, its old master, it seems wrong."

"No, Mary, who better than its former mistress to show our guests around? And why, Arthur, Diana and Sidney grew up there too, you know, and have an intimate knowledge of all its secrets. It must go on, my dear."

"Very well. But it will not be the same, Tom. I do not see what business could not wait."

Here Charlotte noticed distress flicker on Tom's face for a moment before he gave the broadest smile. Charlotte sensed that all was not well. Perhaps he, too, was wishing to avoid Sidney.

"Trust me, my dear, I have business to attend with our creditors and they will not wait."

"Then perhaps, Mary," offered Charlotte, "I may take Mr Parker's place in your carriage. It will save Mr Sidney from making the trip back here and instead he may go straight to Mrs Griffiths' lodgings."

"A very good idea," said Tom and smiled at Charlotte.

"Yes, Charlotte, I would love to point out to you my favourite tree on the driveway in."

It was settled that a message should be sent to Sidney at the hotel that he may go directly to the Terrace and collect persons there, while the others made their way together. By return message, Captain Russell sent his apologies but he could not join them that day. Sidney, however, would do as they recommended. Charlotte sighed in relief – she had spared herself any moments alone with him, whom she dreaded most to meet.

The journey to the Manor House was every bit as lovely as Mary had promised it would be and Charlotte could soon see, before they had even left the carriage, that Mary's heart was yet at her former abode and a sort of melancholy could be deciphered as she greeted it with, "Ye old manor, my old home, I miss you so much."

For her part, Charlotte could comprehend, within her first quarter-of-an-hour, why – such character, greenery, nooks, gardens, birdsong, the river, children running around – none of this was apparent at Trafalgar House. And as Mary walked about rubbing the old walls of the house, whispering to herself, pushing through the old gate into the walled garden and brushing the dust from a bench that they may sit, it was as if she was visiting a dear, dear old friend and recalling their good times together.

The Denhams arrived next and made their own way to the garden and, being familiar with the place from their youth, began pointing out places that had changed or plants they had not noticed before. Soon, they were joined by the remainder of the party. Sidney, Charlotte could see, looked over at her a great deal but was held hostage by the Reverend Hanking who had an unnatural interest in ivy. Arthur, on clearing his throat, took it upon himself to act as guide. He had their attention but for three minutes when Diana relieved him of his duties. He did not seem to mind, for as the group began to stroll along the west wall, it allowed him to linger behind with the young ladies and promise to accompany them on the short stroll down to the river before their picnic. And at the first gateway they passed, he ushered Miss Lambe and Charlotte through and they began the walk.

"They will hardly even notice we are gone," whispered Arthur and with a giggle the other two quickly followed him.

"You spent much of your youth playing here, I suppose?" asked Charlotte, once they were safely away from the garden.

"No," answered Arthur, "not really. I was considered too sick for much time outdoors. But Tom and Sidney, they were out every day. I envied them greatly – climbing trees, fishing and generally doing all that energetic, boisterous boys do."

"Delightful pursuits."

"Yes. They were very close. Inseparable. Or rather Sidney looked up to Tom. He would take Tom's side in everything. Tom could do nothing wrong in his eyes. There, over there. That was a favourite rock pool of theirs. My word, how small it looks now. And over there, that leaning bough, that's where they jumped into the river."

Charlotte was moved by this image of two young brothers, slapping the waters, screaming, splashing each other and scaring away any fish.

"It is a great pity that you could not join them," said Miss Lambe.

"Yes, I thought so too and by the time I was old enough to join them, they were engaged in it less – Sidney was busy with his studies and Tom with his schemes. My parents acquired a dog for me to swim with. Poor Mother and Father! And poor Rover! I had him fifteen years."

As they returned to join the others, Sidney giving them a curious look and Mrs Griffiths a disapproving one, Charlotte found herself joined by a jubilant Sir Edward. He was in the most excellent form she had ever seen him.

"Miss Heywood, may I walk with you to this bench over here?"

Charlotte nodded her consent and they separated a little from the crowd who were now laying out the picnic and trying to organise themselves.

"You are spoken of, a great deal, by a gentleman of our acquaintance. A gentleman who I have found very obliging."

Charlotte said nothing and as Sir Edward was obviously enjoying the element of suspense he was creating, she decided to remain in silence while wondering if he referred to Sidney.

"Why do you not ask me? I will tell you, for I see you are quite wild to know. It is Dr Hollis!"

Charlotte looked at him in surprise.

"Sir Edward, you had everyone believe that you greatly disliked that gentleman."

"Not like him? Why, he is the finest fellow I have ever met. I am very much in his confidence, you know. He has no interest in Lady Denham's estate, none whatsoever, so he was never a threat to me, d'you see? Do you notice how that almost rhymed? If Clara, Miss Brereton, were here, she would have noticed."

Charlotte wondered how much of Sir Edward she could tolerate.

"As I was saying, Dr Hollis is a capital fellow. He does me a great favour with passing messages to Miss ... but, oh my, that is a secret. He has offered to cut me into a deal which is taking place soon, Miss Heywood. Mr Tom Parker is interested also but Dr Hollis says he cannot permit any more investors. How lucky am I? And you, you are lucky too for he has set his sights on you."

"Sir Edward, I do not know what you are talking about."

"Your modesty does you credit, Miss Heywood. I am soon to become independent in fortune and then I may marry where I please. Tom Parker is quite desperate to get in but alas, alack and all that."

"Please, Sir Edward, you are over excited. Let us speak of something else."

"The lady doth protest too much, methinks. You are quite safe in my confidence, Miss Heywood, and equally flattered by the doctor."

The conversation was coarse and Charlotte, though anxious to leave him, yet found herself stuck to her seat. Sir Edward took it as a sign to continue. "Why Dr Hollis speaks of it as certain. 'Sir Edward,' he said to me, 'I shall be a frequent visitor to Trafalgar House for I have my sights on one within.' He was referring to yourself, of course."

Charlotte stood up, curtsied and turned to leave just as Sir Edward finished, "He would have been a great match for my sister but, as I know to my detriment, one cannot prevent a man falling in love."

Charlotte liked very little of what she heard. That a

handsome, wealthy gentleman should take an interest in her was flattering but that he discussed it with Sir Edward, the town crier, at the hotel and while, possibly, under the influence of drink, was most distressing. If the doctor wished to seek her good opinion, he had best act in a more respectful manner. Yes, she knew nothing but good of the doctor. He was honourable and steady, everything that Sidney Parker was not, but if he wished to ingratiate himself to her, to usurp Sidney from her heart and mind, he would have to show more discretion, patience and speak to her directly rather than to her male acquaintances.

Mary, noticing Charlotte approach her, called out, "Charlotte, before you sit down could you please look for Miss Denham and tell her we are about to eat? She went over beyond the big oak. These custard tarts will be ruined if we wait much longer."

"Or Arthur will have eaten them," said Diana.

As Charlotte approached the big oak, she saw Sidney standing very close to Miss Denham. Even as he spoke, Esther stepped in closer to him and laid her head on his shoulder. Charlotte could not decipher the nature of this secret meeting, but when she saw Sidney lay his hand at the back of Esther's bowed head, she knew he was either whispering something comforting or endearing. Despite her promise to forget him, Charlotte could not but be affected. She turned suddenly to remove herself from them but not before she noticed Sidney look up. Had he seen her? She was not sure and told herself she did not care. "What new intrigue is this? What secrecy shown by them both and why? Sidney Parker is nothing to me, and I, no matter how he acts towards me, am very obviously nothing to him."

Charlotte returned to where the others sat on the scattered blankets. When enquiries were made as to the whereabouts of Miss Denham, Charlotte claimed that she had not seen her.

"Oh, look now, there she is," said Sir Edward. "Sister, where did you get to?"

Esther returned on her own and claimed that the day was so fine she looked over the old rose garden.

Mary was pleased and asked if she'd seen Sidney. Esther lied and said 'no'.

Soon Sidney returned and, looking directly at Charlotte, yet addressing Mary, he apologised for his absence and said he had gone up to the Manor House to see if the roof was still in good order.

Charlotte said nothing and found it impossible to look at either Sidney or Esther. Despite Mrs Griffiths' greatest efforts to accommodate all three of her charges on her own blanket, that they may be close at hand and not obliged to share one with any gentleman present, she only managed two, Miss Lambe and the elder Miss Beaufort. Reverend Hanking had insisted on sitting half on hers and half on his own, so that the younger Miss Beaufort was now cast onto the next blanket. She did not seem to mind for it left her next to Sir Edward who recited love-sick poetry and quoted from Shakespeare. Though he spoke it earnestly and with emotion, Miss Beaufort giggled throughout, stating he was very like a theatrical actor she had seen once. At first Sir Edward was flattered until she stated that the actor in question played the part of a drunkard in a comedy performance.

One role Sir Edward was certainly not fulfilling in his

behaviour today, thought Charlotte, was that of the lover of Miss Lambe. His aunt's absence must answer for it. And what had he meant when he said that he would be independent to marry where he wished?

Sidney waited until all others were seated and placed himself, very neatly, kneeling between Mary and Charlotte.

Charlotte ate in silence but was ever conscious of the presence of Sidney at her back and how he might wonder at her silence. They two who had always spoken with such animation and honesty, who had sought each other out as the best company in the room, now sat in silence, side-by-side.

At last the food was finished. Arthur led some of the guests in a tour of the orchard before Diana could follow him, for she was deeply engaged with the reverend on the topic of sitting on damp grass and the evils it produced. Mary joined Mrs Griffiths on her now vacant blanket to discuss her method or attempts at educating her own children at home and Charlotte found herself alone beside Sidney. She made to follow Mary but was held by a quick comment from Sidney.

"You are determined to leave me, I see."

Charlotte sat back again in her spot.

"You are mistaken. I was merely sweeping the crumbs from this corner over here."

"You are silent, Miss Heywood, yet you are talkative enough when in the company of others."

Charlotte attempted another denial. "I assure you –"

"No matter, please come with me to the orchard, where we can join the others."

As Charlotte stood up, her spirits sank again. Everything about this was wrong and full of pretence. She would have to leave, return home to Willingden. How could she tell him that she knew of his mistress? That she had overheard him speaking of her openly, almost boasting, to his brothers? How could she tell him that she could never marry a man who sought his pleasures elsewhere? How could she tell him that she knew of his cruelty and lack of honour with regard to Miss Denham? Of his teasing her here today? Of how nauseous it made her feel? There was no other way about it. She must leave Sanditon.

As they passed through the small gate into the orchard, Sidney took her by the arm, to the side. "Miss Heywood, I cannot bear this. Please tell me what I have done to offend you."

"You have not. I cannot. I must return to Willingden, that is all. I cannot stay any longer here."

"But such a change as this. I cannot fix when I do not know where the fault lies. Please, let me clarify matters. There must be some misunderstanding. Perhaps someone has spoken ill of me. Has another gentleman secured your affections? Miss Heywood, Charlotte, it has been my intention to ..."

"Please, say not another word. Your promises may be spoken freely, easily, to other ladies but I cannot, will not, listen."

"Miss Heywood ... if you speak of Esther, Miss Denham ... if you have seen something pass between us just now, you are mistaken." Sidney pulled her towards him but she managed to pull herself free with a "How dare you?" and, with reddened face, walked briskly to the others now circling an apple tree. Sidney stood staring, equally flushed and frowning, but when Charlotte turned to look back, he had gone.

"Charlotte, come here. Mr Arthur Parker is climbing this tree because I said the apple at the top is the handsomest apple of all," called Miss Lambe.

Charlotte attempted to smile back, as she watched Arthur dangling on a bough to reach the apple. "Someone must catch the apple before it hits the ground. I cannot reach it and must poke at it instead with a stick. There are four of you there. One of you must catch it," he called out.

"I am sure I shall be no good at this," said Miss Lambe as the ladies scattered laughing and took positions around the tree. Arthur, breaking a long, narrow branch, poked the apple and it fell – right into Miss Lambe's outstretched arms. She was delighted and so was Arthur who, once he found his footing on the ladder which he had pushed against the tree, returned to the ground once more.

Jemima offered it to him.

"No, not at all. Finders keepers, Miss Lambe. It was you who spotted it first and you who caught it. I will clean it for you." And Arthur rubbed the apple several times against the chest of his waistcoat and presented it back to a delighted Miss Lambe.

"They are my favourite fruit, Miss Lambe."

"I do love apples myself."

"I knew you would. How can one not? I believe I can make up a poem:

Red, green or in a pie, Apples are a fruit for which
I'd die/
And for the lady, who is the apple of my eye/

If I dare try, she would never say goodbye/
Or else I might cry."

"Good heavens, it is I who will cry, if I must listen to this," thought Charlotte to herself, "and centuries-dead poets turn swiftly in their graves." Then aloud: "Come, Jemima, let us return to the picnic. There is a biscuit we made, using my mother's recipe. I would like you to try it."

"I do like a fine biscuit myself," piped up Arthur. "I can discern all ingredients with only one mouthful."

"A most useful talent, I am sure," remarked Charlotte. Arthur offered an arm each to both ladies and returned them to the picnic fare.

The rest of the afternoon was a penance for Charlotte. Although Sidney was nowhere to be seen and only returned to the group before the agreed departure time, to check his carriage and horses, she was unable to relax at the thought of his being near her again. Then, when she felt that she could not possibly feel more agitated, Mae returned to Charlotte with her telescope, broken into several pieces. Her dearest object, broken beyond repair.

"It was not I. It was the boys but they made *me* bring it back to you."

Charlotte gasped aloud and would have cried but for the audience before her. Mary lamented.

"Oh, Charlotte, I am so sorry. Let me see the maker's mark. I will tell Tom we must replace it."

"No, Mary, there is no need. It is of sentimental value only and Freddie bought it on the continent. I am sure it cannot be got."

"Can it be fixed?"

"I believe the large glass is missing but I cannot tell if other parts are missing too. I will go with Mae to where it was broken and see if I can retrieve more."

Charlotte searched in the grass and found another small piece of the mechanics but she knew that it was beyond repair. Placing all the smaller parts in her reticule, Charlotte returned to the group, noticing that in the busyness of hosting, Mary soon forgot all about the telescope and her interest in repairing it.

"I will hide it in my room and send it to London for repairs when I have saved enough," thought Charlotte. "I would hate for Freddie to see it in its present state. I should never have allowed the children use of it."

The trip back to Trafalgar House was a quiet one, as all the travellers were tired and one amongst them was particularly agitated. Sidney followed behind them to drop his nephews home, who refused to go in any other carriage. As they all pulled up outside the house, Dr Hollis, who was just leaving Trafalgar House, stepped forward to assist the ladies from the carriage. When all seemed preoccupied, he kissed Charlotte's hand.

"You had not forgot that I might call?"

"Sir, I had not forgotten, merely we were otherwise engaged."

Dr Hollis looked up at Sidney Parker who, having witnessed the kiss, could not take his eyes from them, not even as his nephew tugged his sleeve.

"Ah, yes, a visit to the old manor. Tom mentioned it earlier. It has a charming garden, I hear. I rode past it last week and was struck by its likeness to the gardener's cottage on the Hollis estate. Very quaint and agreeable."

"It has an elegance too," added Charlotte in its defence and then fell silent.

"I see," said Dr Hollis. "Well, let us not stand about here. Let me see you ladies back inside your home safely."

As the Parker boys had already jumped down from the gig, there was nothing for Sidney to do as Charlotte was led back indoors, but scowl and drive his horses in a temper, back to his own lodgings.

CHAPTER TWENTY-SEVEN

It took several days and great ingenuity on Charlotte's part to avoid Sidney Parker entirely but it was made easier by the fact that he appeared to stop pursuing her. The doctor, meanwhile, called every morning and although they spoke most agreeably of travel, human nature and the wonders of the world, their relationship did not progress as it might have done if she felt inclined to encourage him more. But she did not. Charlotte knew that she had never met anyone who listened so attentively to her every word, who encouraged her opinions and praised her advice. He was remarkably attractive. It was his presence, his carriage and the way he walked, however, that almost took her breath away at times. He was an object of admiration, even awe. And she knew, when they were in company, others felt that magnetism too. But while her head could be light and her character flattered by his attention, he had never touched her heart, and she believed she had never really touched his. She owned to herself that it was best that she retreat now and put an end to any speculation before it was believed that they had an understanding. Tom Parker, especially, seemed to show great interest in her progress and it was beginning to feel like a pressure and a lie, to allow it to continue any longer.

Charlotte had decided she would inform the Parkers at breakfast one morning of her decision to return to her family, when Tom suddenly announced both of his brothers' departure. Arthur had left already – his sudden removal alarming Diana greatly. He claimed he had been struck with a great idea the day before and so set off with secrecy and determination, promising to return as soon as 'all was settled'. Sidney was to leave today.

"And what a pity when Lady Denham has a dinner party planned for this week. She will not be happy to hear of it."

"I am so sorry to hear of it, Tom. But I had noticed," and Mary looked slyly at Charlotte, "that his visits had become less frequent while Dr Hollis's had become more. You do not think they are avoiding each other, do you?"

"Not at all," answered Tom, missing Mary's meaning. "They are two of the most agreeable men in the country. Sidney is as solid a brother and friend as anyone could hope for and the doctor is now my business partner, or at least he at last permitted me to invest with him. As you can imagine, where money was to be made I could not omit Lady Denham. No, it's merely a case that Captain Russell was called away suddenly yesterday as his regiment is on the move. No time for goodbyes so Sidney gave him his curricle. Now Sidney finds that he must return to town for business. He will say his farewells to the children this morning and take the post-chaise back to town."

Any scenes of 'goodbyes' would be painful for Charlotte so she was relieved that she had planned to deliver the mixed basket to Miss Brereton from her visit to the Manor House. Then she would enjoy the long walk home, being sure to visit the library on the way and not return to Trafalgar House until almost dinner, by which time Sidney Parker would surely be halfway to London. It was cowardly perhaps but she could not risk an encounter while she had not yet learnt to regret him entirely.

Charlotte was quite alarmed at finding Clara not improved but rather worse than before.

"Miss Heywood, how good you are to me. How few visitors I have."

"I am sorry to hear it. Had I known, I would have visited more often."

"Oh, I do see Lady Denham and Miss Esther every day but that hardly counts. And Sir Edward. Well, there was a time ... but enough of that now. It is in the past. Sir Edward, I have no doubt, continues to lure Miss Lambe with his charms. I cannot blame him I suppose. But I had expected him to at least enquire after me – to have cared enough as to whether I lived or died."

"I believe I heard that Lady Denham forbids him to call upon you."

"Yes, but that is no excuse. He may have sent a note."

"Through his sister?"

"No, she is not allowed, and is truly not a great friend of ours, if the truth be known."

"I see. Had the doctor not passed messages on his behalf? If you wish me ... I know it is not to be encouraged perhaps but ... I can take you a note from him or give him a note from you."

"It is too late. It is too late," said Clara, waving her arms. "Too much has happened since … He may go off and marry his heiress bride now. Too much has happened. He should have sent me word before."

"Do not make yourself anxious. In truth, you look well. I am sure you will be downstairs before too long. I believe you should insist with the doctor that you should return downstairs. Too much isolation and inactivity is not good for one."

Clara looked through the open window, into the distance.

"They will announce an engagement soon, I daresay."

"I am no expert in love, Miss Brereton, but even if Sir Edward did pursue, of which I saw little evidence, it does not guarantee that he will be successful."

"Do you think not? I am sure she would not be able to withstand him for long."

Charlotte almost laughed aloud. "Thankfully, we do not all look out at the world with the same eyes. I do believe Miss Lambe is quite safe. Or Sir Edward is quite safe, whichever way you choose to look at it. There was no one as distraught as Sir Edward when you had your accident."

"One cannot always act when one wishes. There are often obstacles that cannot be overcome."

Charlotte felt a change of subject was desirable and forced herself to exaggerate. "You are feeling improved. As I mentioned, your looks are excellent."

Charlotte did not know how to follow Miss Brereton's puzzling line of talk and wondered had she, perhaps, also hit her head in the accident. Instead she attempted to raise Clara's spirits with talk of the gardens at the Manor House and a tale she saw in the paper of a large sea creature swept up on a beach nearby.

Charlotte, tired by Clara's nonsense talk, had hoped, on quitting Sanditon House, for solitude for the remainder of the day. She had much to contemplate but almost immediately she met Miss Denham, walking alone, in the same direction as herself and they were obliged to join together and speak. The conversation soon turned to Miss Brereton.

"I declare there is absolutely nothing the matter with her," said Miss Denham. "I believe she is pretending so that I may be stuck with my aunt instead. Day in, day out. I believe I will go out of my mind. That is why I am out walking on my own, like this, that I may have a few minutes' peace."

"The doctor says that she is unsound," answered Charlotte.

"In many ways, I dare say she is, but not in health."

"We must surely give some credit to the doctor's opinion."

"He seems to have a very good opinion of you," smiled Miss Denham. "Of course, I thought of him for myself when he first arrived but I soon saw my charms did not work on him." Miss Denham looked coyly at her companion but, to Charlotte's relief, changed the subject.

"My brother does not go well with Miss Lambe and it renders my aunt furious. I believe he had tried at first but seems to have given up. He still cares for Miss Brereton, the fool."

"You believe them to be in love?"

"Both are silly enough. They attempt secrecy but anyone

who has eyes can see it and I believe he gets someone to pass his notes to her. He has told me so himself. Their happiness would be assured for they would delight in their mutual silliness and feel sorry for the rest of us mere mortals. All would be fixed in an instant, if they knew an inheritance was secure."

"You believe so?"

"I know so, but my aunt prefers us to feel uncertain in that regard. She once joked that she may leave us a tea set if she chooses and her entire fortune to her two milch asses. She has the means to raise us up or to at least give us hope but she had rather not. If I were sure that something would be bequeathed to me, Captain Russell would not have broken my heart."

"Captain Russell?"

"Yes, as I told you before, I was very much in love and we were on the verge of an engagement when he left, suddenly, last summer."

Charlotte stopped in her tracks. "But it was Sidney Parker who broke a promise to you."

Miss Denham laughed heartily. "Sidney Parker! Sidney Parker! Why, we are like brother and sister."

"But everyone expected the engagement. You pointed to him by the hearth."

"No, I pointed to Captain Russell who stood speaking to him. Sidney and I have always been teased about getting married but I would not do it to him, nor he to me. There is only friendship between us. He deserves a good wife, I would assure him a wretched life. And besides, I now want only wealth in marriage. My aunt has taught me something."

Charlotte was truly shocked and could only move with hesitation.

"Forgive me, Miss Denham, but I happened upon you and Mr Parker by the oak tree yesterday. It was an intimate scene. He was –"

"He was comforting me. Captain Russell had returned this summer, to discover for himself that my circumstances were unchanged and to ask that I approach my aunt regarding my inheritance. I refused to do anything of the kind. It rendered him angry. Then he asked that I wait for him and not promise myself to another, to enable him time to make his fortune at sea. I told him I would not wait and hence his sudden departure and my tears."

"I am sorry, Miss Denham. It is too cruel."

"You are often sorry for me, Miss Heywood. Do not be. I made the correct decision."

What Charlotte really wanted to do was to return to her room and think and feel all the emotions that were arising for her now. She had misread the situation and thought Sidney cruel for treating Miss Denham so badly. She had been wrong about that, but what of his mistress? There still was his mistress. The ladies turned back and walked on in silence with only an occasional laugh from Miss Denham and a "Sidney Parker indeed!"

When they had returned again to the Terrace, Charlotte was readying her excuse to leave when Miss Denham pressed her to take tea with her at the hotel.

"Oh, please say you will. I am so thirsty and I am sure I will look very strange sitting there on my own. We are more respectable when we are together. I wish to delay returning to my aunt for as long as possible."

As Miss Denham had been so open with her, Charlotte felt she could not refuse. Once inside, they were led through a large dining hall. It was noisy and people sat either alone or in groups at various tables and benches, waiting to be served food and drink. They were led to a small snug area where rows of cubicles ensured a small party may have privacy and although the noise was too loud for comfort, the departure shortly after of a large group of men hired for the construction work brought a quieter mumble to the room.

Their tea had not long arrived and Charlotte was reflecting on how nice Miss Denham may actually be as a friend, when the door opened and Dr Hollis entered. He approached them on noticing them, stopping just briefly at the cubicle in front to nod his head in salutation, and was by the ladies in an instant.

"Ladies, what a pleasure it is to meet you here. I was unaware you frequented this establishment. May I join you?"

And without waiting for a response, Dr Hollis sat down.

They had chatted pleasantly for a few minutes when a servant from Sanditon House came up to their table and directed his speech to Miss Denham.

"Begging your pardon, ma'am, but Her Ladyship has sent me out to find you. She has mislaid something and wants you home at once."

Esther stood up and begged forgiveness of the other two.

"This, I fear, is what my life has become. Excuse me, Miss Heywood, Dr Hollis."

As Miss Denham left, Charlotte stood to leave also but was prevented from doing so by Dr Hollis sitting back down again and, in doing so, blocking her exit.

"Surely it is not inappropriate for us to continue our conversation and finish our tea."

"I think it best if I leave. I must go to the library."

"It will be closed now until the afternoon. Sit with me awhile. When else might we get such an opportunity?"

"Very well, for a few short minutes."

"I can see, Miss Heywood, that something bothers you and I want to assure you of my support as a friend, confidence as a professional doctor and interest as a person who finds you … well, more of that later."

"You are always kind to me, Doctor, but I assure you there is nothing wrong with me."

"There may be nothing wrong with you but there may be something wrong with others. Tell me, is your time here at Sanditon going as you wish?"

"No. You have extracted it from me now. It is not but only recently so. Sanditon itself is a wonderful place."

"In and of itself, I agree. But the people? How shall I say it? I find them quite strange myself."

"I am a little confused with regards to some."

"But you are such a wonderful judge of character. I can tell these things. Then you must let me guess. Is it Lady Denham? Has she tried to make you buy her asses' milk? Has she been unkind?"

"She is mean and arrogant. She has been unkind to me only once, but it is not her."

"Then the Reverend Hanking has bored you with his talk?"

"No," Charlotte smiled at last, "although his public displays of attention to Mrs Griffiths make me quite ill, it is not him."

"Then it must be Arthur and Diana Parker with their sores and diseases."

"No, I assure you, it is not. Though they are ridiculous, exceptionally ridiculous in so many ways, it is not them."

Now Charlotte felt relaxed and enjoyed this game they played. His teasing, fun questions amused her and he delighted in her answers. She would play along, for it cheered her up considerably.

"I won't believe it to be Tom and Mary Parker. I dare you to find anything ridiculous and irksome in that example of marital bliss."

"Marital bliss may indeed be when a wife has not the strength of character to stand up to a husband. Where his fanatical schemes are taken too far, she sits back and watches and tells him he is marvellous. He sees only his vision and completely disregards his wife's. He is too impetuous and she, too soft."

"My word, Miss Heywood, you are severe. But I cannot disagree with a single comment you have made so far. You are very observant, I can see. I should hate to hear what you may have to say about me."

"You are very pleasing in your manner and clever at encouraging me to say more than I should. That is all I will say for now."

"Then I am only left with Captain Russell and Mr Sidney Parker. What say you of them?"

"I believe Captain Russell to be a shallow fellow, whimsical and cruel. Certainly, capable of breaking a woman's heart."

"Indeed? I hope it is not yours you refer to."

"No. Certainly not. You give me no credit."

"And the dashing Mr Sidney Parker?"

Here was the crux of her melancholy and the doctor had reached it at last but she could not say much.

"He is a good man."

"Nothing else? Is he not a rogue, a scoundrel, a cheat?"

"No, I had believed him to act without integrity in one matter but I was mistaken."

"So he is faultless."

"No," answered Charlotte, "I do not believe anyone can be."

"Then let us pronounce Sidney Parker a perfect gentleman, a man of integrity and honour. Still, Miss Heywood, you do not look convinced."

"Sidney Parker is a rake. He has a mistress in town." Charlotte had it out before she had meant to.

"Indeed. I am shocked."

"So was I when I learnt of it."

Charlotte's voice was now hardly above a whisper and she felt tears rising up within her.

"Some people do not consider a gentleman having a mistress as a very wrong thing," continued Dr Hollis. "It is a very common occurrence in London. I, however, have always disapproved of the practice. It is sordid and immoral and makes a mockery of the ladies in their lives, their wives in particular. A man should be constant in his affections to one woman, and one woman alone. Miss Heywood, perhaps we can talk elsewhere …"

The door to the room swung open and a young man

came to the door and shouted, "London! The post-chaise awaits for those travelling to London."

Then the scrape of a chair at the cubicle in front and the recognisable figure of Sidney Parker arose and walked past their table without looking and left to join the other passengers. His jaw was tense – a cold, hard expression on his face.

Charlotte gasped. He must have heard everything she said. All those cruel comments about his family and friends and, though it may be true, the most damning of all about himself.

Dr Hollis laughed. "Miss Heywood, I wish you could see yourself just now. I had quite forgotten he was sitting there, next to us, quite hidden. Do not look so horrified."

"But he must have heard."

"You spoke only the truth and has he not said similar himself, especially regarding his family? A gentleman, if that is indeed what he is, never eavesdrops. Therefore you have nothing to fear."

Charlotte arose, her stomach quite unwell. "Excuse me, sir."

Dr Hollis made payment for the tea as Charlotte hurried out to where the carriage was just pulling away. She saw Sidney look directly at her and knew without a doubt that he had heard every single word that she had spoken.

The horror that Charlotte felt could not be done away with despite all of Dr Hollis's attempts to pacify her on the walk home. He assured her that she had said nothing *really* bad and certainly nothing new. What did she say of Tom and Mary Parker that was not true? Or was not said of many married couples? He assured her that the other siblings were absolute nonsensical hypochondriacs, the likes of which he had rarely met with, in all his years as a doctor. As for Sidney Parker himself, Dr Hollis had not wished to speak to a lady on such a low subject but he could confirm that she was correct. He had denied knowledge of it earlier to protect her but now he must own that he knew all. Sidney Parker had boasted of his mistress to Dr Hollis and he could also confirm that he had heard something of the matter at Crockfords, his club in London.

This last comment was like having a knife thrust into her lower chest, just below her ribcage. She had hoped it was not true and yet here was confirmation. It made her feel ill. And yet somewhere beneath the horror sat a strange comfort that she had been right, the balm of which lessened the guilt of what she had said, to a very small degree. The feelings she had felt for him were all one-sided; he would forget her, if he had not done so already. She need not feel guilt with regard to his feelings any longer. She would put all her energy into soothing and healing herself. As if reading her thoughts, Dr Hollis took her hand and said, "He really was not worthy of you, Miss Heywood; please do your best to put him out of your mind. Please allow me the honour of attempting to cheer you up and distract you from unhappy thoughts."

"Sir, I assure you I am well. By tomorrow, I am sure it will be all forgot."

"Then I shall come tomorrow to check that it is so."

Charlotte could do nothing but smile. He had not asked her so she could not refuse and even now as she climbed the steps to the house, he accompanied her.

"I thank you, Dr Hollis, for your comforting words. Good day."

"If I may be so bold as to ensure I hand you over to your hosts, then I am happy."

"There is no need, I assure you."

But Tom, who had spotted them from the parlour, just then swung open the door and invited the doctor inside. Charlotte decided to go to her room and heard the door to Tom's study close and the muffled sounds of men talking and laughing, just as she cast herself on her bed. How wretched it felt to feel wretched.

CHAPTER TWENTY-EIGHT

Charlotte repeated what had been said, again and again. Was it really so dreadful, she wondered? Could she diminish its dreadfulness in some way and view herself in a more bearable light? Sidney Parker, of all people to have overheard her; but then, who but he would know that there was something of truth in everything she said? He had always admired her direct manner and even complimented her on it once. Had he not, himself, poked fun at his own family at every opportunity? Was it not almost expected of him at every family gathering or in every letter of correspondence, to say something of jest with regard to his siblings? They almost encouraged it. And as for what she said of himself, no person could be more familiar with the particulars of his liaisons than himself, and had the doctor not confirmed it, that he had heard something of it? She was only saying what was probably spoken about, at large, in London society. The term was 'rake' and he most likely took pride in this description amongst his likewise rakish friends. Certainly, Captain Russell was no paragon of virtue. She may have hurt Sidney's pride, by exposing him in such a manner, but she must excuse herself for she spoke the truth.

But when she recalled what she had said of Tom and Mary, she felt truly ashamed. She should not have spoken of them in such a derogatory manner – those who had treated her like family and shown her nothing but kindness and generosity since her arrival. She could not excuse herself on that count and even though she felt some anger towards Dr Hollis for his ability to draw her out, she knew that she, and only she, had spoken the words. She also wished that she had not used the word 'ridiculous' when speaking of Arthur and Diana. A remembrance of her father speaking to her before she left Willingden came before her now: *"You believe yourself a good judge of character."* How right he was and she blushed at her foolishness and arrogance. Nothing but a determination to cut her trip short could atone for her behaviour. Although Mary would miss her greatly as a friend and companion and Tom would worry at Sanditon losing so many of its summer guests within a few days, she knew in her heart that she could not impose upon them any longer after what she had said. She would write at once to her brother to tell him to send all future correspondence to Willingden and she would wait until after tomorrow night's dinner at Sanditon House to inform her hosts. To do so beforehand would be insensitive.

Charlotte forced herself from her bed and moved with purpose to collect Miss Lambe – anything to distract herself from the dread she felt inside. But her friend, instead of waiting eagerly on the steps, was to be found lying out on her own bed, sobbing in great gulps.

"What on earth is the matter?" asked Charlotte.

Jemima sat up, allowing Charlotte to pass her a

handkerchief and rub her back before throwing herself back down and sobbing for two minutes more.

"The Chesters have sent for me. They will not let me stay out the summer here."

"Oh dear Jemima, they must miss you. I dare say you can ask Mrs Griffiths for another trip to Sanditon next summer, if you found it so agreeable."

"No, you do not understand. Their son is returning from abroad and they wish me to marry him ... before I come of age."

"Oh. So suddenly. Is there a reason they, you, he ... cannot wait until you come of age?"

"My fortune will go to him when I turn eighteen."

"And do you love him? Do you like him? Do you know him well enough to grow to care for him?"

"I know him well enough to know I could never care for him. Nor he for me. He is cold, spoilt and has only ever looked at me with disgust. I am so wretched."

Jemima broke into great fits of tears again and as Charlotte rocked her back and forth, she spied the now wrinkling red apple by Jemima's bed and another idea entered her head. She dismissed it immediately as impossible.

"You must become calm, Jemima. Then we can look at your options. Do try."

Jemima slowed her breathing and dried her eyes and, with the exception of the occasional gasp or shiver, she calmed herself sufficiently to speak clearly.

"Oh, Charlotte, do you think I have any way out of this?"

"I am not sure, but let us look at the facts. Must you do as your guardians wish? Can you object?"

"I believe not. I may say no and they will force me. Since my father died, I have been entirely at their mercy in all matters. They have control over my finances, in so far as they can, until I gain full access to them myself on my birthday in September. That is why they are determined that I marry their son Oliver before then. That way, I will never gain control or independence. I shall be wretched."

"Try to remain calm, Jemima. Perhaps Mrs Griffiths may convince them. I am sure she wishes to remain longer herself. It would give us time. I could ask Mr Parker to speak with his solicitor to find if there was any way out."

"Mrs Griffiths has no influence with my guardians. They pay her generously. She cannot afford to lose their favour or fees."

"Oh dear. What can be done? Have you any other friends with whom you may stay?"

"No, I have not, and as I said I am totally dependent on them until September. Oh, Charlotte, I wish to marry for love."

"But there is not a gentleman yet, Jemima, for whom you care in that way. I have known you since you have come to Sanditon. You would have told me. We all wish to marry for love and if we could only find a way to delay this event, perhaps someday you will meet a man whom you can love."

Jemima looked over at the now wrinkling apple by her bedside.

"There may be … just someone for whom I have begun to have feelings. But it is no use now."

"Good Lord, no!"

Jemima now fell more fully into Charlotte's arms and sobbed furiously.

"Surely, it cannot be Mr Arthur Parker! You cannot possibly love him."

Jemima pushed herself back. "Why can it not be him?"

"You cannot be serious. You mustn't believe yourself in love with the first man who presents you with an apple."

"I know what you think of him. I know that you find him ridiculous and weak. You have often said it and it hurt me so. But he is kind, good-humoured, loyal and brave. It was he who saved Miss Brereton – that was not weak. Perhaps he has not always been strong in standing up to his sister. He is forever told what he should do. In that respect, we have much in common."

Charlotte realised the truth of Jemima's words. "I should not have said 'ridiculous'. I apologise. He is not that."

"All he really requires is an occupation. He may appear idle but it is the natural result of boredom and questioning his own convictions due to always being led by another. He has little confidence in his own abilities."

"You are completely correct, Jemima, and I am mistaken. Arthur Parker has been a generous, friendly and attentive gentleman since his arrival and is indeed worthy of attaching the affections of a lady as sweet in nature as you, Jemima. Forgive me."

Jemima smiled.

"Yes, of course I forgive you. You are the only person who knows excepting Sarah."

"Do you believe he may also have feelings for you?"

"I believe, perhaps, he does. Oh Charlotte, indeed I

know he does. We have met on several occasions in secret when only Sarah chaperoned me and her secrecy is assured. I pretended I was visiting you or going for a walk but we met in the library mostly."

"Jemima! How deceitful of you. I suppose you were left with little other option. Well, you have disproved Reverend Hanking's theory that entanglements cannot happen in a library."

"Do not be cross with me, Charlotte. Occasionally on Sunday mornings when Mrs Griffiths and the Beauforts were off to church, I feigned illness and was left behind. Then, Sarah admitted him and we were alone for a time."

"Oh, do not tell me this, Jemima. I had preferred not to know your secrets. Now I feel a partaker in your dishonesty. Say no more."

Then a moment later, Charlotte asked, "But he did not take liberties, Jemima, when you were alone?"

"Miss Heywood! How could you ask such a question? Mr Arthur Parker is a gentleman."

"Yes, forgive me." And Charlotte thought to herself, "If being a gentleman was a guarantee of virtue, the population in this fair land would not be so high."

Jemima reached for her friend's hand again.

"Oh, Charlotte, what a relief it is to speak of this to a friend. When we last met, I knew nothing of the Chesters' schemes for me. Arthur set off for London with a plan he believed would help establish him in some line of business. He was so very hopeful that when next we met … but now we won't. Oh, Charlotte, my heart is broken."

Following on from her experience at the hotel, Charlotte

felt truly ashamed of the unjust ridicule she had made of Arthur before. Now her friend, Jemima, who had always seen his true merits, was obliged to return to London and wed a man she disliked intensely so that he may take her money and cast her aside. What life, what vices and dreadful torments would await a young woman married to a man such as that? It could not end well.

"Is there anything to be done, Jemima? Have you any other family whom you may turn to?"

Jemima wiped her eyes.

"No, no one. I must resign myself to my fate. I leave tomorrow with my Sarah as companion on the journey. We will be met by my uncle at Tunbridge and travel the remainder of the journey in his carriage. In two weeks' time, I will be wed. Will you do me a favour, Charlotte? Only one thing."

"Of course."

Jemima placed her hand behind a painting on the wall and removed a letter.

"Will you give this to Arthur? It explains everything to him. He is due back in Sanditon today but it is impossible for us to meet, and I leave in the morning. I cannot trust this job to another. Mrs Griffiths forbids Sarah and me to leave the house. She insists we pack at once."

Charlotte hesitated for a moment, then took the message from Jemima.

"Yes, I will hand it to him the very next time I meet him. I believe he is expected to dinner tonight if there has been no delay in his arrival back to Sanditon."

There was nothing for Charlotte to do but to try to support

and assure her friend as best she could. She promised if she were ever visiting Freddie in London, she would come to visit Jemima. She resolved to include a visit to him soon. They pledged to write to each other, despite knowing their correspondence may be intercepted, and with many tears on one side and a troubled heart on the other, they parted.

As she left the Terrace, Charlotte met Miss Denham, her brother and aunt who were on their way to bid farewell to Miss Lambe.

"We have just heard about Miss Lambe. I am seriously displeased with this business," said Lady Denham, looking at Sir Edward who in turn was looking very sheepishly into the distance. "Still, we must make of it what we can. Perhaps she and Mr Chester will visit Sanditon in the future and finally, without Mrs Griffiths' interference, I will convince her to drink of my asses' milk."

CHAPTER TWENTY-NINE

E ven the most daring of pirates would own that a great too much activity was worse than too little. It was this dizzying sense of instability that Charlotte felt now. Last week, all was ease. She was delighted in her friendships and elated with the probability of romance. She could look with satisfaction at the past, contentedness at the present and a most complacent optimism towards her future. But now, all was not as it seemed. People appeared different from how they portrayed themselves, rumours were unfounded and a great many people who were fixed to Sanditon before and whom she cared for, had up and left. Most dreadful of all was Charlotte's conviction that she had somehow contributed to this state of flux.

Charlotte, aware that Arthur Parker was to join them for dinner, entered the dining room twenty minutes early so that she could find somewhere appropriate to hide Jemima's letter. She had nowhere about her person to keep it and she knew it would appear very strange if she were to suddenly bring her reticule to the table. If they were dining elsewhere she could, but not in the house in which she resided. It took her some minutes to find the perfect place beneath a bulky vase on the side table and, even then, she was forced to fold it several times to make it as small as possible. But how, over the course of the evening, she would have the opportunity to pass it to Arthur, she had not the slightest idea. Opportunity, just then, stepped in, as it is sometimes wont to do, and before she quit the room, Arthur Parker himself entered it and alone.

"Mr Parker, you are early."

"Good evening, Miss Heywood. Indeed I am. I have wonderful news which I wish to share with all present and in my excitement arrived early. Diana was quite put out that I would leave before her. I could not contain myself. You must wait to hear all for yourself. You see before you a man of business, but I have said too much. Pray, what is for dinner?"

Charlotte knew she must not lose this opportunity. She snatched the letter from beneath the vase and, taking his hand, pressed it into his palm. He looked confused and alarmed.

"Mr Parker, this is a letter from Miss Lambe. She is to join the Chesters tomorrow. I am sure this letter will tell you more. Please, take it now and hide it before the others arrive."

Arthur did not immediately hide it as she had hoped but stood staring at her.

"Tomorrow? The Chesters? No, this cannot be," and he ripped open the letter and read its contents to himself before pushing it into his pocket. "I must go, Miss Heywood. I cannot stay for dinner. This changes everything. Please give my apologies to all."

Arthur turned to leave but swung back around and took Charlotte's hand.

"You must have been her confidante. I had not known. Thank you, Miss Heywood, for your friendship. Good evening."

Charlotte, embarrassed by a compliment from a man she had wronged, was left to explain to the remaining Parkers that Arthur was obliged to leave urgently. He had not said why but he was quite well and would join them another time. This response was entirely unsatisfactory for Diana's curiosity and it took all Tom's powers of persuasion to convince her to stay for the meal and not rush off looking for her absent sibling.

As she descended to breakfast the following morning, Charlotte resolved to visit Miss Brereton. Surely here she would find one whose circumstances were unchanged – who would not deprive her of sleep and the security of certainty. If any change had occurred, it could only be for the best. She was sure to find the patient much improved, in better spirits, healthier and more cheerful now that Miss Lambe had left. Miss Brereton might even have finally moved from her bed to an armchair by the window or better still, be now up and seated downstairs amongst others. This change, Charlotte felt she could cope with and hope for. To Sanditon House, therefore, she would go.

Charlotte announced her plan to Mary, in case she would like to attend with her, and at first Mary, agreed until, on opening a letter, she jumped in her seat.

"Oh, my word. I do not believe it. It cannot be so. Within two weeks."

Mary's cheeks flushed red and she turned to her husband.

"Tom, Mr Mooney is coming to Sanditon. He is to open his tea room on the promenade within two weeks. He has been approached by an investor and wishes for me to assist him with its establishment. He is anxious not to waste any more of this season. Oh goodness, we do not even have a promenade."

"Mary, this is wonderful," said Tom, taking his wife's hand. "I would have preferred an investor for the fountain but I shall not put off anyone who sees the potential of Sanditon. This is marvellous. Why, there may be more investors to come. Will you allow me to walk with you this morning, Mary, along the Terrace to see which building suits best?"

"Of course, Tom, you may accompany me, although I have already picked out the most suitable building. Is not this wonderful, Charlotte? I cannot believe it. Thank goodness I have all those sketches begun, Charlotte, and plans for menus. Well, I must see to what extent he wishes me to help him. Oh, Tom, I will get all the ladies to visit once he is set up. He comes soon. The centre building beside the millinery shop is ready as it is, with a large window looking out at the sea. All it requires are some tables and chairs. And a small kitchen. I must write back today and encourage him."

Tom, throwing back the remainder of his tea, turned to Charlotte.

"I almost forgot. Miss Heywood, our friend Dr Hollis sent word late last night. He sends his apologies that he cannot visit you as promised today. The wonderful news is that our deal has been struck so he was obliged to rush back to London before dawn and arrange matters with his solicitor. He is to send word by express the day after tomorrow, to let us know what our investment is worth." He rubbed his hands together. "Come, my dear, the magnificence of Sanditon can wait for no man."

With that, the Parkers left Charlotte alone to eat and contemplate the wonderful news she had just learnt. The imminent establishment of Mary's bakery and tea room at Sanditon meant more to her than the fact that Sir Edward, Tom Parker and Lady Denham were to be enriched by Dr Hollis's scheme. Both pieces of news, however, lifted her spirits and she set off to meet Miss Brereton in the comfort of knowing that she would be the first to inform her. One thought that struck Charlotte on her walk was that she did not miss the doctor as she had thought she would. Her only regret in his departure was that she had not clarified her lack of interest before he left.

When Charlotte arrived at Sanditon House and asked to be taken to Miss Brereton, she was surprised to be informed by the butler that Lady Denham had left word that if there were any visitors for Miss Brereton, they were to meet with her instead. Charlotte followed him into the front breakfast room where Lady Denham sat alone, looking to the gardens, through the window.

"Miss Heywood."

"Lady Denham."

"Please sit. You have come to call on Miss Brereton?"

"Yes, madam."

"I am afraid she is indisposed."

"Is she unwell?"

"Yes, one could say she is."

"Then I will call again tomorrow."

"No, Miss Heywood, nothing will likely have changed by tomorrow."

Charlotte nodded.

"I have been blind, Miss Heywood. There is sometimes that in us, which is so focused on what we believe to be important that we lose sight of what really is important. Is it not so?"

Charlotte had no idea of what Lady Denham was speaking but in applying the older lady's reasoning to her own regretful situation, she felt it was true. Who was more guilty of missing what was really important in a person's character than she?

"Yes, Lady Denham, I believe it may be so."

"Yes, yes. Well, let us speak of something else."

Here Charlotte informed Lady Denham of Mr Mooney and his tea rooms. Lady Denham smiled and said all that was proper but Charlotte saw that it did not impress her as it should. Lady Denham was distracted. Informing Her Ladyship of the success of Dr Hollis's scheme would draw a different response but Charlotte felt it was not her place to deliver this news.

The doorbell rang, the certain sign of another visitor.

"That will be Mr Holmes, my lawyer, Miss Heywood. I am expecting him. I apologise that I had not arranged for tea. You will excuse us. Have a good day."

Charlotte stood up and left, feeling that something unusual was occurring, but instead of meeting Mr Holmes she met Miss Denham, looking more solemn than usual and not inclined to delay Charlotte with idle talk. Esther moved directly to join her aunt and Charlotte found herself, not seven minutes from entering the front door, back through it again.

CHAPTER THIRTY

Charlotte returned home, hardly noticing the burst of new flowers on the hedgerow, so occupied she was with all the unsettling events of late. To the loss of her dear friend Jemima, the hatred that Sidney Parker bore towards her and the guilt of all her prejudices overheard, she must now add the sad fact that Miss Brereton was indisposed again. And judging by the solemnity of Lady Denham and her niece, the reason must be a very serious decline in her health.

As she ascended the front steps of Trafalgar House, Charlotte resolved to lie down for an hour. It would revive her before seeing the children and hopefully distracting herself with their play, but as she walked through the door, she could see, on Morgan's face, that all was not well.

"You may wish to join Mr and Mrs Parker in the parlour."

"Very well, thank you, Morgan."

It was completely out of character for Morgan to say any such thing. She assumed it was his way of saying she may be needed there.

When she entered the parlour, she found Diana and Mary sitting on the sofa, Mrs Griffiths sitting opposite them and Tom pacing furiously back and forth. A heated exchange between Diana and Mrs Griffiths was evident and Mary was pleading with both ladies to calm themselves. All stopped and looked in Charlotte's direction when she entered. Mrs Griffiths stood.

Charlotte apologised and was on the point of leaving when all Parkers asked her to join them.

"Miss Heywood, did you know anything of it? You must have. How could you? I trusted you," shouted Mrs Griffiths.

"I am sorry. I do not know what you are talking about."

Mrs Griffiths sat down again. Her eyes were red; she waved a handkerchief as if about to say something but blew her nose instead.

"Miss Heywood," said Tom, "we received word this morning that Arthur and Miss Lambe have run away, have eloped. We assume they have gone to Scotland."

"Good heavens!" Charlotte was genuinely shocked. She had not foreseen this development. In truth, she did not believe Arthur Parker had it in him to instigate such a daring deed. This was the kind of adventure that Sir Edward would talk of, possibly be capable of, but not Arthur Parker.

"Yes, we are equally shocked. Now, Mrs Griffiths, you can see for yourself that Miss Heywood knew nothing of this."

Charlotte sat down next to Mary, deciding not to enlighten Tom to the fact that this statement was not entirely true.

"Are you quite sure?" she asked.

"Yes, there is the letter," he answered.

Charlotte blushed and asked a little too quickly, "What letter?"

"This one." Diana waved it. "He left it for me on my tea

tray so I would see it first thing this morning. It states that he and Miss Lambe were eloping."

Charlotte was relieved that it was not the one she had given Arthur the evening before.

Mrs Griffiths began crying again. "When I checked her bedroom this morning she was gone, and Sarah with her. I have sent an express to the Chesters, that they may be able to intervene at the earliest opportunity or cut them off before Gretna Green."

Charlotte still sat in silence. She wondered at her own feelings. Her heart told her that she did not wish them intercepted, that dragging Miss Lambe back to London to force her into a loveless marriage was far worse than what had occurred. She could not betray these feelings before those presently in the room, especially as she did not know how they felt about it. She soon found out.

"Arthur was taken in, of course," said Diana. "He would never, in a million years, come up with such a scheme."

"How dare you, Miss Parker, insinuate that Miss Lambe had anything to do with this? She is incapable of such deceit. She was kidnapped. Her health is poorly. You had best hope, for your brother's sake, that she does not die on the journey. Mr Parker, you must do everything in your power to catch them. Write to any connections you have. They must be stopped at once. The Chesters will never trust me again."

"I would not trust you as far as the front door," added Diana.

Mrs Griffiths looked as though, had she an umbrella in her hand, she would have hit Diana across the head.

"Diana, please, that does not help," uttered Tom.

Mary calmly added, "I have called for tea. There is no situation that is not made better with tea. We will discuss this in a composed manner and come up with a plan."

Nobody spoke until all had a cup of tea in their hands and Mary began, "I confess, I have something to add that may prove it was not an underhand scheme on either person's part."

All eyes turned to Mary. "Arthur did tell me that his recent trip to London was to follow a very particular line of business. I was most curious but he would not tell me what it was. When I asked why now – why was he entering a business now when he had never desired to do so before? – he answered, for two reasons. The first was that he had finally found a business about which he was passionate and the second was that he believed himself in love and wished to establish himself before approaching the lady in question."

"And had he told you it was Miss Lambe?" asked Diana.

"No, despite all my teasing and pleading, he remained tight-lipped. But I believe we can now safely assume that it was she."

"Mary, I cannot believe you kept this from me," said Diana.

"My dear Diana, I gave him my word that I would not share his intentions with anyone. He feared that if any part of it was shared with his family, they might try to prevent his taking action."

"Well, this puts a different colour on things," said Tom.

"How so?" asked Mrs Griffiths. "A lady, not yet of age, has been taken off without the permission of her school or guardians. It changes nothing."

"Mrs Griffiths," said Tom, "we understand your plight. The Chesters, about whom we have yet to hear a good report, will be enraged and may lay some share of blame at your door. But it is quite clear that had we not been overprotective and interfering in our brother's interests, and had you not been as strict with Miss Lambe, they would not have been forced to consider elopement. They had little choice."

"Then you condone this, Mr Parker?"

"I do."

"And you will not assist me in retrieving them?"

"I will not."

Mrs Griffiths arose and walked over to where Tom now stood by the fireplace. "You are a great disappointment to me, Mr Parker, as is your entire family. I will never think upon Sanditon but as a disappointing point on the Sussex coastline where opportunists dwell. This is not the end of it. The Chesters are very influential people, Mr Parker. They have connections everywhere. Your brother will be hunted down and brought back before this marriage can take place."

Tom straightened himself and then removed the cup and saucer Mrs Griffiths was holding in her hand. "Thank you, Mrs Griffiths. I believe there is little else to be said except that I do genuinely hope that time will enable this situation to be resolved in a way that is satisfactory to all parties involved."

Mrs Griffiths quit the room without another word, followed shortly by an indignant Diana.

"How could you say it, Tom? How could you imply that we drove Arthur to this? If you had let me seek him last evening when he missed dinner, this would not have happened. I would have stopped him. It is he who is the invalid of the two. If the dangers of this journey should kill him, as I have no doubt they will, it will be some consolation to me, that I would have prevented it if I could."

Once Diana quit the room, Mary walked over to her husband and placed her arm about his back and he did likewise around her waist.

"You were quite right, my love. I am proud of you."

"As am I, Mr Parker," added Charlotte.

"If it was not for Dr Hollis's investment, I fear I might have acted differently. Arthur's actions may well have sullied Sanditon's reputation as a respectable destination. I have no doubt that word will spread among the schools. Mrs Griffiths will see to that. I think we will not see many of their like arriving here over the next few years."

"You give Mrs Griffiths too much credit, husband. She is hardly a woman of influence. Remember it took at least half a dozen of Diana's friends to organise her trip here."

"Howsoever," sighed Tom, "when the express arrives in due course, we will have the certainty and confidence to develop Sanditon at speed. No longer will it be, which shall we build first – assembly rooms, formal gardens, a promenade or the Crescent? It will be all at once."

CHAPTER THIRTY-ONE

A troubled conscience leads to a disturbed night's rest. Charlotte arose to such feelings of unease as had her wish the day was done and she on her way home, yet there was Lady Denham's dinner today and breaking the news of her imminent departure to Tom and Mary to be done. How on earth would she get through the day, with such heaviness about her? She had let everyone down, in one way or another, and everything she touched seemed to lead to unhappiness.

For even a moment, she convinced herself that she should leave immediately but then, realising that it would add to Tom and Mary's distress, she felt she had best stay till the morrow. Lady Denham's dinner would be a smaller affair as there was no Arthur or Sidney and no Jemima. She would get through it in some automatic fashion and be done with it and Sanditon forever. Then she would return to Willingden and reflect on her wilful ignorance, her willingness to condemn first before seeking out and choosing the goodness in others, to highlight the ridiculous and make everyone else seem foolish, except herself. When all the time it was she who was the fool.

She was very surprised when after breakfast Tom invited her into his study.

"All this, Miss Heywood," Tom said, as he waved in the direction of his plan of Sanditon, "is where I have invested every penny, every hope and every drop of sweat from my brow."

Charlotte looked but said nothing.

"May I ask a question of you, Miss Heywood?"

"Certainly, sir."

"I have invested everything that I own in a guaranteed investment with your soon-to-be betrothed."

"Everything?"

"Yes, well, almost everything. I have kept Trafalgar House out of it."

Charlotte could not hide her surprise. "Sir, if it is the doctor of whom you speak, there is no understanding there."

"Oh, I am sorry, Miss Heywood, how insensitive of me to speak of your private affairs before you have had a chance to confide in Mary. Ladies do like to keep their secrets."

"Sir, there is no secret, no engagement and no understanding."

"Well, there soon will be, and I am such an ass to mention it to you. Forgive me."

"I do not expect it. But of course, you do not need to apologise."

"Let us forget it for now, Miss Heywood. I apologise for speaking out of place. But back to the crux of our conversation. I have been informed by a gentleman, of whom I could not think higher, and who has informed me of his honourable intentions in the serious matter of matrimony, that I am to make a great fortune very soon."

"You have invested with the doctor. It was my understanding from Sir Edward that he was not ... you were not ... included. When you mentioned you had succeeded, I believed it may have only been a small investment."

"Aha! But that's where Sir Edward was wrong. I finally convinced the doctor to allow me to invest and what is more, I convinced Lady Denham to do likewise and with a share of her estate."

"I cannot believe it. Lady Denham is so cautious, so hesitant ..."

"Indeed she is, and she warned me not to get involved. But both I and Sir Edward worked upon her until finally she signed over something. I, on the other hand, signed over my funds for the buildings and my entire savings."

Charlotte was shocked. "Sir, was this wise? Can you be certain it is safe?"

"Of course I am. Why, Sidney asked me the very same thing and we had a falling out over it. I shall not fall out with you, of course, Miss Heywood, for it is done now. Besides, we know it succeeded. We must just wait for the details of how much we have made."

"Sir, I do not know what to say."

"If you must, please congratulate me."

"Mr Parker, why are you informing me of this?"

"For I had a foreboding when I awoke this morning, a dread, and I could not speak to Mary of any of this. Dr Hollis, being your ... well, being a man we all know to be good ... I just wished to hear from you, yourself, that all is well and that perhaps he has confided in you some part of his plans."

"No, sir, he has not. I know nothing of it."

"Oh, I thought … well, I believed the other day when you spoke of his morals, his honour, his conduct and all that he said, I believed in a way, that you were vouching for him. That I could trust him fully."

"No, Mr Parker, that had not been my intention. I certainly was involved in no part of this and had I known it may influence your decision-making, I would not have said a word."

"But you do trust him?"

Charlotte could not lie and yet, could not admit the truth. Her heart said, "The doctor tricked me at the hotel. In all other matters he was honesty itself but I do feel he tricked me. He may trick others." But what was done was done and she saw little point in causing anxiety in Tom now, when he could not change the outcome anyhow.

"Truly, sir, I do not know what I think any more. I am sure you have made a good investment and Sanditon will benefit greatly from it. If you succeeded in convincing Lady Denham and, I am sure, her solicitor, well then, I am confident that all will be well. Besides, you will know tomorrow."

"Exactly!" Tom's frown was now turning to a smile but Charlotte could still detect a nervous energy and felt she had best be out of doors for most of today and tomorrow, for watching him wait for news could afford her no amusement. Besides, she was now beginning to get a sinking feeling of her own and prayed, rather than believed, that all may be well and that he had not been a fool.

In the afternoon, a message came from Sanditon House.

Tom gathered Charlotte and Mary and read it aloud:

Sanditon House.

Mr Parker,

The dinner this evening is cancelled. Tell the others. What is the point in having dinner when it is just ourselves? With Mr Sidney, Mr Arthur, that army man, Miss Lambe, Dr Hollis and I daresay the school all gone, why should I go to such expense? Next thing, I will be obliged to invite Reverend Hanking just to make up numbers. And that shall never happen. I have heard about your brother and Miss Lambe. What was he about? I am surprised at you for allowing it to happen. At least we had been more honest in our attempts to trap her. I am quite incensed. I expect to see you tomorrow when the express arrives to tell me how goes my investment.

Lady Denham

Tom sighed. "I hope you are not too disappointed, ladies. I daresay it was going to be a quiet affair and we will have just as much fun at home. I will see her tomorrow with good news and she will be her old self again."

Charlotte smiled. Lady Denham's old self was little better than the 'new' angry self that Tom was referring to. She sincerely hoped that Tom would have news of rich rewards for Lady Denham on the morrow so that her own announcement of returning home to Willingden might not disappoint them too much. In the midst of jubilation and celebration, her withdrawal would be lesser felt. She would wait until the express arrived and make her plans known then.

CHAPTER THIRTY-TWO

As familiar as Charlotte had become with finding one person or another joining them for breakfast, without any advance notice, it was a new thing to find Sir Edward eating his toast and greeting her as she entered the room.

"Sir Edward!"

"Good morning, Miss Heywood, and is it not the most promising of mornings? More delectable, more joyous, more fondamondarous than other mornings?"

Charlotte smiled. "I do believe you created that big word, Sir Edward."

"I do believe I did. But what is a man to do when language is insufficient to describe the magnificence of the day?"

Tom and Mary were also in excellent mood. Sir Edward had brought a bottle of fine cognac so that they may celebrate when the express arrived. Charlotte could not but feel that they had set themselves up for a day of anxious waiting. The express might arrive at any time, even at night. Likewise, she was waiting for *their* news so that she may tell them that she too was abandoning Sanditon, in the middle of what should be its busiest season.

Charlotte decided it wise to spend the largest part of the day out of doors that she would not be likewise impatient and on edge. She would offer to take the children to the beach. This was met with delight by Mary, who wished to meet an old friend, and with indifference by the two gentlemen, caught up, as they were, in the greatness that awaited them.

One unusual occurrence or, more accurately, non-occurrence struck Charlotte – Sir Edward did not mention Miss Lambe and Arthur's elopement. She believed he did not care about it, just as he cared very little for the elopers. Lady Denham may think differently but Sir Edward cared not a jot. Then Charlotte recalled his comments at the Manor House. He was to make his fortune with Dr Hollis and marry where he pleased. This may explain his lack of interest.

The day was fine and Charlotte had returned to carrying the children on her back and racing and rolling down hills with them. Why should she try to appear lady-like and refined anymore? Who was there to impress? Was this not more the real Charlotte after all? Was Sidney Parker correct when he said she had nothing to change?

As the children dug in the sand, Charlotte saw a lone figure, riding a donkey, approach her. It was Reverend Hanking. He pulled up beside her, slid down from his gentle equine charge and tied him to a rock beside her. Then without a word of salutation, Reverend Hanking plopped down on the blanket beside her, without being asked. She felt obliged to offer him one of the sandwiches they had not yet begun eating. The reverend accepted.

"Miss Heywood, I heard of the elopement. Mrs Griffiths is furious. Tell me, did you suspect nothing?"

Charlotte had not lied about this subject yet but the direct manner in which he asked was going to require a coy answer or a lie. The former she was unsure she was capable of and the latter she preferred not to do to a clergyman.

"I suspected nothing with regard to the elopement."

"But ..."

"But I did realise just the day before that Miss Lambe had feelings for Mr Parker. That they might elope had not entered my head. I do not think it had even entered their heads. I believe they acted in the moment."

"I believe you are correct."

"Will you tell Mrs Griffiths?"

"Heavens, no! She is the last person I would tell any such thing to. I was merely curious myself. I believe they were correct in what they did."

"Do you really?"

"Absolutely, freedom is the most natural state of man. To suppress, compromise, deny a person, or have them do it to themselves, is not what God intended. The spirit is free, so should the whole person be."

"Thank you, Reverend Hanking. I believe you are correct."

Charlotte thought of when she felt most free. It was not when she was trying to be grander than she was. It was when she was down on the floor, letting Mae jump on her back and pretend she was her horse. It was when she fell asleep in a field or a beach on a fine day or when she read books about faraway lands. It was when she felt she could speak as she wished and not hold her tongue.

"Do you wish to know why Sir Harry gave me the living?"

"Only if you wish to tell me," answered Charlotte, knowing that the particulars of that secret were not even known to Lady Denham.

"We met in Rome many years ago and shared rooms together. He was very wild in his youth but very clever and a great wit, with an eye for beautiful women. I was younger than he by a few years yet a little more steady of character. But only a little. Sir Harry loved Italy yet his knowledge of the language was poor, mine was excellent. I joined a friend in Naples for a number of weeks and when I returned to Rome, I found Sir Harry in a state of torment. He had somehow entangled himself with a local widow and they were engaged to wed. Her family, of course, were delighted and although some friends encouraged him to run away, his conscience bound him to his promise. Then I resolved the problem for him."

Reverend Hanking paused, looking out to sea and said not another word.

"And how, Reverend, did you resolve it for him?"

"I married her myself. Sir Harry was freed of his entanglement and the widow was happy to marry a charming man who spoke fluent Italian. He felt he owed me a great favour. So when my darling widow made me a widower some two years later and I returned to my homeland, Sir Harry offered me the parish on his estate for as long as I lived."

"I am all amazement, Reverend Hanking. I cannot say whether I feel it was totally proper."

"*Proper* is irrelevant, Miss Heywood. Never let *proper* be your guide in anything. It's what feels right that matters."

They sat in silence for some minutes.

"Sir, may I ask you something?" Charlotte lifted some sand and let it run between her fingers.

"Of course."

"I plan to tell the Parkers later that I wish to return home to Willingden. They will be disappointed but I feel I cannot stay any longer. I have been a terrible friend to them. It feels dishonest and wrong of me to remain. I feel it is the right thing to do."

"Ah, but this is a different 'right thing to do'. We must explore it. When you think of it being the right thing to do, what feelings accompany it?"

Charlotte was surprised that he asked such a question but gave what she knew were the true answers.

"I feel shame and guilt. I feel I do not deserve their generosity. I have been unkind. Please do not ask me to say any more."

"And when you return home and think about the circumstances of your leaving, will you still feel guilt and shame, but instead, this time, from a distance?"

"Yes, I believe I will. I cannot imagine thinking back on my time in Sanditon without it being marred by feelings of shame."

"Then I would say that running away is not the right thing to do. It rarely is. It adds 'cowardice' to your already long list of self-flagellating feelings. Why burden yourself, Miss Heywood, in such a way? It is not what The Man Above intended. Have courage. Make amends. Do not carry that burden home with you. That, I believe, is the right thing to do."

The children ran back to Charlotte, declaring that they were starved and she must feed them at once. There was no opportunity for their conversation to continue as Charlotte busied herself while the children caressed the donkey and argued over the best name to give him, settling at last on 'Albert'. When their spread was ready, Reverend Hanking rolled over so that he could make his way to standing in a series of grunts and pushes. "Descending is a great deal easier than ascending, as I am sure Lucifer found out to his surprise."

With that, Reverend Hanking and Albert bid Charlotte and the children goodbye, leaving Charlotte with the discomfort, yet clarity, that often accompanies being told a truth.

CHAPTER THIRTY-THREE

Charlotte and the children made to return to Trafalgar House in the early evening, despite the sun remaining high in the sky. She knew they had been absent for at least four or five hours and as Mae complained of tiredness, they must return home. As they crossed the Terrace they met Lady Denham, walking alone.

"Good evening, Miss Heywood. My, but you are like a nursery maid, scampering about, all red-faced – dragging that basket up from the beach. Those children are making little of you."

"On the contrary, Your Ladyship, I cannot think of a more pleasant way to spend the day. The children have been most obliging in keeping me company."

"Indeed! And is that a good enough reason to be seen in public, quite uncouth? I had believed you improved of late but you are back as you once were. Old habits die hard, I suppose."

"Yes, Your Ladyship, thank heavens they do," Charlotte smiled. "There is sometimes that in us, which is so focused on what we believe to be important that we lose sight of what really is important. Is it not so, Lady Denham?"

"Ah, yes." Lady Denham's stern face now softened. "I see what you have done. Well, well, you are quite right. I had best taste my own medicine." Then, moving closer to Charlotte, "And have you discovered what *you* believe to be really important, Miss Heywood?"

"I believe I have, Your Ladyship."

"Good, well, Lord knows I would most likely disapprove of it but you hold tight to it and do not be swayed by anyone."

The children were impatient and began running home so Charlotte quickly curtseyed and followed them.

"If my nephew is still with Mr Parker," exclaimed Lady Denham after her, "you must tell him that I expect him to call on me."

Back at Trafalgar House, having handed her charges back to their nanny, Charlotte listened out for sounds of jubilation. As she walked past the study, she could hear two male voices within – Tom and Sir Edward. There was nothing to imply that they were in jubilant mood.

Returning her bonnet to her room, she met Mary on the landing. "Oh dear, there is no sign of the express yet, Charlotte."

"There is plenty of time, Mary, is there not?"

"Of course, but a watched kettle does not boil, as is said, and those men are becoming restless."

Just then, they heard a noise at the front door and ran to the top of the stairs to see if Morgan would reveal the long-awaited horseman with news. Likewise, Tom and Sir Edward ran from the study. All were disappointed to see Diana on the steps.

"I have come to enquire about the express. What news did he bring?"

"None, yet," said Tom, "but we expect him soon."

The men retreated back to the room where, from their dishevelled appearance, Charlotte guessed that the bottle of cognac had already been opened.

The ladies united in the parlour. Diana sat next to Mary and took her hand.

"Mary, please forgive the manner in which I left the house yesterday. I was anxious. In truth, I am sick with worry about poor Arthur. My nerves are unsettled, I am all ajitter and I did not sleep."

"Diana, we are worried too. Your anguish and anxiety for his well-being, we feel it too. But we trust he knows what he is about."

"Do you forgive me?"

"There is nothing to forgive, dear sister."

"And will you tell me if he writes, if he sends you word?"

"If such a letter comes, you will be the first to hear of it."

"Thank you," said Diana, and though Charlotte would not have believed it if she had not seen it with her two eyes, Diana broke down sobbing.

"I am the worst sister."

Mary hugged her then, and Charlotte felt she must do or say something. She knelt beside her.

"Miss Parker, I have never met a sister like you – as kind-hearted, as generous of her time and energy. Truly, if I were half the sister that you are, my siblings would be very fortunate indeed."

Diana put out her other hand and squeezed Charlotte's.

"What a state I make of myself," she said, sniffing and pulling out a huge handkerchief to blow her nose.

"Well, now you are here for dinner," said Mary. "Charlotte and I will dress as fast as we can and return downstairs to you."

Dinner was a sober event despite Tom's attempts at humour and all persons evading the one topic they all wondered about. Where was the express? The Sir Edward who sat down to a beef dinner was not the one eating toast in the morning. All exaggerated mirth and word-inventing games were over. The look in his eyes, which he was incapable of hiding, revealed the real fear he felt. He was distracted and jumpy and wanted nothing more now than to get away and speak with his aunt.

"She will be curious as to why she has not been sent word yet."

"There is nothing to worry about, Sir Edward, I assure you. Stay on for another hour at least. It is not dark until after ten o'clock these days."

Charlotte noticed an anxiety in Tom to keep Sir Edward from his aunt but when the latter insisted on leaving and stated that he would return in the morning, Tom felt it best to give him a note to take to Lady Denham. No doubt, he believed, that any outpouring of anguish on Sir Edward's part would lead to unnecessary worry and anger on hers. A few reassuring words were all that was needed.

When Sir Edward had left, Diana broke the silence that followed. "You do have an address for Dr Hollis, Tom?"

"Yes, of course, but please do not imply that he is not to be trusted or that he would pain us by delaying news. I am confident that the express has met with some setback and will be with us presently."

"Of course, I do not imply any such thing. Dr Hollis is the most trustworthy and upstanding of gentlemen. I merely know what injuries and harms may occur when one travels or resides in a smoke-ridden city, through no fault of one's own, of course."

"Of course."

"So perhaps you should send an express from Sanditon to the doctor, enquiring if he is quite well. Sidney, I am sure, would think nothing of assisting him, if he required it."

Charlotte could see by Tom's grimace that Diana's interference, as well meant as it was, was unwelcome. He arose from the table.

"This is most unusual but I must ask you to excuse me. There are still some matters in the study that require my attention. I was unable to deal with them earlier, with Sir Edward present."

All the following day, tensions remained at Trafalgar House. Sir Edward had not returned as promised but sent a note instead that he would be obliged if word was sent at once, when the express arrived. Tom locked himself into the study, not joining his family for any meals. Mary brought him food that remained untouched and asked him to at least respond to the several messages that had arrived over the course of the day from Lady Denham.

Charlotte, as she descended the stairs, heard his response as he shouted at his wife.

"I will not write nor meet with Lady Denham until I have good news to share with her."

Diana called in the morning, accompanied by Esther Denham, who, alarmed by her brother's appearance, came to see if there was anything new she could discover.

All four women sat worrying and drinking tea.

"Mary, my dear, we are among friends and I believe we all know the seriousness of the matter at hand," said Diana. "Of course, there is a totally understandable explanation for the delay. I am sorry to say it in front of you, Miss Heywood, but I am convinced that the doctor has had an accident. Do you know, Mary, if Tom has much to lose?"

"Oh, do not mention 'lose', Diana. There is not and will not be anything lost. Tom stands to gain. Great amounts, he tells me."

"I am sorry to say, Mrs Parker," said Esther Denham, "but in order to gain so much, one must have invested much. I have no qualms in telling you that Sir Edward has put everything he has into it. It is little enough in comparison to some but it is all he has – his savings and the cottage *orné*. He would have put my miserly dowry in too, if I had not forbidden it."

Charlotte then asked, "And do you think Lady Denham has invested much? They convinced her to get involved but perhaps she was cautious."

"To lose even a sixpence would be a great loss in my aunt's eyes," answered Esther. "I do not know what she gave but as she had her solicitor present to draw up legal documents, I fear it may have been the largest investment of all."

The day dragged on in the most miserable fashion. Charlotte took herself off along the cliff walk in the afternoon to break the day but she saw and heard little, so full was her head of worries. Of course, she could not announce her departure now, in the midst of their current crisis. She would have to stay and weather it out, being of assistance, if she could, to the Parkers.

At breakfast the next morning, Tom, unshaven and wearing the same clothes from the day before, joined them. He ate nothing but slumped into his usual chair.

"I will do as Diana said. I will send an express to the doctor. Of course, there is nothing to worry about, but this sitting around is a tortuous business."

"Oh yes, Tom, that is a wonderful idea. Write it at once and I will get Morgan to have it dispatched immediately. At least we will have a response by tomorrow, and who knows, but the other fellow may arrive in the meantime."

But the 'other fellow' did not arrive and on the following morning, the same express returned, tired and frustrated at not yet having been paid, placing Tom's letter back into his hand.

"There was no Dr Hollis, sir, at that address. The landlady said he left three days ago with no forwarding address."

Tom leaned against the wall to support himself. Mary grabbed him and with Charlotte's help assisted him into the breakfast room while Morgan placed coins into the express's hand and sent him on his way.

"We are ruined."

"Do not say that, Tom."

"We are ruined, Mary."

Charlotte removed herself from their company and paced the floor in the drawing room. Should she call for

Diana? Should she send word to Sidney? Who could help Tom and Mary Parker now? A knock on the door announced a visitor. It was, in all probability, Diana, come to learn the latest news, but as she left the drawing room, she just glimpsed the last of Lady Denham's skirts disappearing into the breakfast room. Voices were heard, in particular Lady Denham's as she scolded and lectured Tom. At last, Charlotte saw Tom emerge and remove himself upstairs just as Lady Denham was leaving. He returned ten minutes later with a small bag and set off for the post-chaise at the hotel, without saying goodbye to wife, guest or children.

Mary looked anxious. "He is going to London, Charlotte. He is gone to find the doctor."

CHAPTER THIRTY-FOUR

In the course of the afternoon, Diana arrived, having collected their post from the hotel. Amongst it was a letter for Charlotte from Freddie.

When Diana heard what the express had announced and how Tom had left for London, she said calmly, "Let him off, Mary, let him off. Such is the way with men that they must be scampering about the countryside on adventures every now and then. It is good for him to expend himself after so many days indoors."

"Diana, this is a great change for you. Yesterday, you were just as worried as we all were."

"But that was before I discovered the most useful information. I spoke with the post boy at the hotel this morning and it appears that there were a number of highwaymen intercepting post on all the main routes out of London in the past ten days – both mail coaches and express. Imagine! Highwaymen, in this day and age! The military have been called in to deal with it and they expect fewer instances. The road hither was one of the main points of aggression. I am surprised your express this morning did not say as much. So you see, the doctor is unaware that his message was intercepted and once Tom meets with him in London, no doubt in some club or other, all will be understood."

"Oh, Diana, you do not know what this means to me. I am sure you are correct."

"Of course I am. I will take myself off to Sanditon House immediately and let Lady Denham know. I will take in Denham Park on my way back to say as much to Miss Denham and her brother, who is most likely hiding beneath his bed-covers."

"Thank you, Diana. You really are so good."

Charlotte could see the relief in Mary's face and they even laughed together at the thought of all their wasted anxiety.

"I believe," said Charlotte, "we may have carved trenches into the floorboards with all our pacing back and forth."

Glad to have her head back to herself at last and convinced that she had been too much inside, Charlotte took her shawl and decided to read Freddie's letter out of doors. Not wishing to meet anyone she knew along the Terrace, who might pry into its contents, she decided to go down to the isolated strand, where she had once lain sleeping. Sitting at almost the same spot, she smiled for a moment recalling her walk home with Sidney that day, then recalling yet again his cold look when she last saw him, she wiped away a stray tear and ripped open her letter.

64 Sloane Street,
London.

Dearest Lottie,

Correct me if I am mistaken, but I could not help but sense from your last letter that you are considering returning home to Willingden sooner than you had intended at first. It might be the phrase "I am considering returning home sooner than I had intended" that gave it away. I hope you are well and not sad or disappointed in your friends at Sanditon. Is Sanditon not as exciting as you had hoped?

Well, I may have the solution. Come to me, Lottie, instead. Then you may return to Willingden or Sanditon or Constantinople thereafter. It is with sincerity and urgency that I ask. My role with the count has been made official. It is one of the most respectable jobs that a diplomat can hope for. The only problem is that when these royal folk leave this country next month, I will be obliged to travel with them and remain in Europe for at least two to three years. It is already almost two years since you and I have met and who knows when we may meet again?

So please write back and say you will visit. I am afraid I cannot leave here. You will see how busy I am when you arrive.

With love,

Freddie

Charlotte was torn. She wished for nothing more than to see her brother once before he left for Europe but she could not leave the Parkers now. She could not abandon them. Yet when, if ever, would she see Freddie again? What if he were to die overseas? What if he became infected with a disease on the ship? What if a war broke out and he was imprisoned? With the strain of recent days, her melancholy thoughts spiralled until she imagined him forced into hard labour in Siberia. Finally, she gave way to all the tears that had been stored up – not just for Freddie but for all the hurt, shame and sadness she had felt, in her broken heart, over the past number of weeks.

Despite the relief that this tearful release gave her, Charlotte felt little comfort from the need to choose between Sanditon and her brother. A walk along the cliff to clear her head was required and, as usual, nature, in its majesty, did just that. Of course she must see Freddie and the Parkers would understand if she was obliged to cut her visit short. Why was she making herself so anxious? She need not act today. Freddie did not leave for a few weeks yet. She would wait until the investment crisis was resolved and Tom was back, happy and wealthy, in Sanditon. Such was her resolution when she re-entered Trafalgar House and was met by Mary who, spying her climb the steps outside, went to meet her and usher her into the parlour. "Come, look, Charlotte. Diana is so clever."

Inside, Diana was leaning over the table with a newspaper spread wide before her.

"Miss Heywood, what did I say? We have it here in black and white. Proof, if it were needed."

Diana read out the report which she had already read aloud a dozen times. Now, for Charlotte's benefit, she accentuated words such as "highwaymen", "authorities" and "mounted patrols" and closed the newspaper to "most notably, the road from London to Sevenoaks."

Charlotte was pleased with this additional proof that all was well. The doctor was to be trusted and Tom could have saved himself much worry. The delight on Mary's face was a particularly welcome sign.

"But men must jump to conclusions, of course," said Diana triumphantly. "They have only a fraction of the sense of women. I have written to Sidney, for Tom will be staying with him, and told him of this development. I expect we will have him home in a few days. Now I can give my full attention again to worrying about Arthur. But, Miss Heywood, have you been crying?"

Charlotte had not looked in a mirror and supposed her eyes must be swollen and red. Seeing Freddie's letter in her hand, Diana continued, "My dear girl, is all well? Did your brother send you word of an illness, a death? Do sit down. We will fetch you some tea, some wine, perhaps?"

Charlotte thanked them for their concern and indicated that tea and wine were unnecessary. She hated causing them concern when they, just now, looked so relieved and, therefore, decided to tell them the nature of Freddie's correspondence.

"Why, Charlotte, you must go to him at once. Oh, I would never wish for you to remain here and miss the opportunity to spend time with your brother," said Mary. "What if he were called away early, then you might regret not leaving sooner? We are a small party now, I admit, and I will miss you terribly, but you will return to us next season, will you not?"

Charlotte had not time to answer for Diana joined in.

"And we find ourselves without a gentleman to escort you but I believe, if we put you on the coach here with Old Sam and you write to your brother with instructions to meet you at Croydon, all would be well."

"But Mary, I cannot leave you like this or, at least, until Mr Parker returns."

"Of course you can. Before you joined us, Tom was forever going away on business. I always missed him terribly, of course, but this is very familiar to me and the children."

"And I am here, am I not?" asked Diana. "Mary and I will be quite thick as thieves at a fair. Now, my newspaper and I must make our way to Sanditon House and let Lady Denham know of this."

What a change in emotions for Charlotte – from fear and despair to relief and joy. Promising Mary that she would be back when she could, Charlotte ran upstairs to write to Freddie and begin packing. In her haste, she could not find the broken telescope and hoped that Sylvia had not thrown it out. Begging Mary to send it on when it was found, she bid her farewells to the children, and within two days found herself standing in Freddie's hallway in London.

CHAPTER THIRTY-FIVE

O ver the next couple of days, as she saw little of her brother, Charlotte realised what a lively occupation he was engaged in. There were always events, both public and private, for him to facilitate for his royal charges, meetings, functions and entertainment. He promised her that he would take her to the livelier ones in time. On her first two evenings, Charlotte only met her brother as she readied herself for bed, when apologising profusely and looking exhausted, he promised that he would try to be home to dinner on the morrow.

For this reason, Charlotte was surprised to find her brother sitting at the breakfast table on the third morning.

"Oh, Freddie. How wonderful, you are here."

"Well, it is my house."

"Are you sure it is? You are never here and may have popped in next door by accident."

Freddie walked over and hugged his sister. "No, I can tell it is my home. My ugly dragon door knocker, a gift from Count Von Lamberg, ensures that I never find myself on another doorstep, no matter my state."

"Enough of that talk. I am sure you are tired only and never inebriated."

"Oh, never, sister. That would not do at all."

Charlotte sat down and both spent a good forty minutes talking, teasing, lamenting and laughing in each other's company. At last Freddie arose.

"I am afraid, dear Charlotte, I am away again for another long day. I must change into something suitable for court. I expect the counts' head valet this morning to discuss some expenses. If you would be so kind as to show him into my study and ask him to wait. I will not be long."

Charlotte had just poured herself another cup of tea, while musing at how interesting a life her brother led and how truly happy he was, when a knock indicated that the count's valet had arrived. Charlotte met him in the hall while the housekeeper took his coat and hat.

"Please, sir, my brother has been expecting you. I will show you to his study. He will not be long."

"You must be Miss Charlotte Heywood. It is an honour to make your acquaintance," he said, bowing quite low.

"Thank you," Charlotte smiled as she led him to the study. He was impeccably dressed for a valet, his accent betraying the fact that he was European, and Charlotte mused that the valets she had encountered in her homeland had much to live up to, to reach the standards of the Hapsburgs.

Once in the study, the valet moved straight to Freddie's desk and began moving papers around as if searching for something. Charlotte was astonished and decided not to leave. "I beg your pardon, sir. You may be accustomed to such liberties in your own country but here we do not search amongst another person's private papers and certainly not without their consent."

The man stopped and stood back with a look of shock at this reproof. "Please, I apologise. I will wait for Freddie."

"Mr Heywood to you, if you do not mind?"

Charlotte's opinion had changed. The European valets may be dressed in the finest fashions and have an extremely good carriage and manner about their person but they definitely thought too highly of themselves and forgot their station entirely.

The valet smiled then and moved over to the bookcase where he began reading the titles aloud. Soon he began telling Charlotte of his great love of travel and dependence on Charlotte's brother for organising everything so well.

"I daresay it makes your job easier, that Freddie is such a proficient in all matters diplomatic, linguistic and administrative. He works day and night. He is completely exhausted. I do hope he is reimbursed for his time and efforts, as he should be."

The valet stopped looking at the books to answer her. "So do I, Miss Heywood. His services are greatly valued. I do hope he is adequately paid."

Then he took down a book and before Charlotte had time to point to his impertinence, he said aloud, "I may ask Mr Heywood if I may borrow this volume."

Just then Freddie arrived and bowed. "Your Excellency! I had not expected you."

A look of horror spread across Charlotte's face as she curtsied and uttered, "Your Excellency, please accept my apology. Freddie had said that we were to expect your valet."

Count Von Lamberg laughed. "It was a very good joke,

Freddie," he said, slapping Freddie on the back. "Your sister thought I was my valet and prevented me from examining your papers. She was very angry."

"So you did not find the receipt?"

"I was not permitted to look for it."

They all laughed, Charlotte a little less so, and she left the room as soon as she could. She determined to spend the morning out of doors, to prevent any further encounters with Count Von Lamberg.

CHAPTER THIRTY-SIX

"I have no idea what you said to the count, Lottie, but he was utterly charmed by you," said Freddie the following morning.

"Really? I am surprised. I must have reminded him of an old, cross governess he once had a perverse fondness for."

"Well, whatever it may be, he was enamoured. He laughed all evening, recounting the tale to all his friends, in English and German, may I add, and did not stop until the tears ran down his face."

"I am delighted I afforded him such comic relief."

Charlotte hoped she would not be frequently reminded of this embarrassing encounter.

"And what is more, at the end of the night, he took me aside and offered me a significant rise in my wages. Did you have something to do with that?"

"Oh, heavens!" Charlotte now laughed too. "Perhaps I did, in a round-about way."

"It was the most wonderful surprise. I will treat you to a new ball gown as a thank you."

"Freddie, I do feel my ball gown days have come to an end for now. I have no intention of staying here for the season. I just wish to get home to Willingden and live a quiet life for some time."

"Nonsense! You will accompany me to all the finest balls, theatres and functions. You have become very beautiful, you know."

"Any improvement, if there is any, will be down to the sea air, I dare say. But in earnest, Freddie, I just wish to get home."

"Stay another while and I will convince you differently."

Charlotte was too weary to argue and so she allowed Freddie to believe that his powers of persuasion had worked as he began listing off all the places he intended to take her. She knew in her heart, however, that she must leave.

A sound in the hall indicated a visitor and before long, the housekeeper opened the breakfast room door and announced the arrival of Sidney Parker.

Sidney entered the room and bowed to Freddie and an alarmed Charlotte, who were now standing.

"Brother, may I introduce you to Mr Sidney Parker? Mr Parker, this is my brother Freddie Heywood."

"Pardon my intrusion but I must speak to Miss Heywood in private on an urgent matter. Miss Heywood, is there somewhere we may speak?"

"Of course, Mr Parker," said Freddie. "This is all very unexpected but as luck might have it, I must get to work in my study." Then turning to his sister he whispered, "Do you wish me to stay?" to which she shook her head and he left, saying, "I am pleased to make your acquaintance, sir." Then to Charlotte, "You know where I am if you need me, Lottie."

The door was closed. Sidney moved closer to Charlotte. The memory of last seeing him as he set off angrily from Sanditon almost overwhelmed her and she wished she could run from the room. But the certainty that something must be wrong or he would not be here ensured she stayed put, holding the back of the chair, and turned her gaze to his weary face. *Those eyes.* Those brown eyes that had once shone bright whenever they rested on her face, now looked lifeless and empty.

"Is it Mary? Or the children?" she asked.

"No, Miss Heywood, they are well."

Charlotte sighed with relief.

"How can I be of assistance, Mr Parker?"

"Miss Heywood, my brother Tom is missing and we fear for his safety. I have already commenced a search while Diana, who stays with me now, is orchestrating the logistics and communications from my house."

"Diana, in London?"

"In truth, it is a struggle to prevent her from taking to the streets herself. She suggested your company and assistance would be useful at this time."

"Dear God."

"Please can you come at once, today?"

"You wish me to help?"

"Not I. Diana felt you may be of assistance."

He was here against his will, seeking her out on someone else's instructions. He would not have sought her himself. But Charlotte forced her thoughts back to the situation at hand. The Parkers feared for Tom's safety. Of course she would do whatever was necessary to aid them.

"Yes, I will come. Perhaps Freddie can help."

"Thank you but no. We wish to remain discreet for now. If something occurs in which we feel he may be able to assist, I will let you know."

"Is Mr Parker searching for Dr Hollis? Does he not stay with you? I thought all was well – it was an accidental miscommunication, was it not?"

His look changed and she cringed to think what he must think of her supposed dalliance with the doctor.

"Tom did not come to me. And having searched for him myself when first the news arrived, we have discovered that Dr Hollis is not to be trusted," Sidney looked away from her as he said it. "It will be a shock for you to learn that he moves in unsavoury circles. I am sorry that you must learn of it in this way."

Charlotte knew not how to respond. She could not believe that Dr Hollis had deceived them. How was it possible? He was all that was good. Perhaps they were mistaken. But as she knew nothing of the particulars and disliked the way Sidney implied that it would affect her in any way other than concern for Tom Parker, she held her tongue and gave a brief response instead.

"I will gather some things and be with you presently."

"I must leave immediately, but here is my address. Diana is expecting you." Sidney handed her the card and turned to leave before swinging back around suddenly.

"I must ask, do you know where he might be? Did he send you word? Dr Hollis?"

"No, certainly not. How can you ask me such a thing?"

"Your former intimacy with the doctor may have led one

to think that he had confided in you."

"There was no intimacy, Mr Parker, and no confidences were shared."

Charlotte was visibly upset by the comment. Sidney, half-relieved, half-mortified, looked searchingly in her face.

"My apologies, Miss Heywood, I was led to believe otherwise. It was expected ..."

Charlotte felt all her foolishness in allowing the doctor's visits, flattered as she was, at first, by his treatment of her. If she had rejected his advances as she should have, she would be less involved in this mischief.

"I fear all were mistaken. There was no understanding and now I begin to wonder if his attentions to me were to gain Mr Parker's trust and greater access to Trafalgar House."

Sidney moved back closer to Charlotte again and took her hands. "Please forgive me, Charlotte. You too have been ill-used. I do not know myself anymore. I appreciate your assistance."

Charlotte almost forgot their current crisis in the tenderness of his grasp and how his eyes softened again. Had he forgiven her for all those terrible things she had said? Perhaps not but there was something of their former intimacy in this gesture. Then she recalled his mistress and pulled her hands away. His look was of injury and confusion.

"I will join your sister immediately," said Charlotte.

Sidney turned and left the room, in what mood, she could not tell.

With a racing heart, Charlotte ran straight to her brother's study and, wishing not to alarm him, announced that she would have to spend a few days with her friends to assist them during a troubling time. She could not give him the particulars but assured him that she was in no danger but that the Parker family needed her and she felt she must go. Freddie looked concerned, offered his assistance, placed several bank notes into her hand and called for a hack-chaise. Charlotte packed a small bag and left her brother's home within twenty minutes, in the most contrary feelings to those she had owned when she arrived just days before.

CHAPTER THIRTY-SEVEN

The greeting Charlotte received from Diana Parker could leave her in no doubt as to how highly she was thought of. Diana met Charlotte at the door with hugs so tight that Charlotte almost struggled to breathe. "Thank goodness, you have come. I knew you would. Oh, Miss Heywood, I am such a terrible sister. I feel so helpless."

Charlotte squeezed Diana's hand and looked her in the eyes. "I have never known a kinder, more loving sister than you are to your brothers. You protect them, guide them and generously give of your time and energy for them. Truly they are blessed. Now, how I may assist you?"

Diana cried at this kind statement, telling Charlotte that she would never know what it meant to her to hear it. Inside Charlotte cringed to recall her cruel comments about Diana which she had shared with the doctor in Sanditon. How could she have been so unkind? How could she have mistaken kindness and concern for ridiculousness? It was she who should be crying for shame.

Diana guided Charlotte to the parlour where she had documents laid out on a table, with some note paper, pen and ink and a map of London. At the table also sat a very elderly lady. Charlotte was surprised to see another person there and assumed she was an aunt that she had not been aware of.

Diana placed her hand on the old lady's shoulder and said, "Miss Heywood, this is our former housekeeper at the Manor House growing up, Mrs Dukes, or as we have always called her 'The Duchess'. She lives here with Sidney and looks after his household for him. Mrs Dukes, the lady who has just arrived with me is Miss Heywood."

"Oh, Lord!" said Charlotte.

"What is it?" asked Diana.

"Nothing, nothing at all," answered Charlotte but indeed she knew it was something, something of great significance. Here sat 'The Duchess'. She had entirely misunderstood everything. There was no mistress. Was there ever a greater fool than her?

Charlotte placed her palm into the outstretched hands of Mrs Dukes, whose handshake was strong and warm. Both acknowledged each other.

"You must forgive me, Miss Heywood, for not standing. I am practically blind so I am afraid I cannot see you. I do less of arranging his household than shouting orders at the poor servants but I don't miss much."

"Oh, do not apologise," answered Charlotte, who was trying to make sense of what was unfolding before her. 'The Duchess' whom she had assumed was Sidney's mistress was in fact his old housekeeper, whose health and age made her unemployable and so he had taken her in. This was the woman of whom she had been so jealous. She had judged Sidney so harshly and so wrongly. She had been wrong –

many times wrong – but she had never been as wrong about anyone as she had been about Sidney Parker.

By the fireplace knelt a man, adding wood to the fire. The day was cold, unusually so for August. The man was William, the Parkers' servant and driver, whom Charlotte had met the very first day she met the Parkers, when their carriage overturned in Willingden.

"William. How good to see you."

William bowed. "And you, Miss Heywood. I was afeared you'd not come."

It was obvious that William knew everything of the Parkers' problems.

"I did and hope to help."

"Miss Heywood, my dear, we must get back to this matter. Please, sit here by me and we shall inform you what has been done so far. We know where to leave messages for Sidney. William will take them if we have anything to communicate as all communication, notes and answers come through this house."

The morning was spent looking through locations that had already been searched, hotels, private rooms, inns and the doctors' offices on Harley Street and reading over notes and letters that had arrived from the previous day's queries. It emerged that there was no Dr Hollis currently operating from Harley Street. One doctor had heard of a Dr Hollis based in London but the same man had been struck off the register some years before for negligent practice. This information was confirmed by Diana's friend Mrs Eagleston's letter, which arrived just then, having been redirected from Sanditon, and letting her know that Mrs

Eagleston's sister's husband recalled a disreputable doctor of that name but did not know him personally. It was believed he had gone into industry after failing as a doctor.

"Sidney's priority is to find Tom. I do wish Arthur was here to help him. Sidney has not slept in days," said Diana, once she had brought Charlotte up to date. "He feels he has nothing to go on and assumes that Dr Hollis may have mentioned something to Tom of his location, in passing, and tither he is gone. Today he starts with the gentlemen's clubs. I do not see how we can help him with that."

"Now, Diana, do not be severe upon yourself," said Mrs Dukes, her blind eyes still holding a twinkle of mischievousness. "You are doing wonderfully well. Why, Tom could turn up on our doorstep at any moment and you'll be needed then. What good would I be, on my own, to assist him?"

"Oh my word," exclaimed Charlotte. "Dr Hollis did tell me the name of his club. I had totally forgot. Do you have a list of those in London?"

"Indeed we do," said Mrs Dukes, pointing at her temple. "In here. I know the name of every club and which street it is on."

"Well, what is it?" asked Diana impatiently.

"I cannot recall it exactly but it is something like 'crockery'."

"That would be Crockfords, St James's Street," said Mrs Dukes.

"Oh, Charlotte, how brilliant," said Diana, scribbling some words on paper. "William, take this at once to Sidney and stay with him. It will focus his search."

While pleased that she had been of some use in such a short time, Charlotte could not help but blush at the manner with which she had snapped at Sidney earlier, when he implied she might know something of the whereabouts of Dr Hollis. She had. She just had not realised it at the time and had she patiently reflected on what she did know, instead of interpreting his query as implying she had colluded with the doctor, she might have passed this information on much earlier. Time would tell, however, if it was of use or just another blind alley.

They had not long to wait. About an hour later, while Diana was arranging mid-morning refreshments between responding to messages, they heard a pounding and men's voices from the hall. The door to their room swung open and Sidney, half-carrying an injured Tom, laid him on the nearest sofa. William rushed in behind carrying hats, coats and the bag Tom had taken with him from Sanditon.

"Mrs Dukes, have my doctor summoned," said Sidney urgently.

Mrs Dukes left the room.

Diana, hesitating for a moment, rushed to Tom's side. He seemed only half awake. "What has happened, Sidney?"

"I know little. Let us get him seen to first and talk later."

"Yes, yes. I will bring a cloth and water to wash him somewhat. That shirt is destroyed." It was torn, dirty and had blood stains at parts around the shoulder, on the lower back and around his waist.

Diana left, like a person given the most important mission.

But Charlotte, unfamiliar with the house and servants,

felt there was little she could do to assist. Feeling helpless, she approached the men and knelt near Sidney.

"Please tell me what to do."

Sidney turned and looked at her. He looked at his brother who was muttering all the while, then back at her again. She was mistaken in thinking he would tell her that there was nothing she could do.

"Please arrange for a message to be sent to Mary immediately. Tell her we have located Tom and he is at my house. That should be enough for now. We will tell her more when we know more."

Charlotte was relieved. She jumped up and ran to the writing desk that Diana had been using and began scribbling. A moment later she was finished. She handed William the note, some coins and instructions.

By then Diana had arrived with a pitcher of water and towels. Charlotte moved into the hall as Diana, with Sidney's assistance, undressed Tom and, while changing his shirt, examined his wounds, just as the doctor arrived.

The door across the hallway opened. Mrs Dukes whispered, "Is that you, Miss Heywood? I know it is not Diana for she would not stand still in a hallway."

"Yes, it is I."

"Well, come join me in here. I have had the refreshments sent in here instead. No point us all getting in the way of the doctor."

"Thank you, I will."

Mrs Dukes was quite the opposite of Diana – relaxed, even in an emergency, and smiling, even now. Charlotte was surprised at the turn in the conversation.

"I dare say he had it coming to him, Miss Heywood."

Charlotte was shocked and could not respond. Mrs Dukes sipped her tea and continued to chatter.

"He was always impetuous, was Tom. Always rushing head first into everything, sometimes making mistakes or getting into scrapes that his parents or brothers had to get him out of. Very minor things, mind you, but that has been his way. This is the same thing happening on a bigger scale and with more at risk, but mark my words, he needed it badly. A lesson he might not forget for a while."

They drank on in silence – Charlotte digesting the words of her companion and even daring to admit that, while severe, there may be the slimmest piece of truth in what the old lady said. Had Mrs Dukes not known him all his life? To what extent, she wondered, had Tom contributed to his own ruin? Even so, he did not deserve the severity of it. He was a good man with a loving family to provide for. She prayed that he would find a way back from this.

Charlotte asked if there was anything she could do to assist Mrs Dukes while she was there.

"Perhaps I may run an errand for you or, if you would like it, I can accompany you on a walk to the park or to visit a friend."

Mrs Dukes laughed. "Thank you, child, but all my friends are dead by now, and I don't care much for what's left out there. I am happiest here, as I am."

Just then, they heard a door opening and persons whispering in the hall. It was Sidney, Diana and the doctor.

Charlotte and Mrs Dukes held their cups mid-air, both secretly straining to catch a few words. Charlotte could not

A SEASON AT SANDITON

make it out, confusing the doctor's voice with Sidney's and
finding herself distracted by the busy London street noises
outside. Mrs Dukes had more luck.

"Flesh wounds, bruising and a bang to the head causing
concussion. He will be better in a few days."

"Oh, thank heavens."

They heard the front door open and close and, from the
nearby window, Charlotte saw the doctor don his hat and
make his way down the steps. She felt it was a good time to
join the others to learn more.

She thanked Mrs Dukes and informed her of her plan to
move back to the other room to see if she could assist. Mrs
Dukes smiled and nodded and said she would join them
later. "All this running about, losing fortunes and getting
smacked about the head is a trifle too much for someone of
my age. I will check in on them later and be getting on with
the dinner in the meantime."

Just as Charlotte knocked and opened the parlour door,
Sidney came out to speak to her in the hall. Diana was
kneeling next to Tom, making him drink something that
Charlotte hoped was water.

"May I help, Mr Parker?"

"No, Miss Heywood, thank you, not at present. Tom was
given a sleeping draught. His injuries are not deep – mostly
flesh wounds, but he was beaten quite badly, hence the lack
of mobility and disorientation."

"Thank God it is not worse."

"Yes. I believe we must thank you for sending us to
Crockfords. The head-waiter said that a Mr Parker had
arrived the day before looking for Dr Hollis. At this point,

I passed some coins to him so he was most helpful. He informed Tom that Dr Hollis had been a member once. He then asked Tom to leave. Desperate, I would imagine, and very unlike himself, Tom shouted to the gentlemen present to ask if anyone knew of a Dr Hollis. He told them that he stayed at an inn at the end of the street, if they had information. By now, the head-waiter had called for assistance in having Tom removed from the club. He apologised to me this morning and said that 'we mistook him as a friend of this Dr Hollis, who had run up great debts. Any friend of Dr Hollis would not be welcome here'."

"Oh heavens!" said Charlotte.

"Thankfully, he informed me where Tom was staying. I then found him in his room, in the condition you see him in now, some mischief having befallen him. We must wait until he can tell us more."

"Do you wish me to remain here for a number of days? I had packed as you asked this morning, not knowing the outcome, but if I am in the way here …"

"No, please, if you would remain to give Diana respite. She will resist, wishing to do everything herself, but I can see she has little strength at times and does not eat."

"Yes."

"You may not see her goodness, Miss Heywood, and instead find her exertions to be eccentric and foolish … but she has a heart like no other."

The words struck Charlotte hard. He had not forgiven her.

"I know … of course. I would like to stay, Mr Parker, to …"

But Sidney had already turned and was back again with Tom and Diana, the door closed behind him.

CHAPTER THIRTY-EIGHT

And so Charlotte remained to be of use or in the way, whichever one emerged on any given day. The truth, she admitted to herself, was that the Parkers felt like family to her now. She felt as close to Diana and Arthur as to any relative she knew, sometimes being reminded of cousins in the next village at home. Tom and Mary were like her brother and sister, their children like what she imagined nieces and nephews to be. She felt such warmth whenever she thought of them and such concern when she considered their troubles. Even Mrs Dukes was like a grandmother, spoiling her, coaxing her, teasing her, in an easy manner, just as her own grandparent had once done. It was only with Sidney that she did not feel this familiarity. For him, she felt something more distant, more estranged and yet more tender than for the others. He had, unintentionally and due to her own fault, caused her the greatest pain and she wondered whether, when all this was over and she was to return to Willingden, the remembrance of him would continue to cause her pain, even there.

She wrote again to Mary, stating that Tom would be returning to Sanditon within the week and that she and

Diana would accompany him, for this was agreed as the best course of action. Meanwhile, a letter was also received from Mary, telling them that she was coping well and thanking them for their care of Tom. But the greatest shock came in her stating that Esther Denham had implied that some mischief had been imposed upon Miss Brereton by Dr Hollis prior to his quitting Sanditon. He had paid Nelly to wait outside the room while he attended to Miss Brereton. He may, they supposed, have taken liberties. It was too ghastly to believe and, therefore, Mary gave no credit to the account. But as Diana closed the letter, having read it aloud to Charlotte and Mrs Dukes, they none of them doubted the truth of it.

Once the initial shock subsided, Diana went to Sidney's study to inform him of this latest development. So much of Clara's strange talk now made sense to Charlotte. The doctor was recommending that his patient remain in her room, that she was unfit and her nerves were affected, while his real intention was to seduce her if he could. He had manipulated her, fed her lies and obviously had not passed on the 'secret' notes from Sir Edward, who loved her but by whom she felt abandoned.

At last a note had arrived for Sidney from Arthur. It gave no forwarding address so they were unable to inform him of all that had occurred of late but at least they knew he and his new wife were safe and well. The letter ended with a promise from Arthur to include a forwarding address in his next correspondence.

Freddie called on the third morning of Charlotte's stay. Tom was upstairs, with Diana at his side, very much shaken, sore and despondent. Mrs Dukes spent her mornings in the kitchen as was her preference and Sidney was in his study writing to his solicitor to discover if anything could be done to retrieve Tom's investment. Charlotte was relieved to be alone in meeting her brother. "Oh Freddie, I am so sorry to be abandoning you like this. Did you receive my note? I will be accompanying Diana in removing Tom to Sanditon in a few days' time."

"Yes, are you sure you wish to? I know you are fond of them but had you not planned on returning to Willingden when you had finished with London?"

"Of course, you know I did. I will only stay as long as I am needed then I will go home. It is my duty to the Parkers."

"Do anything rather than feel obliged, Lottie. I am sure they have someone else they can call upon or one of their servants that will do just as well."

"No, Freddie, I am sorry. I meant to say it differently ..." Charlotte continued, "The Parkers are so good. They are the best people I know. I could not stay in London or return to Willingden, knowing their current struggles. I wish to help. It is more than duty. They are like family, Freddie. I care about them so much. Indeed, I love them as I do you."

Freddie squeezed Charlotte's hand.

"Do let me know if I can do anything."

Sidney coughed. The other two stood up immediately. Sidney had not been there a moment before, she was sure of it. But how long had he been there, wondered Charlotte, and what had he heard?

"Mr Heywood, Miss Heywood," said Sidney, "forgive me for interrupting you. I had heard, Mr Heywood, that you were in the house, and I would just like to apologise for my manner of arrival the other morning. Your sister has been of great assistance. And if we may borrow her for some time more, I hope it will not inconvenience you greatly, although I am sure it will. You both must have been looking forward to the next several weeks together."

"Not at all," said Freddie. "She may go to the highest bidder."

Charlotte gave him a sisterly dig with her elbow and all three laughed.

Then they sat together for twenty minutes. They spoke of Tom's health but soon the conversation turned to persons the gentlemen knew in common. Sidney was altered. He was no longer the man who had reproached Charlotte in the hall. He had softened. Charlotte sat confused but pleased. Here he was, seeking Freddie's good opinion and extending an invitation to dinner when things were more settled. It was graciously accepted and Charlotte felt such pride in her brother and delight at their meeting that its remembrance made her glow for the rest of the day. Perhaps Sidney had begun to forgive her and she could hope afresh that given time, former feelings would reignite within him. She was no longer a stranger to her own heart but his, she felt, would require encouragement and the trust that only a full apology and explanation could offer.

But when Sidney joined Diana, Mrs Dukes and Charlotte for dinner that evening, his face appeared troubled. Once the servants withdrew from the room, he explained that he had finally extracted the full story from Tom, who had been reluctant to tell some, and unable to remember all, of the events of the previous days until now. It appeared that two hours after his visit to Crockfords, a knock came to his door and he opened it. Three men stood without – rough looking individuals. They knew his name and said that Dr Hollis had sent them with his best wishes and that the doctor would join them shortly.

"Tom permitted them into his room and what we see is the result of that meeting. Naturally, the doctor did not come. These assailants threatened that if Tom did not leave London immediately and quit seeking the doctor, they would visit him again and with more severe consequences."

The ladies were shaken. Even Mrs Dukes exclaimed, "The rotten things!"

Sidney apologised but felt that they must quit London at once. Tom was sufficiently strong to travel and it was safest that he return home to Sanditon. Sidney could not join them. With his solicitor's help, he wished to continue to work on retrieving something of the doomed investments.

"We have little to go on but as long as there is even the slightest possibility of preventing Tom's ruin, I must try. Would that we knew who he dealt with."

Without a word, Diana jumped up and left the room to commence packing. She understood her mission – to oversee Tom's safe retreat to Sanditon.

Charlotte, before she had an opportunity to check herself, said, "But you will join us in Sanditon? You will not wait too long to join us … I hope."

"My departure will be delayed only by this business. I would wish to be there tomorrow, if I could."

He looked at her. She could not keep his gaze and,

though Mrs Dukes seemed unaware of the nature of their conversation, her presence prevented further discussion. Sidney stood up suddenly.

"I beg your pardon. There is something I must attend to in my study. We will see you all off in the morning," and then a little louder in the direction of his housekeeper, "will we not, Mrs Dukes?"

"Oh yes, to be sure. For I hardly sleep at all anymore. You could set out in the middle of the night and I would be waving you off."

Then he was gone.

As she left the dining room to go upstairs and begin packing, Charlotte heard Sidney in his study as she passed. She must speak to him now. She must have him realise that her cruel treatment of him was due to a foolish misunderstanding. Now that she knew her mistake, she must ask his forgiveness – for that and for her cruel comments at the hotel.

She knocked and was instructed to enter.

Sidney looked up and was amazed it was her. He quickly tried to hide something on his table but Charlotte spotted its glint and knew at once what it was. It was her telescope. All thoughts of what she was going to say left her. She stood in silence.

Sidney also stood and retrieved the telescope, moving to the other side of the table to hand it to her.

"I have just finished repairing it and I believe it is as good as new. There was just one piece that required replacing and the rest went quite smoothly."

"My telescope!"

"Yes. I did not think I could fix it but, indeed, I surprised myself. I asked Mary to take it from your room. Forgive us. I wished to present it to you in the morning as you set off. But now that you are here and have seen it, you may as well have it."

Despite the strain on his face, Sidney looked pleased as he handed it to her.

"Mr Parker, you will never know what this means to me. You are too good."

All her courage left and Charlotte allowed the overwhelming disappointment and heartache of recent weeks to envelope her.

"Miss Heywood, do not cry. Please, do not cry. It is but a trifling thing."

He placed an arm about her and let her head rest on his chest.

"That you would do this for me ... after all I have said ... after I treated you so dreadfully. I do not deserve it."

"Of course you do. I have been tired, the strain of all this, the worry ... I hardly know myself anymore. Doing this for you, well, it has helped to take my mind off things." He seemed to hold her even tighter and whispered, "It made me think of you."

"Mr Parker, I have so much to say ... I do not know what you will think of me ... when I have done ..."

Just then, the door, which was slightly ajar, opened further and Mrs Dukes walked in. Sidney and Charlotte jumped apart.

"Mr Parker, what time are they setting off on the morrow?" asked Mrs Dukes. "I have so much to arrange."

"At first light, Mrs Dukes. I've arranged the carriage. If you could see that they have provisions for the journey, please."

"Are you here too, Miss Heywood?"

"Yes, Mrs Dukes," said Charlotte, attempting to sound calm. "I have just been presented with my old telescope, which Mr Parker has kindly fixed for me."

Mrs Dukes stayed put, evidently waiting for Charlotte to leave with her. The moment to speak openly to Sidney had now passed and Charlotte, forlorn at this interruption, knew that she must quit too. This precious moment was gone.

"Mr Parker," asked Charlotte, just as she reached the door, "is there anything that I can do to assist your search, when I return to Sanditon?"

Sidney looked at her.

"No, no, Miss Heywood, there is nothing ... but perhaps, there is."

He began walking back behind his desk.

"I was just about to sit and write to Sir Edward asking him for details of what Lady Denham and he have lost, that we may include it in our attempts at retrieval. But perhaps you may pass this message on instead. He may send his response to my solicitor, Mr Davis of Gresham Street."

"Mr Davis? Oh my word, was Mr Davis not the doctor's solicitor?" said Charlotte. "No, I am sure it began with a *T*."

"Miss Heywood, you must be confused; it is my solicitor who is Davis. I will write it down for you if you wish."

"We must call for Diana at once. No, I will go to her."

Charlotte excused herself and almost ran up the stairs to

Diana's room, barely waiting for a response to enter. Diana was surprised. "Miss Heywood, whatever is it? Is it Tom?"

Sidney knocked on the door and entered too.

Charlotte asked, "Miss Parker, do you remember the name of Dr Hollis's solicitor?"

"Of course not. How would I know such a thing?"

"But you do know it, just you do not realise it."

"No, Miss Heywood, I do not."

"Can you recall any details from when you first enquired about the doctor at the hotel in Sanditon?"

Diana looked blankly at Charlotte.

"Miss Parker, you discovered some details about him including that he had only posted one letter since his arrival. It was one to his solicitor in London. You mentioned his name."

"Yes, no … I do not know. Yes, in fact, I did." Diana paced over and back and looked up. "It was the only letter he sent from the hotel … the boy told me it was to a Mr Travis, solicitor in London."

They turned to Sidney who placed an arm on each woman's shoulder.

"Ladies, we will only know the significance of this in due course. But I am hopeful. I will notify the authorities and we will plan a meeting with this Mr Travis. Perhaps we can prevent a total loss for Tom and the Denhams. Seize his papers! Who knows? He may lead us to Hollis."

"Do take care, Sidney."

It was Diana who said it but Charlotte wished it was her – that she had the right to show him in words that she too cared what became of him. He looked in her eyes for several moments, as if he could read it there.

While keeping his eyes fixed on hers he said, "Do not worry, ladies. I will send you word."

When Charlotte retired to her room to pack, she knew that sleep would evade her that night. Her heart was thumping fast with the sudden trip they must undertake which was not without risks. But she also owned that not all beats were for themselves; that several, perhaps many, belonged to Sidney Parker – for his safety in attempting to intercept Dr Hollis mixed in with gratitude for the affection she had seen in his eyes when he looked at her earlier. She knew now what her heart was. How could she possibly have considered returning to Willingden when there was even the slightest possibility of winning him back? She was herself again and that gave her strength. She would, as Reverend Hanking advised, not run off but make amends. She felt she had already started to do so. Then her thoughts turned to Freddie and the question of when they would meet again.

It was midnight when all her packing was done and she finally sat at her desk and wrote to Freddie. She would trust it to Mrs Dukes in the morning – to have it sent to her brother's address.

Just before dawn, Sidney and Mrs Dukes bid farewell to Diana, Tom and Charlotte.

"I will be with you soon, within days, I hope," said Sidney.

Charlotte, hoping that this may have been said on her account, sat back in her seat and looked on the broken Tom and anxious Diana before her, as William set the carriage into motion, bound once more for Sanditon.

CHAPTER THIRTY-NINE

On the second morning after their arrival back at Sanditon, as they anxiously awaited news from Sidney, Diana left Trafalgar House and returned within the hour with a guest. She brought with her Reverend Hanking and gave no other explanation than, "At times like this, one must seek the help of God, as well as man."

Charlotte and Mary were already seated in the breakfast room with the forlorn Tom when they entered. None had eaten, none had spoken much and none, with the exception of the reverend, had slept. Guessing as much, the reverend felt it his duty to fortify and rally the others.

"Mr Parker, your sister has shared with me the extent of this dreadful occurrence. But we still have cause to hope. 'Hope' you may feel, at this moment, has no business here. How dare 'hope', you may say to yourselves, march with ill-deserved confidence in the direction of my bosom?"

All looked up at him. Morgan arrived to see if anything was wanted but, sensing the tense atmosphere, immediately retraced his steps back to the kitchen.

The clergyman, buoyed up by their looks of confusion, continued his lesson.

"As was said in Ecclesiastes, *For everything there is a season – a time to break down, and a time to build up; A time to seek and a time to lose; A time to throw away stones, and a time to gather stones together.*"

He paused and looked about for a response. Diana obliged.

"Reverend Hanking, thank you for those soothing words, but I do not see how stones have anything to do with what has occurred."

"Well, they do not really, but essentially what I am attempting to say is that *this too shall pass*, Mr and Mrs Parker."

"Yes, indeed it shall." Diana took the clergyman's words and, leaning across the table to where her sibling sat, repeated them for emphasis. "This too shall pass, Tom, and we will find a way through."

"Not 'we', Diana," said Tom. "Rather 'I'. You none of you have led us to this disaster. It is I who have brought this upon us. Mary," now turning to his wife, "can you ever forgive me?"

Mary squeezed her husband's hand.

"We have each other, Tom, and the children are healthy. That is all that matters."

Reverend Hanking found it a good time to whisper more comforting words.

"As was said to the Corinthians, love is patient, love is kind, something, something, something … It bears all things, believes all things, hopes all things, endures all things. Love never ends."

"Love will not feed us and house us, Reverend. Love will

not put a dowry aside for my daughter or provide educations for my sons. We have lost everything."

"No, Tom, we have not. We have each other and we will return to the Manor House," said Mary. "We must give up this house. The Hilliers are moving away so this saves us seeking new tenants and I do love my old home. The gardens there more than provide for our every need. It is not defeat, Tom. We have not lost everything. Sidney will try to retrieve something too. All is not lost."

Charlotte saw Tom flinch at the mention of giving up Trafalgar House and could not but feel what a crushing blow it would be for him. She wondered at Mary for speaking so frankly of their options in front of all in the room. In her eagerness to make things appear better, Mary could not see what a humiliation this was for him. To her, Trafalgar House was brick and stone but to her husband, it was his finest symbol of success. To abandon it was acknowledging failure. But Charlotte also heard the wisdom of what Mary suggested. The sale of Trafalgar House would recoup some share of their losses and if Sidney could secure something for them, Mary, now acting in the best interests of her family, would make do.

Tom nodded in agreement but did not raise his head from his hands. When at last he did, he turned to Charlotte with reddened, melancholic eyes.

"Miss Heywood, we must be glad that at least you had not become prey to the doctor. I shudder to think what would have become of you. In light of Miss Brereton's situation, please forgive me for any force on my part. I encouraged his visits and his interest. Believe me, I did not know what he was."

Charlotte shook her head.

"Oh, do not blame yourself, Mr Parker. You are in no way to blame for what that man is. It is a credit to you, that you had no idea, no misgivings, that you are so kind and trusting of everyone."

"No, Miss Heywood. It was poor judgement on my part. I had been blind in my over-enthusiasm, my greed. I was not astute enough, clever enough to be a man of industry and business. I had but a boy's dream. I was a fool. There was a time, simpler times, when people were satisfied enough that they got by. Would I had that time again, I would not have lifted a finger to further Sanditon."

Tom put his head back in his hands but was forced to lift it again immediately by Charlotte's almost angry response.

"Enough, Mr Parker. That is not true. You were made for these times. And these times need people like you. The world changes and evolves and there is something in us that seeks its improvement. You had a vision and you made something where there was nothing. You have prospered Sanditon and all those who live there. Do not give up because you have been disappointed. Return better than before."

"An express, an express at the door. Just now!"

Tom sat sunken in the chair. Diana rushed to open the door and hurried back with a confused look on her face.

"It is for Miss Charlotte Heywood."

All were surprised except Charlotte herself who ran to meet the man and take the letter from him.

"I am to await a response," said the man at the door.

Charlotte opened the letter. It was only half a page. She read aloud:

Sister,

We are coming. Almost immediately! Respond at once. I will arrive on Thursday to arrange matters for the others. They arrive next week. Can all be arranged in time?

Freddie

Charlotte took a quill from Mary's writing desk, scribbled something on the back, folded it over and handed it back to the express. "My brother will pay you, when you deliver this."

The express mounted his horse and rushed off at speed. All eyes rested on Charlotte, even those of Tom who had been snapped out of his melancholy.

Miss Parker spoke first.

"Dear Miss Heywood, is all well? Who is coming where and who is ill? An express is never sent unless it is a matter of life and death."

Charlotte placed one hand on her ribcage and the other on the back of the chair that stood before her. Taking a deep breath, she then smiled.

"My brother Freddie is coming to Sanditon. He brings a party from the ruling houses of Europe – Count Von Lamberg who employs him, a baron from Liechtenstein, an Austrian viscount and an Italian prince amongst other lesser aristocrats. I have just responded that we can accommodate them. We must act at once."

Tom listened to Charlotte with his head resting on his two hands but spoke not a word.

Mary was flushed. "Can this be? Really can this be? We must act immediately and make of it what we can. Tom, come, we must speak with Lady Denham. This is marvellous."

Tom said nothing and remained as he was.

"I must secure the best houses on the Terrace," said Diana, "at once!"

"And the hotel, Diana," said Mary, "we must speak to the hotel about rooms, dining and an assembly or several assemblies. We must learn how long they will stay. How many servants they will bring."

"Heavens bless your brother, Miss Heywood," said Reverend Hanking, clapping his hands. "As Marcus Aurelius, emperor of Rome, would say if he were sitting amongst us now, Man is born for deeds of kindness."

Mary and Diana moved to kneel by Tom.

"Brother, please, you must rally yourself. Do you not see, all is not lost?"

Charlotte approached him too. "Mr Parker, please, I have just answered my brother and thanked him. I have assured him that Sanditon is the perfect seaside location for them. They were to go to Brighton but now come here instead. Please, exert yourself, sir. There is not a moment to lose. Sanditon needs you, the trades people, farmers and builders need you to lead this. They depend upon you."

Tom looked up with tears visibly gathering in his eyes, his voice unsteady.

"I am humbled, Miss Heywood. I cannot believe what

you have done for this family and for Sanditon. I can never repay you."

"Sir, your kindness to me has been payment enough."

Tom breathed deeply, sniffing, coughing and gathering himself. Then, when nobody expected it, he jumped up from his seat. "I know what we must do. We will call the Crescent 'Von Lamberg Crescent'. 'Waterloo' is too common. There is a Waterloo this and that in every town. But what other place along the English coast will have a Von Lamberg Crescent, answer me that!"

They all laughed and hugged.

"I must put an advertisement in the newspapers immediately. To get the word out. Everyone will wish to come and dance with European gentry. Imagine all the mothers and their unmarried daughters! But first, I must inform Lady Denham."

And with that Tom Parker grabbed his wife's coat in error and ran out the door.

CHAPTER FORTY

S hortly after dawn, three weeks later, Charlotte walked
on the beach with only her telescope for company.
She had slept but two hours. The Sanditon House
Ball, held the night before, was hailed by Count Von
Lamberg as the 'most exciting evening' he had spent since
leaving Europe. This praise, taken by Lady Denham as
a compliment entirely to herself, had equally delighted
everyone in the room and Charlotte, who had been the
chief orchestrator in getting him to Sanditon, allowed the
tearful pride on Tom Parker's face to keep her from her
sleep. It was generally agreed that it was a night like no
other. Only the absence of one particular gentleman could
dampen Charlotte's spirits, on the few occasions she had
time to reflect on it.

Count Von Lamberg had danced a great deal with
Esther Denham to the delight of her aunt (whose frown
rested firmly on the face of any other young lady who dared
to stand up with him). Esther looked radiant and, as she
walked past, Charlotte could hear Miss Denham confidently
chatter in German, French and Italian – a sure sign that
she was engaging her charms upon her royal companion.

Meanwhile, the rest of his party looked quite determined to spend the evening dancing, especially to the livelier tunes, which saw not one lady left seated. Even Freddie coaxed Lady Denham to her feet, though she swore she had not danced in twenty years, while Diana Parker danced with a young baron from Salzburg until he begged her to stop. Everything about the ball had been a triumph. Indeed, all that had occurred in the past three weeks since Charlotte received Freddie's express had breathed new life into the declining bathing place and now, in the after-glow of a wonderful ball, Charlotte allowed the satisfaction of knowing she had helped her friends wash over her.

The weeks had not been without some strife, however. Tom and Mary had lost heavily. Sidney had succeeded in finding Travis and preventing their losing further but Dr Hollis had already escaped London with much of their savings. Tom resigned himself to leaving Trafalgar House. It must go, he admitted that, but he could live out the rest of this present season in it, which was comfort enough for him. To oversee this new success of Sanditon, that the promise of their European visitors offered, gave fire to his vision once more. As hoped, the hotel filled up and was heaving with activity, carriages full of guests arriving and leaving, dinners and seaweed baths offered. Five new bathing machines were ordered, and fishermen and farmers could hardly keep up with providing produce to the hotel and guest houses. The Terrace buildings were fully occupied and the library subscription list had increased five-fold. Even William Heeley could boast of selling not just another pair of blue shoes but yellow, pink and green slippers too in addition to his other stock. When Tom was not bringing home such uplifting reports he was busy instructing builders at the recently commenced Crescent.

Mary was pleased that she would be returning to live, once more, at the Manor House but, like her husband, she owned that she would be in the heart of Sanditon almost daily. For now she had a tea room to support in any way she could. Her dream had come true and the mysterious investor turned out to be none other than her brother-in-law, Arthur Parker, who had at last found an area of business he felt passionate about. They had received a letter the week before, revealing all, and indicating that he and his beautiful new wife, Jemima Parker, were to arrive within the fortnight to inspect the tea room menu and asked if Diana would be so kind as to find them suitable lodgings.

Diana Parker had found additional zeal in the midst of this thriving Sanditon. Everywhere she looked, she was needed. Sanditon's very success depended upon her and, therefore, she was practically a fixture at the hotel, greeting guests and having all their needs met, before they had swallowed their first cup of tea. Reverend Hanking, observing her enjoyment in her usefulness, found reason to quote Marcus Aurelius once more:

But true good fortune is what you make for yourself – good fortune, good character, good intentions and good actions.

The reverend had also attended the ball at Sanditon House the evening before. He brought with him a humbled Mrs Griffiths who found a moment, over the course of the evening, to apologise to the Parkers. She had been angry, she acknowledged. She had lost the Chesters, who were her main source of income. The Beaufort sisters had been sent for, to return home, by a mother who was determined to choose their husbands and feared they too might elope. Mrs Griffiths had several days and nights of torment, fear for the future and confusion as to how she would begin again at Camberwell with so few pupils. But her dear, dear friend, Reverend Hanking, had helped her through her dark night of the soul. She had come out the other side, and had decided, with his advice and encouragement, to establish a new, smaller, summer establishment at Sanditon. Here she would arrange dance classes for young ladies, give lessons on etiquette and decorum, instruct in languages, hire musical instruments and arrange painting classes '*en plein air*'. Naturally, Reverend Hanking would continue to offer her students lessons in theology, Latin and philosophy.

The greatest change, however, in the past three weeks was in Lady Denham. At some point, shortly after Tom's departure in search of Dr Hollis, she changed her will. Perhaps witnessing the damage caused to her young cousin Clara, as well as the stupidity of Sir Edward in his desperation to be financially independent, had led to her change of heart. One report indicated that it only occurred after a lengthy visit by Reverend Hanking. But as neither party ever commented on the matter, it was believed to be untrue. Calling the Denhams and Clara before her, she said words to the effect that she may, herself, have prevented some of the unfortunate events of late, had she assured her family of their future security. Sir Edward would inherit the house and estate and, as she would not be alive to witness it, she hoped he would not run it into the ground in one generation. Clara and Esther would each receive a fortune of thirty thousand pounds – Esther that she may marry as she wished and Clara, that she would marry Sir Edward. All were astounded. Sir Edward, Lady Denham decided, must marry Clara, to return her to respectability and him to common sense, although she held out little hope of the latter. And it must happen at once. She would arrange for a carriage to take them away to her cousin, a bishop in Oxford, who would oversee it all. This was the condition she laid down and one that delighted the young people. For in addition to actually being in love, Sir Edward realised that if he could not be Clara's villain, then he must be her hero. Charlotte learnt all this from Esther, who had come to tell her and the Parkers almost as soon as it happened.

"But what of Lady Denham's own losses?" asked Mary. "We believe she signed over a great deal to Dr Hollis."

"This is the best part of all," laughed Esther. "I asked her this myself and this was her response: 'I had my solicitor in the room, if you remember, as all those gentlemen stood around and while they were excitedly talking to Dr Hollis, we switched the contracts. Dr Hollis will have discovered by now that he is not the owner of any share of my estate but of two milch asses.' She laughed as she said it. 'And if he wishes to return to Sanditon to claim them, I will be waiting for him.' We could not believe it."

"But I was present," said Tom. "We looked over the document."

"Yes," replied Esther, "before she swapped them."

"This is marvellous. I cannot say how relieved I am."

Tom's voice betrayed his emotions. "In truth, I felt so terrible because I believed I had lost her much. Now this is comfort indeed. But Sir Edward, he did lose?"

"Yes, of course, everything, but at least he now has an inheritance to look forward to."

"Well, I never! Lady Denham and her two milch asses!"

Everyone laughed.

"But I still cannot believe that she did not fall for his scheme. I believed we had convinced her at last."

"That would not be the first time you underestimated a woman, Tom," said Mary.

"That is the truth," said Tom.

Esther explained. "My aunt said that she knew from the first moment she laid eyes on him, what he was."

"I do not doubt it," said Mary.

"Her oversight was in trusting a poorly paid chambermaid not to take bribes," continued Esther.

With the morning sun now breaking through the clouds and the beach noisy with the sound of hungry gulls, Charlotte, beginning to tire at last, finished her musings with a sigh. The lightness she felt of no longer carrying the self-loathing and shame of before was great. She had learnt her lesson and had done her best to make amends. In three weeks' time, she would be back again at Willingden, where she hoped the soothing balm of home and family would console her sore heart in respect to the only regret she had left – that of not making amends with Sidney Parker. If he had truly loved her, however, he would have returned to Sanditon long before now. She had expected to see him, so sure she was that he would follow her, once his dealings in London were finished. His business was done, they had received confirmation as such a fortnight before, but he had not come. He had chosen to stay away. She needed no further proof that where once they were on the verge of admitting how dear they had become to each other, they were now forever distant. That ship had left port, no more to return.

It was time to return to Trafalgar House. Her limbs ached but she would join the others for breakfast soon and rest for the day. Freddie had promised Tom to join them later for dinner. As she turned to walk again the length of the beach, she realised that, this time, she was not alone. A male figure walked towards her – one she recognised at once. It was Sidney Parker.

CHAPTER FORTY-ONE

S
he must meet him. There was nowhere to go except into the sea or over a sand dune. Even if he was merely going for a walk, he was now close enough to recognise her and yet he did not avoid her. He did not turn back as she half-expected. They would meet. They would talk. How would she bear it? What would he say?

"Good morning, Miss Heywood."

"Mr Parker."

"I trust the telescope is put to good use?"

"Yes, I thank you."

"You are returning to Trafalgar House? May I accompany you?"

Charlotte nodded acquiescence. At least, she thought, they would be side-by-side and not face to face. She had no doubt she looked haggard from her night of revelry and lack of sleep and would talk nonsense from her confusion and fatigue. She would say little.

"Did you enjoy the ball last night, Miss Heywood?"

Charlotte said nothing – a 'yes' might be misconstrued – that she had forgotten him already, but a 'no' would be a lie, for she had enjoyed it greatly. Oh, if she were only thinking clearly.

Sidney smiled. "But I can see that you did."

"Yes," Charlotte offered at last, "it was a very pleasant evening."

He was looking quite tired himself and unshaven. He must have just arrived that morning. But if he had cared what she thought, he would have been at the ball himself. He knew of the ball. If there was even a smite of interest in her on his part, he would have been there, asking her to dance, looking on jealously if she danced with another, making it known that he wished for them to begin again.

As if he read her mind: "I could not attend the ball, I am afraid. I had hoped I could. I hoped to be here two weeks ago. But Mrs Dukes had a fall."

Charlotte turned quickly to face him. "Is she well? Has she been greatly injured?"

"It was a bad fall but she is mending well now and can finally move again, with some effort. I could not leave her."

"Of course. You did not send word to Tom or Diana? I am sure they would have mentioned Mrs Dukes' fall."

"No, I could not. I know how Diana would have fussed and left immediately for London with notions and potions. And I did not wish to worry Tom. He has had enough to worry about of late."

"Yes. You were right."

They walked on again.

"I had to be sure she was out of danger before leaving her ... She likes *you* a great deal."

"Oh, dear Mrs Dukes, she is such a warm soul. And to think what I thought she was at first."

Now Charlotte stopped again to face Sidney. This must

be done and done now, while they were alone and while her mind was not quite her own. She must speak freely to him, no matter the cost to herself. She owed him this much.

"Mr Parker, I believed, wrongly, when I overheard you speak to your brothers of 'The Duchess', that you were referring to your mistress. Miss Denham had suspected that Captain Russell had a mistress in town. Unfortunately, all the time she spoke of him, I believed it was of you she was speaking. That it was you who had disappointed her, you that had broken her heart, you that had a mistress in town. Unfortunately, Dr Hollis confirmed the rumour to be true. He claimed to have heard something of it at his club and that you had boasted of the affair. I was convinced you were a rake of the worst kind."

At first, during her speech, Sidney had looked shocked, then amused, but on hearing mention of Dr Hollis, his jaw tensed and he looked away. "I no longer wonder at your treatment of me, if this is what you believed. As for that doctor ... is there no limit to the damage he has tried to cause my family ... or me?"

"I only realised my error in confusing you with Captain Russell shortly before you left for London. Even still, I was convinced that you were returning to your mistress."

Sidney looked back at her for some moments and then a smile broke over his face. "Until you met Mrs Dukes, 'The Duchess', at last and realised your mistake."

Charlotte placed her hands over her face. "I am mortified. I had totally misunderstood your character, which has always been good. I believed myself to hate you."

Sidney moved closer and gently removed Charlotte's

hands from her face. "Do not worry. I see now that your hatred of me was completely founded on misunderstandings. You are not to blame."

Charlotte wondered if she should now try to remove her hands from his. But a moment later, she decided that she should continue to confess all that had been troubling her. She would not pull away and hurt his feelings again as she had done in London.

"When you overheard what I said at the hotel about your family and friends, I was so ashamed. Please be assured that I felt the wrong of what I had said almost immediately."

"I was angry. Yes, I was at first. But when I reflected on what I heard, there was truth in some of your opinions. Some were even opinions I had myself professed on occasion. What really made me angry was how the doctor, who knew where I sat, led you in his questions, setting you up to say things that you may have wrongly believed."

"As much as I despise the man, he is not fully to blame. I prided myself on being an excellent judge of character and cared not how unkind I was in the description of others. It emerged that I was not such a discerning judge after all. I believed myself superior to the company I kept in Sanditon. It was too late when I realised that that same company was, in fact, superior in everything that truly mattered – courage, kindness and friendship. Others, I later realised, who had all the appearance of excellence, were devoid of a single good deed or thought."

Sidney kept Charlotte's gaze. "Your hands are cold." He rubbed them briskly, then removing his jacket said, "Allow me," and swung it over her shoulders. It was true.

Charlotte was now cold, hungry and tired but she was also exhilarated from the relief of unburdening herself at last and spending time so close to the man whose gaze was beginning to offer her hope again.

"You are like one of my beach treasures."

"I truly believe it and have all the appearance of one – washed up and discarded."

"No – beautiful and unique, with your own charming story. Would that I were part of that story … Miss Heywood … Charlotte, we will return at once for you are cold, but please let me be assured of one thing. There has been no understanding or courtship between us. We have avoided each other for longer than we sought each other out. I was rejected rather than encouraged. Yet, I hope, you will allow me … us … to begin again. Will you return with me to Trafalgar House as my intended? Will you consider allowing me to make my intentions known? Will you be mine?"

He held her hands tightly in his, lowered his forehead to touch hers, never looking away.

Charlotte, pragmatic and not given to the whims and sensibilities one reads about in romantic novels, took a moment to reflect. As a girl, when she had imagined the moment that her beloved would declare himself, she had imagined herself looking her best, sitting elegantly in a drawing room, composed and sure of herself. Her beloved, a handsome and, at least, clean-shaven gentleman, would be down on one knee. She had not envisioned walking along a beach, with sand in her shoes, her hair half-falling down from the night before, hungry, tired and half-delirious from exhaustion … but this would do. It would have to do. This moment was her moment, their moment, and she would not change a thing about it. It was perfect. Sidney loved her as she was. He always had.

Sidney used this pause to search Charlotte's face and, finding encouragement enough in her smile, bent his head to embrace her. No words could better convey their mutual affection than this act, which began with hesitation but soon left them in no doubt of the other's feelings.

When next Charlotte found she could speak, she uttered the words, "Yes, Mr Parker. Yes, Sidney. I will walk by your side into your brother's house and yes, by all means, make your intentions known."

With hearts relieved of heaviness and replaced with delight, Charlotte and Sidney slowly returned to Trafalgar House. At the door, they were greeted by an equally dishevelled Morgan who had also been in attendance at the ball. He raised an eyebrow at their linking arms and wondered at Miss Heywood handing him a telescope but shuffled out of their way so they might enter the breakfast room – there to meet their family and friends within.

Despite sharing their news in a timely fashion, with those who loved them best, Sidney and Charlotte soon learnt that they were not the first persons in need of congratulations that morning. For moments after the ball, Reverend Hanking had, very carefully, lowered himself on to one knee before Mrs Griffiths. And quoting Aristotle, he asked her if she too felt that 'Love is composed of a single soul inhabiting two bodies'. Once she concurred and helped him to his feet, they agreed that while others may follow, they were most certainly the happiest couple that season at Sanditon.

THE END

www.ingramcontent.com/pod-product-compliance
Lightning Source LLC
Chambersburg PA
CBHW030758210726
48290CB00002B/313